Home of the Double Cross

Jerrell Speller

(2019)

Author Contact Information:
Facebook/Jerrell Speller (TrackLife)
Email/JPay.com Jerrell Speller #1391669

CONTENTS

~

Home of the Double Cross

Acknowledgements

~

First and foremost I have to acknowledge & show my gratitude to the Speller family along with my beautiful baby girl Ivyona. Since day one y'all have been with me through thick & thin & to this day y'all are still by my side fighting the storm with me, words can't explain my love & appreciation. The Williams family my love goes out to you all as well, from Fayetteville NC, to Hampton VA. All of my rounds from across the tracks, Nino, Mann, TJ, Humble, Lil Wes, Y'all are the definition of "Tru friends" who keep it solid. Nino I tilt my hat to you big dawg they don't make em' like you no more I swear they don't. Keep doing what you doing, you got the hood on your back and you making VA look good. All of the original certified Park Place families, the Foxes, Askews, Matthews, & Hawkins, I send my love out to you all as well. Jessica Holiday, even though we went our separate ways once we got older I still got nothing but big love for you lil moma. The entire Corporation Family from the North side of Richmond all the way to Park Place in Hampton, there will never be another family like ours & Brandon Robertson I salute you. My sister Jalisa and her group of successful, beautiful, independent, home girls who I granted the name #prettygirlgang. Y'all keep killing the game & putting on for our black queens across the nation. Women like you put women of color on a pedestal & I respect that. Last but not least I have to send my love to "lil miss Wicked," even though we have our differences you know I can't 4get about you girl you gon' always have a place in my heart, you know who you are..

Home of the Double Cross

CH/1.

~

On a cold November evening in the drug infested neighborhood known as Park Place in Hampton, VA sat a young hustler named Gator in his hunter green Cadillac STS. Backed into the rundown driveway of his mother's house on Childs ave with the seat laid back, he let the oversized blunt filled with purple haze ease his mind as he rap along to the Pimp C song "Top notch hoes." He was so caught up in his own thoughts that he forgot Angel was sitting in the passenger seat next to him until she nudged him on the shoulder to pass him the cup of syrup they were sipping on. Damn lil daddy you was zoned out won't you? Gator didn't reply, he just gazed at her through his half closed red eyes and cracked a smile flashing his full set of shiny gold teeth.
Gator liked Angel in his own special kind of way mostly because she was different from the rest of the women he was dealing with, she was a hustler. She never asked him for money on a regular bases, never confronted him about all the other women he was dealing with, and most of all she turned him out in the bedroom giving him the game on how to "fully" please a real woman. Angel's pussy was the first piece of pussy Gator ever ate and after a few rounds of her showing him how to master her body Gator became a pro, even bringing her to multiple orgasms just from eating her pussy. The only thing stopping Angel from making Gator her man was their age difference. She was 22 and he was 17 but she was so in love with his style and sex game she figured she would just enjoy the ride while it lasted.

There was also a flip side to Angel, she had what the Ghettos across America called KP, short for killer

1

pussy. Almost every nigga she dealt with ended up dead or missing. Her pussy was rumored to be so good that whoever she was dealing with would kill the next man even if he thought she was fucking him. That big monkey in between her legs was definitely a trap for niggas.

As Gator continued to stare an Angel with that devilish grin through his cloudy red eyes, she already knew what was on his mind so she added fire to the flame by licking her soft full lips while cocking her legs up exposing her other set of phat lips through her black leggings.

"I'm telling you girl don't write a check yo ass can't cash, cause the way I'm feeling rite now we might not make it to the house," said Gator as he grabbed at his growing manhood through his jeans. Angel stared at him seductively then replied, "Shit you the one still talking." Feeling as if she was challenging his ego, without another word being said Gator put the cup down, leaned over to the passenger seat, and began passionately kissing her soft lips while at the same time gently massaging her pussy through her tights.

Just as he began to slide her thong to the side and feel the softness of her warm phat cat he heard three loud knocks on the driver side window. "What the fuck?" was the first thing that came out of his mouth. The first thought that came to mind was one of the local jack boys had caught him slipping. Gator quickly grabbed his snub nose .44 and aimed it at the window ready to shoot his way out of a sticky situation but once he finally got a glimpse of who it was through the partially fogged up window he breathed a sigh of relief realizing that it was only Rhonda, one of his most loyal customers.
Rhonda what the fuck you doing sneaking up on me like that, you know you almost got yo ass shot!

2

"Why you ain't call me first?" asked Gator as he put his pistol in the middle console. Child I ain't got no more minutes on this phone and the pay phones at the corner store is broke.

"Now I got $32 look out for me I'll be back once my old man get off work at 9", said the foul smelling woman as she leaned through the driver side window of his Cadillac. Gator reached down into the pocket of his boxer briefs a pulled out a freshly cooked ounce of butter bage crack and broke her off a fat $40 piece. Gator never bagged up his work because that was a sure way to get a distribution charge if ever caught. As he dropped the piece of crack in her hand resembling a piece of buttery popcorn, a huge smile spread across her face as she realized how big it was. Thinking fast she quickly ripped off a piece of the brown paper bag she was carrying her Wild Irish Rose in and wrapped the product in it so she wouldn't lose it. Thank you baby boy I'll be back. Y'all be careful now its two rollers at the corner store parked side by side talking to each other, they might be ready to roll through.

"Aight good looking out Rhonda, said Gator as he rolled the window up to keep the heat from escaping his warm car. You think they gon' roll through here on some bullshit? Asked Gator as he placed his bag of crack back inside his boxers.

"I don't know but if they do just pass me the shit and I'll stash it on me," said Angel nonchalantly. There was a few seconds of silence between the two before Gator responded, "I wish it was that easy lil moma but if you can stash this on you then you a bad muthafucka. Gator reached down behind him in the backseat and reemerged with a Chinese SKS as Angel looked at him in disbelief. Really Gator?

"You mean to tell me you been riding through the city all day with a fucking assault rifle in your back seat?" said Angel as she crossed her arms over her chest while resting her back up against the passenger side door.

"Come on Angel don't act like you don't know how it is out here, rather get caught with it then without it," said Gator with a straight face. Angel shook her head once again while staring into his eyes. Truth be told she actually admired him and wanted what was best for him, the last thing she wanted to see was him end up with a life sentence, or gunned down in the streets.

Y'all young niggas with this beef shit is ridiculous. Let me ask you something Gator, how you expect to get money and go to war at the same time? Gator looked at her as if she were speaking a foreign language as he took a sip from the Styrofoam cup. What the fuck you mean how am I gon' get money and go to war at the same time?

"Shit so far I'm doing aight, I'm stacking my bread while at the same time giving these niggas the business," said Gator with a wicked grin on his face. That was another reason why Angel was so cautious about getting into a serious relationship with Gator. He was reckless and still on that hot boy shit. She figured if they did get into a relationship and have kids Gator wouldn't live to see their 5th birthday.

With thoughts of Gator running through her mind she turned her head and began gazing out the window to hide the emotions written all over her face, that's when she noticed an unmarked police car creeping up the street with its headlights out. Looking to her left she notice another one creeping up the Ave toward them except this one had its side spot light on flashing in between rows of each house as if he were looking for someone. Gator was in the driver seat with his head

4

leaned against the head rest enjoying his high from the
purple haze and codeine. With his eyes closed and
rapping along the music he was oblivious to what was
going on around him until Angel turned the music off
and made him slouch down in his seat so they couldn't
be seen.

The unmarked police car with the spot light
slowly crept up in front of Gator's mother house where
they were parked and put his spotlight on both sides of
the house. Once he saw that it was clear he then
proceeded to put the spotlight on Gator's Cadillac.
Gators heart skipped a beat because he knew shit was
about to get real as his sweaty palms clutched his assault
rifle tightly. Gator please don't do nothing stupid them
people go'n kill you baby it ain't worth it, pleaded Angel
as she tried to talk some sense into the trigger happy
young man before her eyes. Gator didn't respond he just
put his index finger to his lips signaling for her to stop
talking.

Ten long seconds passed by which seemed like a
lifetime, then by the grace of God the police car finally
pulled off and the two of them were able to breathe
again.

"Let's get off this hot ass strip and go to my
place for the rest of the night," said Angel.

"Aight cool," replied Gator nonchalantly, but on
the inside he was grinning from ear to ear because he
knew what that meant, he was about to be knee deep in
that sweet pussy all night long.

Angel only lived a few doors down so there was no need
for them to drive to her place. As they stepped out of the
Cadillac the cold November air chilled their bodies,
causing Gator to stuff his hands into the pockets of his
black North Face hoodie where his hand rested on his
.44 bulldog. Ever since his lil soulja T2 got robbed and
shot up a few months ago coming out of the corner store

5

Chicken & Pork, Gator had been on high alert, especially after dark. He had witnessed too much death and bloodshed in his short 17 years on earth so he refused to be a victim of gun violence, especially if he could prevent it.

"I ain't cook nothing so if you want something to eat you shit outta luck," said Angel as she threw her keys on the kitchen counter before heading to her bedroom to change clothes.

"Got damn well at least give me the number to the Chinese food place," said Gator as he sat in the living room rolling a blunt. A few minutes passed before Angel returned to the living room wearing a pair of burgundy boy shorts that exposed the bottom of her ass cheeks, with a white snug fit Polo tee shirt that hugged her titties and stomach perfectly.

As she sat down next to Gator on the couch she threw the brochure at him with a hint of attitude and aggression behind her actions. Unfazed by her antics, Gator proceeded to place his order over the phone but he couldn't help himself as he kept glancing at her through the corner of his eyes. Angel was a bad bitch at 5'8 145 pounds with smooth coco brown skin and an ass like Trina. Looking at her reminds you of the reality TV star from Love & Hip Hop, "Yandi." Even when she was mad she was still sexy, if not more.

Once Gator ended his call he lit the blunt then casually made his way over to Angel with his eyes glue to her thick thighs which were laced up with baby oil. "You ain't getting no ass tonight so don't even think about it," were the first words that came out of her mouth as if she could read his mind. Gator looked at her and smirked. He was a smooth young dude and as sharp as they came so he knew exactly where this was coming from and how to get around it.

"I know you ain't still trippin off that shit that

6

happened in the car?" asked Gator. Angel didn't reply she just kept flicking through the channels as if she didn't even hear him. Look Angel you knew what type time I was on before you started dealing with me so don't turn your back on me and leave me standing in the rain when shit get real. Angel looked at him as if he had just disrespected her with his last statement. Gator I would never turn my back on you, that type of shit don't even flow through my blood, and besides that ain't even the point.

By now Gator had stopped what he was doing and gave her his full attention as he looked into her dark brown almond shaped eyes then asked her, "so what's your point then? There was a few seconds of silence in the air before Angel responded, "my point is you could've gotten yourself killed and you think that shit is cool, like you don't even give a fuck." Right then and there was the moment Gator knew that Angel had feelings for him and cared about him deeply. She always had her guard up and made sure to let it be known that they were only fucking and that their relationship could go no further so now Gator was confused.
I feel what you saying lil moma just know that I was go'n kill them muthafuckas before I let em take us to jail. Angel couldn't help but crack a smile at his remark and once she lightened up Gator knew he had her so he went in for the kill. As he passed her the blunt he began slowly kissing on her neck while making a sensual trail all the way down to her pierced belly button. Once he pulled her thong to the side he began planting soft, wet, kisses all over her pussy lips causing her to tense up and softly call his name.

After about 20 minutes of him taking her to ecstasy and two orgasms later Angel was stuck and couldn't keep her legs from trembling. She had never in her entire life had her pussy ate with so much passion and Gator knew it. Gator sat there grinning and shaking his head, amused at her because she was literally stuck in the same position with her legs wide open laid back on the couch.

"You aight lil moma?" asked Gator. Angel didn't respond she just looked at him and gave him the finger. Once Angel regained her composure she slowly made her way in between his legs and began removing his pants and boxers. With his semi hard manhood in her hand, she began stroking him while softly licking and kissing the head at the same time. Satisfied with how hard she had him she gathered as much saliva in her mouth as she could and in one gulp got almost all 8 inches of him down her throat. After only about five minutes of her pleasing him orally Gator had to put his pride to the side and make her stop. Her sloppy blowjob on top of her erotic moaning while staring into his eyes was enough to make him erupt like a volcano.

"What's wrong lil daddy you aight?" asked Angel mocking him from earlier. Gator didn't reply he just grabbed her hand and motioned for her to straddle his lap. Riding his dick while kissing on his neck made Angel's pussy wetter by the second. Thinking of a move she once saw on a porno, she spent around on his dick and began riding him reverse cowgirl.
Using her knees for leverage, she bounced her big brown ass up and down on his dick like she was in a Luke video. The sight of her pussy swallowing his dick up and down like that was driving Gator crazy! Feeling his manhood growing bigger inside of her and knowing he was on the verge of cumming, Angel picked up the pace causing Gator to explode deep inside of her while she also reached her own orgasm spilling her sweet juices all over his lap.

The next morning Angel was up cooking breakfast listening to her Gangsta Boo album, "Best of both worlds." This wasn't something that she normally indulged in after a night of sex, but Gator had put it on her so good she had to show him her appreciation and let him know that he was definitely on his job. Gator's phone had been ringing nonstop all morning but the grade a pussy along with the grade a weed had him in a coma like sleep. Sensing that he was missing important calls Angel brought him his breakfast in bed then began licking a trail from his belly button all the way up to his neck.

Feeling her warm, soft, tongue caress his stomach Gator opened his eyes and was ready for round two, but the constant vibrating of his phone brought him back to reality as he put Angel on hold and began taking his calls. The first call he took was one of his runners, Money Mike. Money Mike what's the word? Damn nephew I been calling you all morning you straight?

"Like a white line in the street, talk to me," replied Gator. Aight look I'm on Hemlock, JB got $60, Net got $20, and lil Willy got $ 37, said Money Mike eagerly anticipating his early morning blast.

"Aight I'm on Childs, meet me on Angel's back porch," said Gator.
It was 9am on a Friday, Gator knew money was going to be jumping all day so he got on his grind early. Gator had strong clientele so he didn't have to stand on the block, all he had to do was answer his phone and he would make anywhere from $1,000 to $1,500 a day. Early bird get the worm, that was a saying he got from his right hand man Poncho and he ain't never lied. For the next three hours he directed all of his traffic to Angel's place and she didn't mind because she was able to squeeze in another round of mind blowing sex.

9

CH/2.

~

       It was around 1pm when Gator made his way back down the street to his mother's house. Gator lived with his mother Ms. Darliene, along with his 13 year old sister Natasha. He and Natasha barely ever got along due to the fact that Gator was always picking on her and constantly putting her in wrestling moves, but that was just how he showed his love. In all actuality Gator was her favorite sibling but she would but she never let him know such a thing.

Gator also had a 15 year old brother named Deyshawn and a 19 year old sister named Latreice. However, they were not living with them at the moment because Latreice had went off to college to study criminal justice, while Deyshawn was sent to North Carolina a few months ago to live with his aunt to avoid going down the same path as his older brother Gator. Gator was real close to all of his siblings and he showed his love to all of them in the same way, by getting on theirs nerves while at the same time making sure they had what they needed.

       "What's up chump," said Gator to his little sister Natasha as he walked past her at the kitchen table and mushed her on the side of her head almost knocking her grilled cheese sandwich out of her hands.

       "Stop playing all yo life, I'm telling moma," said Natasha as Gator made his was down the hallway to his mother's room.

What's up old lady? Hey my lost child where you been at all morning? "Down the street at Angel's house," replied Gator. He knew his mother didn't care too much for Angel but the way she was putting that veteran pussy

10

and head on him his mother was just going to have to be mad. Ms. Darliene cut her eyes at him then replied, "You and that damn Angel."
What's wrong with Angel, Why you don't like her? Asked Gator as he sat down next to her on her bed and began devouring her bag of potato chips as if they were his. Boy don't eat all my chips, I walked to the store to get those chips personally for myself.

"Why you ain't drive my car?" asked Gator. Boy the store ain't nothing but a hop & skip away, besides, I seen something in your back seat that I ain't wanna see, said Ms. Darliene as she shot her oldest son a cold stare.

Gator fell silent because he knew his mother had seen the assault rifle he left lying in the back seat of his car. Even though she knew what he did in the streets, he always tried his best to keep it out of her sight out of respect, so whenever she ran across one of his guns in his room or caught him making a sale outside, it struck a nerve in him leaving him with a guilty conscious. His mother was cool, but at the end of the day there was still a level of respect that needed to be shown.

"So tell me why you don't like Angel," said Gator with an inquiring mind. Ms. Darliene took her eyes off of the computer screen she had been focusing on for the past twenty minutes then looked her son square in the eyes. First of all she too damn old for you, second of all I'm trying to figure out what the hell she want with my 17 year old son, third of all, "aight moma you got it, I get your point," said Gator wishing he had never brought up the subject.

"Yea you better get my point, cause I be damned if you end up like the last three dudes she was with, I heard about that girl," said Ms. Darliene as she tilted her head and looked at him over the brim of her reading glasses. Gator tried to play it off as if he didn't know what she was talking about, while in his head thinking to himself," Shit I see why niggas kill over that pussy."

"So what you doing on the computer anyway?" asked Gator trying to change the subject.

"Filling out some applications," replied Ms. Darliene as her fingers continued to type on the laptop. Applications for what? Asked Gator. For a two bedroom apartment, "I'm thinking about getting one uptown, they have some real decent ones up that way," replied Ms. Darliene. Two bedrooms? How you gon' make that work when it's three of us? Because Gator the two bedroom apartment is for me and your sister.

"So what you saying you kicking me out?" asked Gator as he made firm eye contact with the woman who birthed him. Ms. Darliene looked at her son through watery eyes then told him, "No son I'm not putting you out, I'm just letting you go." You wanna be grown and sell drugs then that's on you, but I can't let you put you little sister in harms way any longer. It's too much traffic going on in front of my house, I'm tired of your customers knocking on my backdoor waking up out of my sleep, and you got these fast ass girls running in & out of your room all hours of the night.

"What kind of example you think you're setting for your thirteen year old sister?" asked Ms. Darliene with great emotion behind her words.
Once again Gator fell silent. She was right, what kind of example was the setting for his little sister? His mother walked up to him and gave him a comforting motherly hug before saying," I love you baby, but until you start living right I can't have you living under the same roof with me and your sister, it's just too much of a risk, I hope you understand. Gator left his mother's room with a tear in his eye but the willingness in him to prevail refused to let it drop.

Once inside his room Gator turned on his favorite Boosie song "Going thru some thangs," then went into his closet to put together an outfit for the day. After a nice hot shower Gator got dressed in a pair of black Evisu jeans, grey suede Nike boots, black tee shirt, and his black & grey leather Avirex jacket. Throwing on his black skully as he grabbed the keys to his Cadillac and his .44, Gator walked out the front door hoping the rest of his day would bring him some sunshine.

Ever since Gator was a young boy it seemed as if the odds were against him but he always prevailed. Born December 4th 1989 in the height of the crack era, Gator was destined to be a hustler. Brought up in the "Pine Chapel Projects," the most notorious projects in Hampton or Newport News back in the early 90's, Gator witnessed and encountered more traumatic situations before the age of 7, then your average person at the age of 18.

His Mother's apartment was "the spot." Since his father wasn't in the picture, mama had to get it how she live. Selling dinners, liquor, and running a poker table out of 323 Freeman Dr. was how she put food on the table and clothes on the backs of her four youngins. With that hustle came a hefty price tag because the young, quiet, observing Gator, saw a lot and learned a lot.
The drug dealing environment was contagious, Gator witnessed everything from sexual acts being committed for drugs, to fiends getting assaulted for being short on payment, to his mother's boyfriend being shot 11 times as he lay on the couch sound asleep right in front of 6 year old Gator. Needless to say, all of the traumatic situations he witnessed, along with the grooming of the older hustlers, made him the man he is today.

Over the next couple of hours Gator sat in his Cadillac at the basketball court just getting high while trying to get his mind right. He knew what his mother was saying was true he just couldn't wrap his mind

13

around the fact that she was abandoning him. His thoughts were interrupted as his right hand man Poncho pulled up beside him in his black Monte Carlos bumping Lil Webbie's song "G Shit."

"My nig what's the word?" said Poncho as he turned the music down and flicked the ashes from his blunt out the window.

"I can't call it mane just getting my mind right," said Gator barely making eye contact with his day one comrade.

Poncho had been knowing Gator for the past seven years so he knew when something was bothering his lil soulja. After parking his car Poncho jumped out of his ride and joined Gator to see exactly what was going on with him. What's the word lil daddy I see you all hied up usual, "you need to stop popping those pills while you sipping that syrup that shit will have you late my nig," said Poncho out of sincere concern for his childhood friend.

What's up tho you aight? Asked Poncho.

"Yea mane shit crazy right now, moma talking that bullshit bout putting a nigga out," said Gator as he took a sip from his cup of syrup then passed it to Poncho. Damn lil bruh, so what you gon' do?

"I don't know mane, I know it may sound crazy but, I'm considering moving in with Angel for a few weeks until I find my own place," said Gator as he stroked the hair under his chin. Come on Gator you supposed to know the game baby boy. If you move in with Angel shit is gon' change between y'all and 9 times out of 10 that lil no strings attached relationship y'all got going on is gon' get real complicated.

Gator took a long pull from the blunt and let it linger in his lungs before he spoke, "so how you think I should play it?" Well you know you always welcomed at my spot. Either that or get a decent lil hotel room for about a month and see how it play out from there.

"It ain't like you hurting for cash so you'll be aight," said Poncho giving his friend some words of advice.
Poncho was right, Gator was sitting on a nice piece of change to be only 17, so he took what he was saying into consideration and decided to roll with it.

"What's up tho mane we hitting Pure Pleasure across the water tonight, you fucking with us?" asked Poncho as he began to exit the car. I don't know mane its Friday, money been jumping all day I might pull an all-nighter and get the rest of these two ounces off, plus I ain't really in the mood for no club tonight.
Lil bruh you got to get up out the hood sometime mane, what's the point of having money if you can't enjoy it?

"Oh best believe I enjoy my money," said Gator with a wicked grin on his face. Yo ass crazy mane, well look I'ma hit yo line a couple hours before I slide out so let me know by then. Aight bet, said Gator as the two dapped up and parted ways.
Poncho was Gator's right hand man along with Jux. He was also a big brother figure since he was 20 and Gator was only 17. Poncho was what you called a "true hustler," he was smart. He always kept bond and lawyer money, always thinking before he made a move, was well connected in the streets, and most of all he stayed out of jail. So to sum it all up, Poncho was winning.

Poncho took Gator under his wing once he saw that he was about his paper and lived by morals and principles at such a young age. When Gator first started hustling he was buying already cooked up crack from the older hustlers from around the way but the quality was garbage. Poncho saw the ambition and dedication in the young hustler so he taught him how to cook his own crack and make it so potent that his life would change overnight. Not to mention he witnessed him get down with that pistol play on several occasions so he knew he was about his business and he respected that.

Later on that night Gator pulled up to Pure Pleasures dressed to impress. Draped in a black Prada sweatshirt, white Tru Religion jeans, with a pair of high top black Prada sneakers. To top it off he had on all of his jewelry which consisted of three yellow gold chains, five gold rings with diamond clusters, and his yellow diamond earrings which he like to prefer to as "Lemon heads." He wasn't in the mood for Angel tonight so in the passenger side of his ride was is lil gutta bitch, "Ma Ma." Gator had been fucking with Ma Ma on and off for the past three years, dating back to when they first met at Hampton High school in the 9th grade.
The first day Gator laid eyes on her in the cafeteria he knew he had to have her. It was something about her that stood out as she sat at the table by herself eating her pizza and French fries looking like she didn't have a care in the world. At 5'6 135lbs with smooth caramel skin, and thick golden brown hair with black streaks that complimented her skin tone, she had definitely caught his attention.

Making his way over to her table the first thing he noticed were her exotic looking hazel eyes as she shot him a cold stare insinuating that she didn't want to be bothered. Unfazed by her playing hard to get tactics Gator sparked a general conversation with her and once her guard came down and the laughter and smiles came out he knew he had her. As he was getting to know her he noticed she had a tattoo on her arm that read "NAS" so Gator asked, "Damn lil moma you must really be a big fan of Nas? Ma Ma looked at him strange then replied, "Naw why you say that?" Looking at her arm then back at her Gator replied, shit you got the man's name tatted on you, I thought you was a die-hard fan. Ma Ma cracked a smile showing her two gold slugs

16

before replying, naw lil daddy, NAS is short for "Niggas ain't shit."

Gator sat back thinking to himself, "yea I'm feeling shawdy already." The more he got to know her it began to feel like she was a female version of himself. Over the next six or seven months they became close, actually closer than expected.

The only thing that was keeping Gator from making her his main squeeze was the fact that she had a reputation for giving up the pussy if your paper was long enough, she was a bit "promiscuous." Gator kept her on his team because she was loyal to him and down for whatever. When Gator came home from upstate and was down bad on his luck, she put together the perfect home invasion for him by setting up a well-known drug dealer from around her way for him to rob. Every since then, she and Gator were click tight.

Once inside the club he noticed Poncho in the back by the pool table getting a lap dance by a sexy dark skin girl with two long cornrows that stopped at the crack of her ass. He also had another stripper sitting right next to him whispering in his ear while rubbing on his chest. Feeling like he was missing out on the action Gator casually made his way to the back with Ma Ma on his side to join Poncho.

"Damn big bruh you done started the party without me," said Gator as he lustfully eyed the two half naked strippers Poncho had entertaining him. "You already know what time it is my nig, who this you got with you?" asked Poncho referring to Ma Ma. Oh this Ma Ma, said Gator proudly.

"Oh okay that's Ma Ma," said Ponch with great enthusiasm behind his words. He had hear about her through Gator but he never brought her around. Every time Gator would get high off the ecstasy he would talk about Ma Ma, that's how Poncho knew he

17

had a thing for her. Sitting down eyeing her 5'6 caramel frame Poncho understood why Gator never brought her around, she was beautiful.

"Where Jux I thought he was coming out tonight?" asked Gator causing Poncho to snap out of his lustful gaze.

"Mane shit he probably somewhere fucking with a lil broad you know how he is," said Poncho. Jux was also Gators right hand man, He and Poncho were similar in certain ways. Jux was laid back, Never too flashy, and considered a ladies man, but at the same time he had a temper like a bubble and if you bust it you're in trouble. He was also know to be on his GQ shit. Unlike Gator and Poncho who only seemed to attract ghetto fabulous women, Jux was on a whole another level.

Jux would pull up out the hood with women from college universities, women who worked for the government, women who dealt in real estate, women with checkbooks, credit cards, and assets. Even though he was only 20 years old he was working the game like a true veteran. Gator and Poncho didn't know how he was bagging women of that caliber but they definitely admired it.

Gator and Poncho ordered up two bottles of Hennessey at $350 apiece and the real party began. As Ma Ma showered the two strippers with ones the two other beautiful strippers joined them, causing their section to turn into a girl's gone wild segment. Twenty minutes later Jux strolled through the double doors and the four of them had a ball as they gulped down shots of Hennessey while smoking blunt after blunt of OG Kush. Master P song "Thug girl," was blaring through the speakers of the club when Gator looked up and spotted someone who looked real familiar on the other side of the room. He thought his mind was playing tricks on him at first so he took off his black and gold Versace shades and just like he thought it was the same dude who shot his lil soulja T2. As Gator inhaled the high grade Kush smoke he stared the young man down and thought back to when his lil soulja almost lost his life.

Just a few months ago 16 year old T2, Short for "Trained 2 go," a well-respected killer from Childs Ave, was walking out of the corner store Chicken & Pork, when he was robbed and shot point blank range by a gang of jack boys from the other side of the tracks. The beef stemmed from an incident a year ago when he and Gator were shooting dice downtown Newport News at Ma Ma's place when words were exchanged over a money dispute. Hearing the heated argument Ma Ma came rushing into the backroom to get the group of rowdy teens out of her house because she knew how Gator and T2 could get, but she was one second too late. Not the type to argue and having a short fuse for the bullshit, Gator pulled out his .40cal Sig and unloaded hot slugs into anyone who was in reach, while T2 joined the action emptying his .38 special into one of the teen's back as he tried to flee the scene. Leaving two dead on the scene and one paralyzed from the waist down, it's been war ever since.

His first thought was to walk up to him and push his shit back leaving his brains on the poorly decorated wall but just then he remembered he had left his gun in the car. This wasn't his part of town so the bouncers didn't know him well enough to let him in with his gun. Gator was deep in thought when Jux walked up beside him and passed him a bottle of Remy Martin. What's the word, look like you got something on your mind, you straight? Asked Jux.

"Bruh that's one of them Chestnut niggas who robbed and shot T2," said Gator never taking his eyes off of the target. Where he at point him out, said Jux. Right

19

there with that black skulky on standing by the Dj booth.

"Shit what up, we can go over there right now and smash him, said Jux. Naw bruh I got a better idea, said Gator as he signaled for Ma Ma to come have a chat with them. With the plan set in motion, Gator, Jux, and Poncho sat back and let Ma Ma work her magic.

After about fifteen minutes of the two of them flirting back and forth, they casually made their way outside to the parking lot and headed to his candy apple green box Chevy. Stalking their prey like a snake patiently stalking a rat, the three men waited outside by the dumpster for a few minutes before making their move. Gator had to get his Mac11 out of his car while Jux and Poncho already had their snub nose revolvers on them that they had somehow snuck in the club with them.

"Damn girl suck that dick just like that don't stop," said Wax as he lay back in his driver seat enjoying some of the best head he ever had in his life. With his head leaned back and eyes closed trying to savor every moment, he never noticed the three trained killers creeping up on the side of his car until it was too late. The first burst of bullets from the Mac11 lit up the night as they ripped through his chin sending chunks of his mouth and lower face flying in the passenger seat, while Jux and Poncho stood on the other side unloading there .38specials into his chest, face, and neck, leaving a crime scene so horrific one would've mistaken it for a scene out of a movie.

"Got damn y'all could've at least warned a bitch before y'all started shooting, now I got that bitch ass nigga blood all over my new Chanel dress," said Ma Ma as they quickly walked back to Gators Cadillac. Gator couldn't help but crack a smile at his lil ride or die chick while admiring the gangsta inside of her. There wasn't too many females who could play the position she was playing, that was that New Orleans running through her blood.

The next morning Gator lay in bed with Ma Ma sound asleep after a night filled of drugs, liquor, and wild sex. Hearing four loud knocks at his hotel room door he quickly snatched his 12 gauge pistol grip shotgun off the dresser and looked through the peep hole. Realizing that it was only Poncho he took his finger of the trigger and opened the door.

"Mane put some clothes on and put that big ass gun up it ain't nobody but me," said Poncho as he walked through the front door. By now Ma Ma was waking up so she passed Gator his pants then made her way to the bathroom to take a hot shower wearing nothing but a pair of laced panties with a tank top.

"What's up with baby girl? That lil ass fat as a muthafucka," said Poncho as he carefully watched her soft caramel ass jiggle with each step she took to the shower.
You know that's my lil gutta bitch mane, she claim she don't wanna fuck with nobody but me.

"Aww mane there you go with that handcuffing shit, I ain't tryna make her my girl I just wanna fuck her," said Poncho hoping is right hand man would give him the green light. I ain't even gone give you the run around bruh, that's shit a dead issue. Baby girl pussy too good to be sharing, "she got that good creole pussy that got a young nigga hooked!" said Gator as the two shared a laugh.

"What's the word tho, I know you ain't come through this early for nothing," said Gator as he began to break down the Kush weed on a $20 bill. Oh yea let me get that Mac. I already talked to Ray he on standby ready to buy all three guns from last night for a crazy number then he gon' shoot to NY, and sell em to his people for double.

21

"Come on Poncho you know how I feel about my Mac, I ain't tryna get rid of it just yet," said Gator as he dreaded the thought of getting rid of his rare sub machine gun.

"So you must be tryna go down for a homicide cause if you get jammed up with it that's exactly what's gon' happen," said Poncho with a straight face.

"Plus I got something better lined up for you," said Poncho with a wicked grin on his face. Oh yea what you got? I'll bring it by here later on this evening after I drop my old lady off at work, said Poncho as he placed Gator's murder weapon in a book bag then made his way out of the hotel. Gator knew Poncho was right but he just had to try his hand. He had been in numerous gun battles with that same Mac11 and came out on top every time. Some things were just hard to let go, and that was one of them.

Laying in the bed with Ma Ma Gator couldn't help but to think about the murder they pulled last night. The sight of Wax brains and skull fragments on the interior of his decked out old school brought a slight smile to his face as he blew the Kush smoke out of his nose. Right then and there he began thinking of his lil soulja T2 and decided to call his mother to see how he was holding up.

Hey Ms. Jackie what's going on? Hey Gator I'm glad you called, I just get off the phone with Tyquan and he asked about you. Oh yea, how he doing, he aight? Asked Gator. Yea he doing better, they just took him out of the medical block a few days ago and put him in population.

"He walking a lot better since they took those two bullets out of his back, so he's just taking it day by day," said Ms. Jackie. Oh okay I'm glad he doing better, I got some money for him too, I'll drop it off a lil later when I come around the way.

"Okay Gator I'll see you when you get out here," said Ms. Jackie before ending the call.

Gator felt his lil soulja's pain but at the end of the day its consequences when you thuggin. T2 was shot 5 times with a Tech9 leaving two bullets stuck in his back. If it wasn't for the rusty Tech9 jamming up he would've ended up with a hell of a lot more holes then just five so he was actually lucky. However, when he was in route to the hospital and they were trying to save his life, the paramedics found 19 grams of crack on him landing him a sentence of 18 to 24 months.

After another round of intimate Thug passion, Ma Ma and Gator were showered, dressed, and on their way out the door. As Gator pulled up to her project building she looked at him puzzled, "I thought you were taking me shopping," said Ma Ma as she reached over and turned down the music. Look lil moma I got some important business to handle but I'ma still take care of you like I said I would. Reaching into his deep pockets Gator pulled out his dope man knot and counted out $500 in all twenties then handed it to Ma Ma as she quickly stuffed it into her Chanel handbag trying to keep her nosy neighbors out of her business.

"I appreciate what you did for me last night that was some Trill shit," said Gator as he looked her in her puppy dog hazel eyes meaning every word he spoke. Yea well you know I'll do anything for you Gator, "but don't you ever in your fucking life ask me to do no shit like that again," said Ma Ma with a piercing look in her eyes. Gator couldn't do nothing but respect her mind, she was as Trill as they came.

So when you gon' make some more time for me so I can take care of him? By now Ma Ma had her hand on his crotch massaging his manhood through his jeans while staring into his soul with her enticing eyes and Gator couldn't help but crack a smile. I'ma get with you

23

in a couple days but check me out I need you to
understand me. About last night that shit stay between
us.

"You already know how the game go so if I hear
you been running your mouth you already know what
time it is," said Gator with a straight face.
A wave of disbelief and rage overwhelmed her body as
she sat there thinking to herself, "how far do I have to go
to prove my loyalty to this nigga?" Really Gator? Are
you fucking serious? By now the tears had welled up in
her eyes to capacity as she stared at him feeling the up
most disrespected by his blatant comment. Did I run my
mouth when I set up big Twan for you to rob? Did I run
my mouth when you and T2 killed those two niggas in
my aunt house a year ago? "Naw you kept it solid," said
Gator. I know I did cause I'ma Trill bitch. How many
times I gotta tell you I ain't nothing like the rest of them
bitches you be dealing with, I'll kill for you and I'll die
with you, but the fucked up part about it is you don't
even realize it.

Gator sat in the driver seat lost for words as his
mind digested the heart felt words she had just dropped
on him. He knew she was a soulja and was as Trill as
they came but sometimes you just gotta test the waters.
Attempting to mend her broken heart Gator leaned over
and kissed her on the lips then gently wiped away her
tears.

A few hours later Gator made his way across the
tracks and pulled up in front of Angel's house. Her front
porch was crowded as usual, with a mixture of hustlers,
smokers, and around the way hood bitches tryna smoke
up a young playa weed all day, so Gator decided to sit in
his car to avoid being harassed by the Felisha's of the
ghetto. Sitting in his Cadillac waiting on Poncho to pull
up, he began to pour himself a cup of syrup, it had been
almost two days since he had any codeine in his system

so the first few sips sent chills down his spine and relaxed his whole body. Moments later Angel stepped out of her house about to make her way to the store until she spotted Gator sitting in his car blocking her driveway.

What's up Lil daddy?

"So you was just gon' sit out here, block my driveway, and not come speak?" asked Angel in a playful but seductive tone as she leaned through the passenger side window.

"Girl you know I was gon' come holla at you, get in," replied Gator as he hit the unlock button for her. As Angel sat down on his soft leather seats her sweet fragrance lingered in the air causing Gator to lean over and kiss her on the neck.

"Damn you smell good girl," said Gator as he inhaled her Jimmy Choo perfume. You know Gator a real woman is always supposed to smell good for her man, you would know that if you had a real woman instead of a lil ass girl.
Gator began to smirk as he took a sip from his Styrofoam cup. He knew what she was insinuating but he didn't respond. In his eyes a true boss bitch shouldn't have to send shots to get her point across, her actions alone should be enough to secure what she wants. Besides, going tit for tat with a woman is something that a man of his caliber never indulges in.

This what I wanted to talk to you about, "you know your boy Wax got smoked last night at Pure Pleasure," said Angel as she sat in the seat sideways so she could make full eye contact with him while reading his body language. Wax?

"Who the fuck is Wax?" asked Gator trying to play it off like he didn't know who she was talking about. Boy stop playing dumb with me Gator, "Wax," the nigga from downtown who shot lil T2.

"Oh yea, how you find this out?" asked Gator trying to see exactly how much she knew.

"Shit you know how the streets talk, they say whoever killed him had to know him, and it was probably a personal vendetta cause they damn near blew is whole face off, could barely recognize him," said Angel as she began to feel empowered by telling the story.

Damn that's crazy, said Gator as he took sip from his cup then passed to her. Yea that shit is wild but the crazy part is they say the last person that was with him was that girl Ma Ma you be fucking with, and they tryna say she had something to do with it. Now this caught Gator's attention and struck a nerve as he locked eyes with her to see if she knew more then what she was revealing.

"So what else did they say?" asked a curious Gator. There was a few seconds of silence and uncertainty in the air before Angel replied, "That's all I heard."

Gator sat there in deep thought as he hit the blunt while thinking about what Angel had just dropped on him. He knew Ma Ma was a true soulja and would die before she even considered turning rat, he wasn't worried about her, he was more so worried about Angel.

"How the fuck did she know all of this?" is what Gator asked himself as he glanced at her out the corner of his eye.

His thoughts were interrupted by the vibration of his cell phone. Poncho what's the word my nig? I got that thang ready for you, where you at?

"I'm on Childs in front of Angel's crib," replied Gator before ending the call. A slight smile spread across his face as he wondered what kind of gun Ponch had for him. He knew whatever it was it had to be something exclusive because Poncho only dealt with

26

high quality firearms.

"Oh lord, there you go with that damn grin on your face," said Angel. You and that damn Poncho y'all keep some shit going. Gator cracked a smile then let his hand linger on her thigh as he slowly pulled off giving her a ride to the corner store.

No more than five minutes later Gator was pulling back up in front of Angel's place with Poncho right behind him.

"What's up mane, what you got for me big bruh?" said Gator as he stepped out of his Cadillac and approached Poncho who was parked behind him in a black Yukon. Jumping out of the SUV with a green duffle bag, Poncho led the way as they made their way inside Angels place.

I told you I had something better for you than that old ass Mac, said Poncho as he pulled out a brand new fully equipped AR15 with a 50 round clip. Gator examined his new assault rifle with a wicked grin on his face feeling like a kid on Christmas morning. Got damn Poncho you came through on this one, this the same type shit the S.W.A.T. team be using.

"Yea you know I do what I can my nig," said Poncho feeling proud that he made his lil soulja's day. Its three extra clips in the bag and if you flip that switch right there on the side it will switch it from semi-automatic to fully automatic.

"Poncho I don't know why you sold that boy that damn gun, you know he ain't got no mind, and he already got too many guns as it is," said Angel as she stood in the kitchen seasoning her pork chops with a disapproval look on her face. Shit he aight, one thing I learned in these streets is that you can never have, "too much money or too much guns," said Gator as he finished off Poncho's sentence for him.

"What's up with Ms. Jackie, she still got some

percocetes for sell?" asked Poncho as he scrolled
through his call list checking his missed calls.

"She should, let me call her and make sure," said
Gator as he pulled out his cell phone and hit her on
speed dial. Hey Aunt Jackie you still straight? Yea baby
but I only got a half bottle left, they been flying like hot
cakes so you better come get em. Ms. Jackie was the
local pharmacy for the Ghetto. Due to her age and health
issues she was constantly getting prescriptions for
percocets, codeine, xanez, etc., and she didn't mind
selling them to get a few extra dollars on the side.
Don't get lost out there in them streets Gator, you got me
in here cooking these pork chops for you, your ass better
come back. I got you girl damn calm down, I'll be right
back once I grab these pills, said Gator as he proceeded
to put his jacket on. Yea you better, "cause I'm tryna do
that reverse cowgirl thing again tonight," said Angel in a
whisper like tone but Poncho was still able to hear her.
Reverse cowgirl! Damn lil bruh you doing it big like
that, blurted out Poncho letting them know that their
secret was out the box. Gator couldn't help but crack a
smile as he grabbed his Glock off the table then passed
her the blunt he was smoking before walking out the
front door.

Ms. Jackie lived on the next street, Spruce St. so
instead of driving they decided to walk through the cut
by the train tracks. As soon as they hit Spruce they
spotted Ms. Jackie on her front porch drinking a glass of
Alize with a few of her friends.

"There go my nephew, come give your aunt a
hug," said Ms. Jackie felling the two glasses of Alize she
had already consumed.

After about 20 minutes of them enjoying each
other's company while floating off the percocets, they
never noticed the dark blue Nissan Altima that had
pulled up across the street. "Gator you know who this is

in this car right here?" asked Poncho as he clutched his P95 Ruger under his sweatshirt.

"Naw I don't know who that is bruh," replied Gator. As soon as he went to asked Ms. Jackie if she was expecting company he noticed the sudden movement in the backseat through the tinted windows.

Y'all go in the house Ms. Jackie, said Gator as he continued to stare down the mysterious Nissan. Boy I'm grown I, before she could get out another word all four doors flew open and all hell broke loose as the four gunmen opened fire on any and everything that was in their path. Gator and Poncho quickly drew their weapons and began firing back as the quiet dead end street turned into a scene they were both too familiar with.
With the sound of gunfire erupting and windows being shattered by the high powered assault rifles and sub machine guns, Ms. Jackie tried to get up and run in the house but was struck in the lower back and the back of her head with a Calico. Seeing Ms. Jackie get shot like that in front of him turned Gator into a madman. Walking up on the gunmen like he was the devil himself, Gator sent shot after shot from his .40cal Glock until his 30 round magazine was empty, hitting two of the gunmen on sight dropping them in front of the Nissan.

As the other two gunmen jumped into the car desperately trying to flee the scene they were met with a barrage of gunfire as Poncho hit the cut and chased them down. Running behind the van in the middle of the street, Poncho sent his last 11 shots through the back window hitting the driver several times in the back causing him to crash into oncoming traffic. The impact of the head on collision had very little effect on the passenger as he hoped out and ran, barely escaping with his life.
Running back down the street to where Gator was at, Poncho's heart went out to his right hand man as Gator

knelt down on one knee next to Ms. Jackie crying silently while trying to convince himself that she was going to be okay.

"Gator we gotta go bruh the law on their way out here we ain't got that much time!

"I can't leave her out here like this we gotta get her to a hospital," said Gator. Looking at the top left side of her head missing Poncho knew that Ms. Jackie was gone and it was no bringing her back. Once Poncho finally got Gator up off the ground he walked over to the two deceased gunmen lying in the middle of the street and went to put his signature stamp on them with two shots to the head but his gun only clicked, so instead he spat in both men's face before running off through the cut.

CH/3.

~

Over the course of the next few weeks Gator hid out in an upscale hotel on the outskirts of Richmond just until the streets died down some. A quadruple homicide in a drug infested neighborhood with over 80 shell casings left on the scene had the ATF and Feds crawling all over it. The funeral for Ms. Jackie was one week after her murder. Gator didn't attend because he was still too fucked up about the entire situation however, he did pay for the entire funeral with the help of Poncho and sent T2 a nice piece of change to help ease his mind.
Ma Ma had been on his mind a lot lately so he sent for her to come chill with him and keep him company while he was laying low. His 18th birthday was in a few days so since wasn't the mood for partying he figured he would just kick back get high and explore the tender body of his ride or die chick. While resting in the king size bed with nothing on but his Ralph Lauren boxers, Gators' phone began to ring. The only calls he had been taking were those of his mother, Jux, & Poncho, but Angel had been blowing him up all weekend so he decided to take her call figuring it was important.

Angel what's the word? As soon as Ma Ma heard the name Angel she stopped rolling the blunt and cautiously looked at Gator to see what was going on. She had heard some wicked stories pertaining to Angel but she knew how Gator felt about her so she tried her best to stay clear of that topic. "Shit you tell me what's up, you the one that's been MIA for the last two weeks," said Angel with a slight attitude in her tone. Come on girl you already know what time it is, I'm ducked off right now. Yea I can see that, so who you with? asked

Angel as if she were is mother or his woman.

I'm with Ma Ma, why what's up? As soon as Angel heard the name Ma Ma her face turned sour. As much as she hated to admit it, she had caught feelings for the young hustler, and all of that good dick he was feeding her was beginning to fuck with her mind.

"I see you must really be feeling this Ma Ma girl, y'all been spending a hell of a lot of time together lately," said Angel with a hint of animosity in her voice.

"Yea that's my lil soulja but what's up with all these questions?" asked Gator as he was becoming irritated with the conversation.

You know what Gator fuck it. I called you to let you know that my uncle got a pint of syrup he tryna get rid of and you were the first person who came to mind so where you at? It had been two whole weeks since Gator had any codeine in his system and as bad as he wanted to pour up and get the monkey off his back, he just couldn't chance it. He didn't think Angel would turn him in to the authorities, but at the same time when there's a $10,000 reward for any information leading to an arrest, you had to be cautious about everyone. Look I'm out of town right now just hold it for me until I get back. There was a few seconds of silence on the phone before Gator heard the dial tone; Angel had hung up on him.

Sitting down trying to enjoy the breakfast that the five star hotel had prepared for him, Gator could sense that something was on Ma Ma's mind.

"What's up lil moma look like you got something on your mind, you aight?" asked Gator as he cut into his fluffy pancakes with his butter knife. Ma Ma sat there for a minute contemplating on whether or not she wanted to open that door and speak on another woman, but at the same time she felt he had the right to know. Look Gator it ain't really my place to be speaking on other women who you deal with, but at the same time

I wouldn't feel right if I didn't bring it to your attention. Wiping his mouth with a napkin, he leaned back in his chair then replied, "Talk to me."

I'ma cut straight to the chase, your girl Angel ain't right, I don't think she can be trusted. I know you probably heard all of the stories about niggas killing one other behind her pussy, but they ain't the only ones doing the killing. Angle used to deal with one of my older brothers' friend named Fat Pat. Fat Pat was getting some serious money when he met Angel and my brother told him to fall back from her because she was treacherous but Fat Pat wouldn't listen, he thought my brother just wanted her for himself.

One day my brother had called Fat Pat because he needed to re-up so Fat Pat told him to meet him at his spot. Once my brother got there the front door was halfway open and he found his friend in the bed ass naked with two gunshots to his head and his whole stash emptied out. Word got back that Angel had fucked him to sleep, killed him then ran off with over 80 grand. Gator had hear a similar story but he thought it was all a myth.

"I know you gon' do you Gator just be careful when you dealing with her," said Ma Ma as she walked over and sat on his lap while caressing the side of his smooth chocolate face. Gator sat there and inhaled the Kush filled blunt as his mind absorbed everything Ma Ma had just brought to his attention. He always knew in the back of his mind that Angel had the potential to be a shysty bitch, but he also knew that she would never try to pull that shit on him off the strength of the type of bond they shared, not to mention she knew first hand that he was a stone cold killer. With a lot weighing on his 17 year old mind Gator crushed up three xanez bars, dropped it in a bottle of orange juice, and sipped away until he dozed off.

Over the next couple of days Ma Ma and Gator explored one another's body as if they were the last two people left on earth. Ma Ma pleased Gator in ways of which he never knew existed, and in return Gator met her match as her fulfilled her every wish and command. Gator learned a lot about Ma Ma during their time spent together in Richmond. She opened up to him about her life story letting him in on things that she had never revealed to anyone before, even her most vulnerable moments.

Ma Ma was born in 1990 in New Orleans Louisiana, raised in the Magnolia projects of uptown. Her father was a well-known pimp throughout the South but he was never in her life. He would fluctuate throughout the South pimping different groups of women two or three years at a time than once things got too hot or money slowed up he would relocate leaving his women to fend for themselves.

Ma Ma's mother was a heroin addict and a prostitute. However, she wasn't always like that , she used to be a fun, loving, outgoing, young lady full of life, until she met Pretty Tony who turned her life upside down. Once he got her hooked on heroin and was satisfied with the amount of money he made off pimping her, he left town leaving her with a heroin addiction, prostitute lifestyle, and a 7 month baby girl.

A day in her life that Ma Ma would never forget is when she came home from school one day in the fourth grade and her life was drastically changed forever. Sitting in the living room drinking a bottle of Night Train was her mother Pearl along with one of her dealers as ten year old Ma Ma walked through the front door. Attempting to make her way to her room she was stopped by her mother before she could make it down the hallway. Hey my sweet baby, your moma needs your help, do you love your moma? asked Pearl as she continuously tapped her foot on the floor as the long Camel cigarette hung from her dry lips. Shaking her head up and down the innocent ten year old girl replied, "Yes."

Well look baby I need you to take this man in your room and be nice to him, if you love mommy you will be nice to him and do what he says. Ma Ma didn't know what was going on but she knew whatever it was it wasn't right. With tears welled up in her eyes as the dealer escorted her to her bedroom, she tried her hardest to fight the man off with her little fist while screaming for her mother's help but it was to no avail as he overpowered her, locked her room door, and had his way with her.

Over the course of the next few months whenever her mother didn't have enough money for her heroin she would use her ten year old daughter as a cash crop to get high. After months of having her mind, body, and soul, broken down into pieces so tiny that no one could find them, she decided to save her own self as she came home from school one afternoon with a gun in her book bag refusing to be a victim of this man's filthy fetishes any longer. Three days later her mother needed her to "be nice" to Black again, little did she know, her ten year old innocent daughter had a surprise waiting for the sick child molester. As Black closed the door behind him and proceeded to take his shirt off, Ma Ma reached into her book bag pulling out a .25 automatic hand gun and repeatedly unloaded shot after shot into her molesters' chest, stomach, and face, until her tiny fingers were no longer able to squeeze the trigger. Thinking fast she took all of his cash out of his pocket then caught a Greyhound bus to her aunt's house in Virginia where she never looked back.

Ma Ma was hesitant about revealing her past to Gator because she figured that he may look down on her, but in all actuality it drew him closer to her. The more he learned about her the more he felt her pain and struggle. Gator didn't realize it but he was also slowly falling love. The following day they decided to hit the city and do some shopping just to get some fresh air and get out of the hotel room. After a couple hours of them touring the city Gator began to get agitated. The two weeks without any codeine in his system was starting to get the best of him and Ma Ma sensed it. Picking up on his body language she went on and asked him, "what's wrong Gator, you need a cup don't you?" Gator cracked a slight smile and shook his head from side to side then replied,

"It must be written all over my face ugh?" Ma Ma laughed then replied, "yea it definitely his."

"I might be able to help ease you mind I just hope she ain't change her number by now," said Ma Ma as she searched through her purse for her phone. Who you calling? asked Gator. My sister Tammy, that girl plugged in with damn near everything she should be able to point us in the right direction, said Ma Ma as she scrolled through her call list.

About 20 minutes later Gator pulled up in the driveway of a teal green duplex house with old paint chipping off the sides in the Highland Park area of Richmond. Once inside Ma Ma was greeted with hugs and kisses from several different women who were all beautiful but one in particular stood out the most catching Gator's attention. With dark green eyes, smooth rich butterscotch skin complexion, and jet black crinkly hair that she wore in a Mohawk, to say she was beautiful was an understatement. "That gotta be her sister," said Gator to himself as he discreetly eyed her breathtaking 5'9 frame.

Tammy was Ma Ma's half-sister, they shared the same father but not the same mother. Tammy was five years older than Ma Ma and was born and raised in

Memphis. Just like Ma Ma's situation Tammy's mother was a victim of her father's seduction and pimp game. The only difference in the situations was that once Tammy's mother gave birth to her she cleaned her life up and never touched another drug or sold another ounce of pussy again. Her father Pretty Tony also lived with them until Tammy was about 5 or 6, unlike in Ma Ma's case which he abandoned her mother and her at only 7 months old.

Growing up on the North side of Memphis Tammy got involved with the drug game early at just 16. Off the strength of her father's name alone who was originally from Memphis, she was able the move freely through the trenches and soon began to catch the eye of the notorious Vice Lords. After putting in work on the shysty streets of North Memphis for several years, the Vice Lords noticed it and offered her a seat at the table that would ultimately change her life forever.
Seizing the opportunity to gain money, power, and respect, Tammy took the slums of Memphis by the horns and ruled with an iron fist. What they didn't expect was the amount of mayhem, destruction, and bloodshed, she would bring to the city once in the position of power. After four straight years of brutal, senseless homicides, and enormous amounts of heroin being distributed throughout the city, Tammy's name began to fluctuate amongst the Feds so she hoped on a plane and moved east to Virginia to avoid being indicted.

"Tammy this is Gator, he's the one I've been telling you about," said Ma Ma introducing the two. Hey Gator nice to finally meet you.

"So you're the one that's been giving my sister the run around all these years," said Tammy with her hands on her hips as she stared Gator up and down. Gator looked over at Ma Ma for an explanation but all he got was a smile as she shook her head from side to side.

37

From that statement alone he could tell that they had been having conversations about him, he didn't know if that was a good thing or a bad thing.

After they all got acquainted Tammy called Gator into the kitchen to discuss some business.

"So what's up lil daddy what you tryna get?" asked Tammy as she leaned up against the refrigerator with her arms crossed over her chest.

"Shit I'm tryna get a whole pint if you got it," replied Gator. Walking over to the cabinet by the sink, Tammy bent over right in front of him giving him a full view of her cornbread fed phat ass. The top of her purple thong could been seen as she bent over damn near touching causing Gator to get slightly aroused but he had to remind himself she was Ma Ma's sister and quickly pull himself together.

Gator was surprised to see her emerged from up under the sink with a whole case of syrup.

"Damn girl I aint know you was on like that," said Gator with a bit of surprise in his tone. Just as she put the case down on the counter she looked up and the two of them locked eyes for a brief moment. Gator was caught up in the moment and mesmerized by her beauty. It was something about those almond shape dark green eyes that had him in a trance and Tammy must've felt something herself cause she was found herself lost in his gaze as well.

Their unspoken chemistry was interrupted as Ma Ma walked into the kitchen and handed him the blunt she was smoking. "I ain't interrupting y'all business am I? Asked Ma Ma. Naw baby girl you good. I ain't know your sister was rocking like this I should've been linked up with her. Gator ended up buying four pints of syrup at $700 a piece which was a lookout for him cause he normally paid $1,000 flat for one pint.

Over the course of the next couple hour the three

38

of them at soul food, took shots of Remy, and laughed and joked as if they knew each other their entire lives. Finally feeling comfortable enough Tammy decided to ask Gator the question she had been contemplating on asking him the entire evening. She knew a hustler when she saw one and she figured they could make a lot of money together. Let me ask you something Gator, what you know about the heroin game? Gator looked at Ma Ma with a screwed up face for an explanation. Wiping her face with her napkin then taking a sip of her cold water Ma Ma casually replied, "she good people, you can trust her."

For the next half hour the two of them discussed heroin prices, quality, and trafficking mechanisms, as if they were in Wall St. By the end of the conversation Gator had agreed to purchase 4 and 1/2 ounces of heroin for 9 grand and in return she would front him another 4 and 1/2 on consignment. Gator would end up with 9 ounces of heroin with a street value of close to 50 grand. He only had 13 grand to his name so he was taking risk by spending such a large amount on the dope, but he figured if the dope was as raw as she said it was then he would make a killing so the risk was well worth taking.

CH/4.

~

Over the next 6 months Gator ran through the streets of Hampton like he owned them and just as Tammy assured him, the heroin was so raw that he ran through the first 9 ounces in only eight days. Gator had the streets on lock in a matter of weeks. He had so much traffic fluctuating back N forth on Childs ave that he had to set up another trap house on Spruce St. just to manage the heavy flow of traffic. Gator broke down every ounce piece by piece and dealt strictly with dope heads while Poncho and Jux sold weight to small time dealers throughout the city causing them to take over and rule with an iron fist.

After about a year run minus a few losses, things began to fall in place for Gator and his team. He was now purchasing a brick and a half of heroin on his own and no longer dealing with the hand to hand break down part of the game, it was too time consuming. Every time he would re- up he would drop 4 and a 1/2 ounces off on Angel which was twice a month. In return she would bag up the heroin in bundles and make around 25 grand every two weeks for him. At the end of the month he would collect his money from her while giving her a well-deserved cut of 15 grand so at the end of the day everyone was eating.

"Why you keep dealing with this bitch? I told you she was shysty," said Ma Ma as they pulled up on Childs ave in his brand new smoke grey S550 Benz to collect his money from Angel. Look Ma Ma, Ima tell you like I told you before, she pull that shit on them weak niggas who she feel can get over on, she know better than to even think about pulling that shit on me.

She know I'll kill her and everybody she's with if she cross me, said Gator with a hint of arrogance behind his words. Aight Gator you got it, it's your world, said Ma Ma as she threw her hands up gesturing he had won. Here roll this blunt while I step in here handle this business, I'll be right back, said Gator as he handed her a box of dutches and an ounce of sour diesel before exiting the car.

Gator entered Angel's house without knocking because now he was like God in his hood and had the keys to the city. Once inside he was greeted by Angel's home girls, Auriell, Chocolate Ty, and Stacy. Ladies, Ladies, what's the word, y'all aight? asked Gator as he gave each woman a friendly hug. Yea we good, but I would be doing a whole lot better if I had some of this in my life, said Chocolate Ty as she grabbed a hand full of his manhood through his white Evisu jeans. Go head girl I ain't fucking with you Chocolate Ty, said Gator as he cracked a smile then made his way down the hallway. Making his way towards Angel's room the sound of shower water running could be heard coming from her bathroom. Knowing it was Angel inside he slightly opened the door telling her to hurry up and that he had places to be. A few minutes later Angel entered her room wearing nothing but a towel as Gator sat on the edge of her bed sipping a cup of syrup. Damn girl it took yo ass long enough, you knew I was on my way over here why you ain't have my shit ready for me? Angel didn't reply she just reached into the top of her closet and threw a Foot Locker shoe box at him then casually replied, " you gon' stop underestimating me one of these days."
Once Gator finished counting the money and put her 15 grand to the side, he stood up to hand it to her but was thrown off guard when he noticed her ass naked on the bed with her legs wide open playing with her perfectly trimmed pussy. Come taste your pussy, then I want you

to hit it from the back, "said Angel as she began to massage her clit. Gator watched her closely as she put on a show for him by fingering her tight wet pussy, while slowly licking her Hershey colored nipples.

Walking over to the bed to assist her and get an early quickie, he remembered that he had Ma Ma in the car waiting on him.

"Why you stalling baby boy this pussy ain't go'n fuck its self," said Angel as she continued to lay in the middle of the bed with her legs wide open.

"I can't even fuck with you right now I just remembered I got Ma Ma in the car waiting on me," said Gator with a hint of disappointment in his voice. Truth be told it was like night and day when it came to Angel and Ma Ma. With Angel he could have his way with her, bust on her face, tea bag her, hit her in the ass, with Ma Ma it was more of a sensual thing.

Ma Ma? Fuck Ma Ma, I know she can't suck your dick better than this, said Angel as she sat up on the edge of the bed pulling Gator closer to her while unbuckling his pants. Once his manhood was free from his boxers and in her hand she wasted no time taking all eight inches of him into her warm mouth in one gulp. Sucking and stroking him at the same time Gator had to admit she had the best head he had ever ran across. Every time he would look down at her, his entire dick would disappear in her mouth and reemerge 10 times wetter than before. After about six minutes of her relentless super head attack, Gator could no longer take it as he filled the back of her throat with his warm thick nut causing his knees to buckle.

Sitting on the edge of the bed licking her lips and fingers like she just had a bucket of Kentucky fried chicken, Angel had just dominated Gator and she didn't even know it. The way she put that head on him had him weak in the knees ready to tell her he loved her! As she lay back on the bed with her legs open softly patting her fat cat she asked him, "so when you gon' come back and take care of this business right here?" As bad as he wanted to say fuck Ma Ma and take a dive in the big juicy pussy he just couldn't.

"Yo ass crazy girl, Ima slide through here later on tonight and fuck with you," said Gator as he zipped his pants back up, still trying to pull himself together. Gator couldn't resist Angel, she was like a dose of heroin to a recovering addict. He knew she ain't mean him no good, but to leave her alone was easier said than done.

Back inside the car Ma Ma sat patiently waiting on Gator as she inhaled the Kush smoke while listening to her favorite Aaliyah song "At your best." As much as she disliked the fact that he was dealing with Angel, she accepted it and played her position accordingly because she knew Angel was bringing in close to 50 grand a month for him so she would never come between him and his paper. She just wished that he would understand where she was coming from and look at the bigger picture, but when it came to Angel he couldn't see past that big monkey in between her legs.

As the day went on Gator and Ma Ma rode through the city picking up money and dropping off dope all the way from the Rip Rap area of Hampton, to the downtown area of Newport News. A lot of hustler stop doing business after dark and were skeptical about serving other dealers in neighborhoods such as Queen St, Shell Rd, Park Place, and downtown Newport News, but Gator didn't give a fuck. He was well respected by the killers and robbers because he had been putting his murder game down since he was fifteen. Not to mention he kept Ma Ma at his side at all times and he knew if shit got thick she wouldn't hesitate to slang some iron with him. That's why he loved her so much, her loyalty to him had no limitations.

Around 2am. Gator decided to hang it up and hit the after hour spot for some drinks. The Moonlight wasn't your typical after hour spot, some would even consider it a death trap. A shabby rundown building only big enough to fit 40 or 50 people, one way in one way out, was home to the hustlers, robbers, killers, and Alley cat bitches after 2am. Bitches were fucking in the pissy bathroom for $50, the bartender was selling drinks for $10 pieces of crack while getting high in the back, and the task force was known to do a random sweep through and shake everybody down. Despite all of that, it was still a "Gangstas Paradise."

Gator was a regular at the moonlight. He had been going there since he was 15 so he was well acquainted with the owner and bouncers, meaning he had plenty of clout. He and his team were never searched at the door so they were fully armed at all times and that's what Gator loved about it the most.
Pulling up to the parking lot in his pearl white .745 on 22 inch rims, one could say that the 18 year old hustler, baller, Gangsta, cap peeler, was definitely feeling himself. Minutes later Poncho pulled up beside him in his grey Rang Rover blasting Lil Boosie, "Swerve on em," with a back seat full of Hampton University bitches who were all turned up to the max yearning the attention of a real street nigga. As Gator sat in the Parking lot waiting on Poncho to finish rolling his blunts so they could all enter the club at the same time, he decided to check his voicemail.

The first message was from his mother, "hey baby I ain't seen or heard from you in the past few days, I'm just checking on you making sure you still alive. I'm cooking a big dinner Sunday make sure you stop by and bring Ma Ma with you." Gator glanced over at Ma Ma and cracked a smile, thinking to himself, "yea she must be the right one cause moma don't fuck with none of my

44

other girls. The next message was from Angel, "danm Gator that's how you do? Its 11:53 I been waiting on you all night, call me when you get this message. Third message; "Yea Gator it's me Angel, its 1:17 and you still haven't returned my call, looks like you stood me up for the second time in a row, and I even cooked for you. I don't know what you take me as, but I ain't one of them bitches to be played with."

Gator shook his head from side to side and told himself he was done fucking Angel. She had made it clear several times that their relationship was strictly sex so why was she trippin? Right then and there Gator decided to keep their relationship strictly business and stay out of her "K.P." He wasn't feeling the wave of unsteady emotions Angel was bringing to the table, so to avoid a catastrophe before it occurred, Gator had to leave her alone.

Stepping out of his .745 with Ma Ma on his side Gator looked and felt like a mill ticket. Dressed in a in a grey Chanel sweatshirt, white Evisu jeans, with a pair of suede grey high top Prada sneaker. Ma Ma was also killing the game rocking a pair of burgundy Dolce & Gabbana jeans that hugged her small waist and Apple bottom ass perfectly, a burgundy and black Gucci collar shirt, with a pair of high rising Gucci sandals that complimented her entire wardrobe. Her thick, wavy, goldish brown hair, was now tied up in a bun the way Gator liked it.

Once inside the club the six of them made their way to the back by the pool table where they normally post up at and were greeted with daps and hugs by the other hustlers and night life women. Once the DJ noticed Gator and Poncho in the building he gave them a shout out and started playing a gang of three six Mafia, Master P, and Boosie, that's when the real party began. There were only two strip poles in the small rundown shack but

45

that meant nothing as strippers began coming out of the wood work, even dancing on tables to get the attention of the two young ballers. You see, in the Moonlight, anything goes, so once Gator and Poncho started popping rubber bands, they turned their small section in the back of the club into a girl on girl orgy show.

With blunts of OG Kush and sour diesel being passed back N forth all night, everything was all gravy in the Gangstas paradise as Ma Ma stood in front of Gator holding his hand while slowly grinding her soft ass all over his growing manhood. Looking out the corner of her eye as she as she gyrated her hips to the rhythm of the Master P song "Bounce dat ass," she spotted Angel along with her three sidekicks strolling through the door. Ma Ma knew Angel had a bit of animosity in her heart towards her, but hey, it wasn't her fault. The way she saw it, as long as Angel stayed in her lane there would be no static.

CH/5.

~

       Sitting at the bar Angel ordered her and her friends all double shots of Hennessey. She was tired of sitting in the house waiting on Gator to come put that Track Life dick on her so she decided to step out and snatch her another young baller to get her mind right. Angel was a bad bitch who had her paper together so other hustlers were dying to get a taste of that sweet pussy, it was just something different and intriguing about Gator that made her feel like every other man was just in the way.

Her thoughts were interrupted by Chocolate Ty as she walked up behind her and put her arm across her shoulder, "girl look there go Gator right there." Angel turned around in her bar stool and got a salty taste in her mouth when she saw Gator and Ma Ma hugged up rapping along to the Pimp C lyrics. Her eyes saw red as she thought about walking back there causing a scene but that would've been childish and below her character. Ordering another round of drinks for herself and her girls, Angel took a deep pull from the Kush filled blunt then said to herself, "that's aight, I got a trick for his ass."

Ch5/ The following few weeks for Gator and his team sailed by smoothly. Tammy kept her word and was consistent with the product, while he, Jux, & Poncho, were like the Hot Boyz in '98. Gator had surprisingly stuck to his word and fell back from fucking Angel, he assumed that she would show resentment, or get on some childish shit and start acting a fool, but surprisingly she was cool with it.

Leaving the car dealership across the water in Virginia

Beach, Gator had just purchased Ma Ma a brand new Lexus LS400. There was no way in hell she was going to dealing with a hustler of his caliber and not own a car, Gator didn't rock like that. Being that it was close to the end of the month Gator decided to call Angel and check on that bread. After dropping 40 grand cash on the Lexus for Ma Ma, he had to get that money right back.

Angel what's the word, said Gator as he floated his S550 up the interstate with Ma Ma behind him. I'm cooling, sitting here counting this money up, said Angel and wrapped a rubber band around the last stack of money.

"Okay cool, we looking?" asked Gator. How we looking? Naw lil daddy you mean how "I'm" looking. Gator pulled the phone away from his ear and looked at it as if he had heard wrong.

Look girl stop playing with me, I'll be at your crib in bout twenty, have that ready for me. Angel began laughing in his ear on the other ended of the phone. You really think I'm playing don't you? Well let me make myself clear, that 46 grand I made for you this month is MINE, those three AK47's you left in my closet are MINE, and that half brick of dope you stashed under my sink is MINE. I told you I ain't one of them bitches to be played with but you just wouldn't listen.

Gator hung up the phone, threw it in the passenger seat and did about 100mph down the interstate all the way to Angel's house. With his snub nose .44 glued to his hand Gator had murder written all over his face as he recklessly pulled up to her house knocking over the two green trash cans she had out front. Jumping out of his car with gun in hand, Gator stormed through her front door but was surprised when he saw that it was empty, furniture and all. Thinking fast he ran to the bathroom to see if the half brick of heroin was still under the sink and just as he expected, it was gone.

48

Days, weeks, then months had passed by and there was still no sign of Angel. Word around town was that she had fled to Atlantic City with her new man and was running through Gator's money like there was no tomorrow. He thought about putting a nice piece of change on her head but after taking a big lost like that he decided against it.

Laid back in his three bedroom condominium he shared with Ma Ma in Virginia Beach, Gator let the purple codeine ease his mind as he and Ma Ma watched "Waiting to exhale" on their 60 inch flat screen. Just as he was about to nod off again from the effects of the potent codeine his cell phone rang, bringing him back to reality. Big Jux what's the word my nig? I can't call it mane, I been out here politicking and networking for the past few days and I was able to scrape up some good info for you. Sensing that it was something important Gator sat up and was all ears as he removed himself from Ma Ma's arms who was now sound asleep. I'm listening big bruh, talk to me.

I found out who Angel ran off with, some jack boy from Aberdeen named Tone. I guess they ran through that 50 grand while they were down there splurging in Atlantic City now they back in VA. Oh yea? I need an exact location, said Gator as he inserted the 50 round clip into his AR15. You see that's the thing, I know they're back in town but I don't know exactly where, but with a little more time I'll be able to come up with something. Oh yea before I forget, that nigga Tone she fucking talking real crazy too, "talking bout he gon kill you when he see you," said Jux as he and Gator began to laugh.

"Yea she been putting that "KP" on him, he don't even know he bout to dead right along with that bitch," said Gator as he and Jux continued to laugh.
If Angel thought her taking those three assault rifles

49

from Gator was going to leave him unarmed or put a dent in his artillery she was sadly mistaken. Gator collected guns like a stripper collected high heels. He had all type of shit from Calicos, to Saiga 12 semiautomatic shotguns, to mini 14's, and didn't mind using them.

Over the next few days Gator was on the hunt for Angel and whoever was in her vicinity. Lurking through the city in a low key Buick with his fully equipped AR15 and two .38's, Gator was on a mission. Poncho & Jux both had told him to fall back and let her come to him but Gator refused to entertain that idea. In his mind he would feel like a cold pussy if he just sat there and did nothing while waiting on her to show her face.

After a five day stretch of being on the hunt with no shower or sleep, Gator decided to hang it up for the day and go regroup. All of the ecstasy pills he had been taking to keep him awake and alert was beginning to take a toll on his mind and body so the last thing he wanted was to get pulled over for falling asleep at the wheel. With the type of record he had along with the arsenal of firearms in his possession he would be looking at 15-20 years easy.

"Damn baby you look like shit," said Ma Ma as Gator walked through the front door and dropped his duffel bag on the floor by the couch. "I feel like shit," replied Gator in a groggy tone of voice. While Gator indulged in a much needed long, hot, shower, Ma Ma fixed him a plate of hot food and rolled him a king size blunt filled with sour diesel and dipped in codeine just the way he likes it. It had been almost a full week since she last felt him deep inside of her so her young ripe body was body was yearning for his affection in every kind of way.

Showered and well fed, Gator lay back in his

king size bed with nothing on but his silk Armani boxers taking pulls from the Boss Hog blunt Ma Ma had rolled for him.

"You have any luck today?" asked Ma Ma as she rubbed his entire body down with lotion beginning with his feet.

"Hell naw, it's like that bitch hiding up under a rock somewhere," replied Gator as he flicked the ashes into the ashtray. Well, don't let it stress you out, you'll find her.

"In the meantime just sit back, relax and get your mind focused on me," said Ma Ma as she finished rubbing his body down then gave him a peck on the lips. Ma Ma made her way to the shower to go freshen up. She had plans on giving Gator a night of Thug Passion that would rid his mind of all the worries and stress he was carrying on his young shoulders. Popping the seal on her new $600 Christian Louboutin perfume, she sprayed a light mist on her neck and wrist before slipping into her two piece Dolce & Gabbana bra and panty set. All freshened up while looking like she belonged in a "Straight Stunntin" magazine, Ma Ma made her way to the master bedroom but was filled with great disappointment when she noticed Gator sound asleep snoring with the blunt still hanging from his lips.

The next morning Ma Ma woke up around 9am and Gator was still knocked out. Looking at how peaceful he was sleeping she figured he needed the rest so she let him sleep in while she hit the city and made a few errands. After picking up a few appliances for their condo Ma Ma decided to place a call to set an appointment at her nail salon where she was a regular at. Just her luck there was an opening slot for her in the next hour so she made her way to "Pearls elite palace" in the Ocean view area of Norfolk.

Pearls elite palace was a high end salon where

you had to have a nice piece of change to acquire their
services. It was to home to a lot of independent, money
driven women with careers, but there main source of
clientele were women of big time drug dealers. Ma Ma
had been a regular for the past year so all of the women
who worked their treated her like family.
Sitting back in the plush suede sofa scrolling through a
XXL magazine, Ma Ma waited patiently for her stylist to
call her name. While reading an article on Alicia Keys,
she just so happen to glance up and notice a familiar face
walking through the front door. Not sure if her mind was
playing tricks on her or not, she double looked and sho
nuff, it was Angel. Telling her stylist that she had a
family emergency to attend to and that she would
reschedule her appointment, Ma Ma quickly left the
salon.

"Look at that scary ass bitch," said Angel talking
to her boyfriend Tone. The only time she go hard is
when that nigga Gator around, you catch her by herself
she softer than baby shit. The shysty couple shared a
laugh as they joked about how Ma Ma ran out if the
Salon as soon as she caught a glimpse of Angel.
Sitting in the parking lot of the salon Ma Ma desperately
tried calling Gator several times but got no answer.

"He pick the perfect time not to answer his damn
phone", said Ma Ma as she repeatedly tapped her finger
on the steering wheel. Thinking of what Gator would
want her to do in a situation of this sort she went with
her first instinct.

About forty five minutes later Angel was exiting
the salon with her freshly manicured nails and Tone
right behind her. It was Wednesday so her and her girls
were stepping out to the popular club, "The Alley" for
wild out Wednesday. Waiting on Tone to unlock the
door as she examined her nails she never noticed Ma Ma
crouched down creeping up from behind until it was too

late. The first two bullets from the snub nose .38 special ripped through her back while the third one struck her in the neck causing he whole body to lock up as she awkwardly fell to the pavement. Never being in a situation like this before Tone was distraught as a he frantically fumbled with his pistol trying to get it out of his waist band but was too slow as Ma Ma ran on the other side of the car and gunned him down.

Around 2:30 in the afternoon Gator was just waking up. He looked around for Ma Ma but she was nowhere in sight so he picked up the piece of folded up paper on the nightstand which read,(Good morning my love, I stepped out to run a few errands and to get my feet and nails done, I know how you like to kiss on my pretty feet and suck on my manicured toes while you're deep in my guts with my feet resting on your shoulders so I wanted to get them extra nice for you, Love Ma Ma.) Gator couldn't help but crack a smile as he thought to himself how on point she was and how she knew him like the back of her hand.

With Ma Ma on his mind he decide to call her just to send some love her way. As soon as he picked up his phone he realized that he had seven missed calls from her, causing an eerie feeling throughout his body. Hoping nothing was wrong he hit her number on speed dial and waited for her to pick up.

After calling him several times back to back she finally picked up. What's up baby you aight? Asked Gator. Yea I'm good but I can't talk right now, meet me at the house in twenty minutes. Aight, say no more. As Gator went to hang up he heard her voice coming through the other end of the receiver, Gator! Yea I'm here what's up? I love you.

The ride was silent for the first ten minutes with the exception of some old smooth Shirley Murdock playing as Gator floated his .745 up the interstate to who

knows where. After she had given him the rundown on
the whole situation and how everything transpired, the
only thing he could think of was how she had put her
freedom and life on the line for him. Right then and
there he knew she was the one who he wanted to spend
the rest of his life with and he would go above and
beyond to protect her and keep her safe.

"You aight?" asked Gator as he reached over
and gently rubbed his hand up and down her thigh. Yea
I'm good, said Ma Ma as she glanced at him through
watery eyes while trying to wear a fake smile on her
face. Angel's life wasn't the first life she had taken but
for some reason it felt like it. Back when she was just ten
years old she was forced to take the life of her molester
but this was different.
Laying in the bed of a low key hotel on the outskirts of
D.C. Ma Ma was awaken by the constant ringing of
Gators cell phone.

"Gator baby wake up, your phone been ringing
all morning," said Ma Ma becoming irritated with the
constant ringing. Her words fell on deaf ears as Gator lay
in bed slightly snoring from one too many xanez bars the
previous night.

Ma Ma had been dealing with Gator since they
were 15 so she knew exactly his to get him out of one of
his deep sleeps. Peeling the covers of his half naked
body she slowly wrestled his manhood out of his boxers
and began stroking it slowly while planting soft wet
kisses all around the tip. Once she felt him move a little
she took it a step further by licking it with a wet slow
rhythm starting with his balls and ending with the tip of
the head.

By now Gator was fully awake sparking the
blunt on the nightstand that he was too high to finish the
previous night. " Oh Naw don't stop now, you wanted to
wake me up now I'm up, said Gator as he lay back

resting his head on the pillow yearning for the sensation of her soft pretty lips all over his manhood. You know I always finish what I start but right now I think you need to call Poncho cause he been blowing you up all morning, " I got a feeling its important," said Ma Ma dreading the news that Poncho might have for them. Moments later Gator was on the phone with Poncho. Big bruh, what's the word my nig? "Mane I been calling you all morning tryna give you the scoop, where you at?" asked Poncho. Shit I'm ducked off right now Ima just text you the address. What he say baby? Asked a concerned Ma Ma as Gator ended the call. You know we don't talk over no phones, he should be up here in about 3 or 4 hours, said Gator as he began texting him the address.

As Ma Ma finished brushing her teeth she walked over to the bed and sat next to Gator. "So what do you think is so important that he gotta drive 4 hours just to tell you," asked Ma Ma. I don't know, but whatever it is it can't be good.

Ma Ma sat there in silence for a few seconds before picking his hand up and placing it in the palm of her soft hand. As she began Caressing his hand while staring into his eyes she told him the realest shit ever. Listen to me Gator, When I say I'll ride for you and I'll die with you, I mean it from the bottom of my heart. I did what I did cause that bitch stepped out of line and crossed you, and I know you would've did the same for me. I don't give a fuck about nothing in this world, as long as I got you I could die tomorrow and be fine with it.

Staring back into her puppy dog hazel eyes, Gator wiped away a single tear as it slid down her left cheek. Truth be told he was a little choked up by her heart felt words as he felt his eyes began to water up himself. Without another word being said he leaned over and began passionately tongue kissing her as if he would never see her again. Caressing her soft Bcup breast, Gator made his way to her neck and began planting soft kisses from one side of her neck to the other while massaging her clit through her laced panties. Gator was about to do something he had never done before in his life; make love.

Hold on baby let me go grab something I'll be right back, said Ma Ma as she got up and went to the kitchen area of the room. Moments later Ma Ma returned with a bottle of Hennessey and a bucket of ice from the mini bar and began to pour Gator a drink. She had didn't know what lie ahead for her future so she wanted her time spent with Gator to be filled with nothing but pleasant memories as she prepared the water in the hot tub while scrolling through her playlist to find some soothing music to ease their minds. With the hot tub filled up with warm bubbly water and the sound of Monica's song, "Why I love you so much" playing softly in the back ground, Ma Ma led Gator to the tub and began to undress him. I told you I always finish what I start, said Ma Ma as she began planting soft, sensual kisses all over his body.

Gator sat there in the hot tub admiring her fully nude 19 year old body as she stood in front of him. There wasn't a blemish, stretch mark, or scar in sight which gave off a look of youthful innocence. Her perfectly shaped Bcup breast sat up firm on her chest complimenting her slim waist and apple bottom ass. Ma Ma didn't have the fattest ass, but it was enough for Gator.

For the next couple of hours they made love to one another as if there were no tomorrow. They used the hot tubs as their personal playground, nothing was off limits. From eating her pussy as she sat on the edge of the tub, to hitting her from the back as she held on to the water knobs while calling out his name. On the verge of tapping out, Ma Ma straddled his lap and rode him into ecstasy as she held on to the back of his neck while softly moaning in his ear causing him to explode deep inside if her tight warm pussy.

After two long rounds of sensual love making, Ma Ma sat on Gator's lap in the hot tub as he sipped Hennessy from his glass while she traced her soft French manicured fingers up and down his chest. "You want me to pour you a drink?" asked Gator? "Naw baby I'm good, I'm still floating on cloud 9 from all that good loving you been giving me," said Ma Ma with a smile on her face. As she lay her head against his chest while listening to the rhythm of his heartbeat Gator felt a connection like never before, he was in love.

The two of them dosed of in each other's arms to a light sleep, so close and peaceful they could feel each other's heartbeat. Waking them up out of their blissful sleep was four loud knocks at the door that startled the two as they quickly jumped up. Glancing at his phone Gator noticed he had three missed calls from Poncho so he quickly called him back assuming it was him at the front door.

Hello? Mane stop banging on the door like that I'm putting some clothes on right now! Said Gator as he slid into his Ralph Lauren sweat pants. Shit that ain't me knocking on your door, I'm still bout 15 minutes away I was just calling to get the room number.

Right then and there Gator's heart skipped a beat, he knew exactly who was on the other side of the door. Dropping the phone to the floor he quickly made his way to the nightstand and grabbed his .40cal Glock. Checking the clip and making sure one was in the chamber as the pounding on the door continued, he made his way to the peephole to see how many were out there. Sensing something was wrong Ma Ma came rushing out

of the back with her baby 9mm in hand. "Gator baby
stop it ain't worth it," said Ma Ma as she realized who
was standing on the opposite side of the door. Gator
turned around and replied, "Ain't worth it?" We in this
shit together through thick & thin, said Gator with a look
of pure rage mixed with sincerity in his eyes.

I'm just saying baby this might not be the end,
we might be able to, and before she could finish her
sentence the front door came crashing in as U.S.
Marshalls and ATF agents swarmed the room with guns
drawn. Get on the fucking ground now drop your
weapons! Gator and Ma Ma locked eyes as she pleaded
with him to put the gun down. Baby please put the gun
down I love you too much to lose you, I need you WE
need you. Her last statement caught Gators attention
causing him to raise an eyebrow. We? Yes Gator I'm
pregnant with your child.

For the next few seconds they stared into each
other eyes ignoring the commands of the officer as if
they were the only two people in the room. A single tear
slid down her left cheek as she dropped her pistol to the
floor and began to hug and kiss the love of her life as if
she would never see him again. Their sentimental
embrace was cut short as the officers violently snatched
Gator out of her arms while viciously slamming him
face first on the ground and cuffing him. I got you girl
don't worry bout nothing, Ima take care of you! Said
Gator as he lay on the floor of the hotel room looking
into her beautiful eyes. Those were the last words
spoken before the two of them were escorted out of the
room and placed in separate police cars.

Two weeks later Gator was released on a 15
thousand dollar bond, but Ma Ma wasn't as lucky. She
was charged with one count of first degree murder and
one count of aggravated malicious wounding, facing the
rest of her life behind bars. Angel had died on the scene

before the paramedics could arrive, while Tone on the other hand had survive the shooting but was still in the hospital listed as critical condition. Despite the fact that he was on his death bed, he was still able to identify Ma Ma as the shooter to the authorities' leading to her arrest. The first person who Gator linked up with when he was released was Tammy. Being that she was Ma Ma's family he felt she deserved to know everything that transpired, and along with her street smart and well connections he felt they could come up with a plan together.

"So how you wanna handle this situation?" asked Tammy as she navigated her candy apple red Mercedes Benz G- Wagen truck through the heavy D.C. traffic. Shit it ain too much to it, as far as I know that police ass nigga Tone is the only one who can identify her as the shooter, so without him they ain't got no case. Them people talking bout giving her a life sentence Tammy, "a fucking life sentence," expressed Gator with great concern in is voice as he stare out the passenger side window thinking about Ma Ma and their unborn child.

"Did she tell you she was pregnant?" asked Gator.

"Pregnant?" repeated Tammy just to make sure she heard right.

"Yea you know, pregnant, like when a woman gives birth to a child," said Gator sarcastically.

"Boy I know what the fuck you mean," Tammy snapped back. But to answer your question no I didn't know.

Truth be told Tammy was a bit jealous that Ma Ma was carrying his child. The first time she and Gator met she felt a connection with him out of this world, it was all in the eyes. For those first few seconds that they locked eyes in that kitchen over a year ago, that was all it

59

took to acknowledge their unspoken chemistry.
Gator would make a trip twice a month to Richmond to
purchase his heroin from Tammy. It would be times
when they would have lunch together at a nice diner to
discuss business and Tammy would find herself slowly
falling for the young hustler. His charm and charisma
brought a gleam of light into her dark world for the time
being, but out of respect for her sister she kept her
feelings to herself and respected their relationship.

  All the money in the world couldn't buy Tammy
love. It wasn't as if she were some love struck woman
who was in a desperate search for love while yearning
the touch, affection, and connection of a real man, but at
the same time she wouldn't mind it. Tammy was tall,
beautiful, successful, powerful, and treacherous, which
in return intimidated most men. The average man doesn't
feel comfortable if his woman makes more money than
he does, the average man doesn't feel comfortable if his
woman drives a better fleet of cars then he does, and
most of all the average man doesn't feel comfortable if
his woman's name holds more weight than his. So with
all that money, beauty, power, and respect, she was still
missing something; Love.

  Pulling up to the driveway of a home that looked
as if it belonged in Orange County California
somewhere Gator got confused, "I thought we was going
to your place," said Gator while looking around at the
surrounding six figure homes. Looking at him through
her Fendi sunshades with a slight smirk on her face,
Tammy replied, "This is my place." That house on the
North side that's just where I run my business, you never
shit where you eat, said Tammy as she climbed out of
her G wagen truck then hit the alarm as she made her
way to the front door of her $600,000 home.
Tammy insisted that Gator stay with her for a couple
weeks until things died down and they came up with a

plan to avoid Ma Ma from spending the rest of her life in the penitentiary. Refusing to let the love of his life die in prison Gator got Ma Ma the best lawyer money could buy with the help of Tammy referring him to her elite defense team. On top of Gator putting a 15 thousand dollar bounty on the head of the prosecutor's star witness, Gator felt there was no way she wouldn't prevail.

The first couple of weeks of Gator staying with Tammy were pretty normal between the two. Gator would get up every morning around 7am sharp, then drive to Hampton to conduct his business, and make it back to Tammy's place before the streets got too hot. Tammy still conducted her day to day business out of her trap spot on the North side while running her beauty salon on broad St, however, going into the third week things seemed to take a slight turn.

As Gator returned from making his daily drop offs and pick-ups he sat in Tammy's living room with stacks of money on the table counting up his profit for the week. Gator!

"I'm in the shower I left my towel in my room can you bring it to me?" yelled Tammy from upstairs. Aight hold on! Replied a frustrated Gator. Her interrupting him like that made him fuck up his count, now he had to start all over. Putting the blunt in the ashtray Gator made his way upstairs with a slight attitude while mumbling under his breath, "this bitch always need something."

With her soft fluffy violet color towel in hand, Gator entered the bathroom but was thrown off guard once he saw the shower curtain pulled all the way back exposing her wet, honey colored, heaven sent body. Gator stood there in awe as he admired her beautiful body while trying to control his growing manhood. Gator was snapped out of his lustful daydream by

61

Tammy's voice, "Boy don't act like you ain't never seen this before.

"Naw I ain't never seen a body like that," replied Gator with a slick grin on his face.
Tammy smirked as she stepped out of the shower and grabbed the towel from Gator while standing so close to him he could smell the Dove body wash seeping from the pores of her wet, naked, body. Her boldness turned Gator on even more, the confidence and cockiness she possessed while staring him down was a show of assertiveness mixed with aggression which had the young hustler lost for words. Without another word being said, Tammy walked right past him, entered her room, and began rubbing her body down with oil while Gator made his way back downstairs. As he lit the blunt back up and let the purple haze ease his mind, the first word that escaped his lips were, "temptation is a muthafucka."

CH/6.

~

Later on that evening Gator met up with Poncho at the local strip club Liquid Blue, to do some catching up. Gator arrived there before Poncho so he ordered up a bottle of Remy' and kicked it with the bartender Claudia to buy some time. After about twenty minutes flirting back N forth with the pretty brown skin purple hair woman, Poncho finally showed up.

"What's the word my nig?" said Gator as he pour Poncho a glass then slid it to him. Poncho took a sip and let the fine brown liquor heat up his insides before replying, "I just got word that Tone got out of the hospital a few days ago." Oh yea? So what's the status?

"He been out the hospital for a full 72 hours and ain't nobody put a hole in his head yet?" said Gator. You see that's the thing, ever since he got out of the hospital he been MIA. Word his he got whiff of the bounty you put on his head now he scared shitless, you know Murdock been watching his spot for the past two weeks and he ain't seen a soul.

Gator sat there in deep thought pondering on ways to find Tone. He had six months until Ma Ma's court date so that meant he had six months to locate and murder the rat.

"You know what, take the bounty off his head," said Gator as he pour himself another round. Poncho looked at him like he was crazy before replying, so what you gon' let him live? Yea for now, but once he found out I took the bounty off his head he'll feel like the situation died down then eventually pop back up on the scene, trust me; and besides a broke nigga like him can't stay on the run for too long, said Gator as they both shared a laugh.

"So what's up with Ma Ma, how she holding up?" asked Poncho. Yea she good mane I went to go see her the other day. "That's my heart, my round, my other half, my soulja, I think I finally found the right one big bruh," said Gator with a smile on his face. Yea you better cherish that girl cause I'm telling you what I know, it ain't too many women out there that's go'n keep it solid and ride with you to hell and back like your girl, said Poncho with a straight face.

Speaking of Ma Ma let me tell you bout her sister Tammy. I'm in the living room earlier today minding my own business and she call me upstairs to bring her a towel while she in the shower. So I open the door and hand it to her, this bitch standing in the shower with the curtain pulled all the way back just staring at me.

"For real mane?" asked Poncho with a hint of excitement in his voice.
Yea bruh, that's my word, replied Gator with a straight face.

"So did you fuck her?" asked Poncho. Hell naw mane I can't do Ma Ma like that, especially when she sitting in jail facing a life sentence behind me and my bullshit.

"I see you finally learning, I like that bout you my nig," said Poncho with a look of approval on his face. Mark my words though, if you give in to that temptation and start fucking her, that's gon' be your downfall, remember that.

Over the next two hours Gator and Poncho drank glass after glass of Remy' while just kicking it and enjoying the drama free atmosphere that the night had to offer. Poncho had the make it home to his old Lady cause she had been blowing up his line all evening so the two of them left the club about an hour before closing.

Jumping into his S550 tipsy and feeling good, Gator hit the highway and let Boosie do the talking while he vibe to his album "Ghetto Stories."

Once inside the house Gator made his way to the kitchen to fix himself a late night snack. The purple haze he had been smoking all night on top of the entire fifth of Remy he and Poncho had manhandled had him with a bad case of the munchies.

"Long night ugh?" asked Tammy as she sat at the kitchen table wrapping up individual stacks of money with rubber bands. "Yea you can say that," replied Gator as he reach into the top cabinet looking for the jar of peanut butter. Gator tried his best not to look at her through his half closed red eyes because he knew if they locked eyes she would see that he wanted her as bad as she wanted him.

Keeping the conversation short Gator continued making his peanut butter & jelly sandwich while occasionally glancing at her through the corner of his eye.

"I cooked earlier, I made you a plate it's in the oven, I know that lil sandwich ain't gon' fill you up," said Tammy as she noticed him making a sandwich that would barely fill up a ten year old.

"Yea you definitely right," said Gator with a slight grin on his face as his stomach began to growl.

Getting up from the barstool Tammy made her way over to the oven to get his plate for him wearing a black & red Miami Heat basketball jersey that stopped right at the bottom of her ass cheeks. What spiced up the moment even more is when she bent over to get his plate out the oven showing that she had on no panties giving him a full glimpse of her fat pussy lips from the back. Gator couldn't help but stare and wonder what it would feel like to be up inside of that fat pussy all night long, but he quickly erased the thought out of his head

65

remembering the words Poncho dropped on him.

"I hope you hungry," said Tammy as she sat his plate on the counter in front of him which consists of fried pork chops smothered in gravy, homemade mac N cheese, along with a side of fully loaded mashed potatoes. Gator couldn't help but crack a smile thinking to himself how on point Tammy was.

After the mouthwatering meal they took shots of Hennessey and smoked a few blunts while watching Gators favorite movie "Friday," just enjoying one another's company. While sitting on the sofa relaxing Gator didn't realize it but Tammy had slid over closer to him and he naturally put his arm around her shoulder leading her to lean her head up against his chest. Sitting there with Tammy like that reminded him of the times he and Ma Ma would sit up together on a late night and sip syrup until they doze off in each other's arms. Just the thought of Ma Ma alone brought a wave of guilt over him causing him to remove his arm from around her shoulder while sliding over a bit to create some space between the two.

Checking the time on his cell phone which read 3:18am. Gator decided to make his way upstairs and start on the letter he was supposed to be sending out to Ma Ma. Aight Tammy I'm bout to hang it up for the night, "I gotta write Ma Ma and send it out first thing in the morning," said Gator as he yawned while stretching his arms out. Tammy knew since he was thinking about Ma Ma that she was losing her shot at the young hustler so she stepped up her game, she wanted to see how much he truly loved Ma Ma.

Before Gator could get off the sofa and make his way upstairs, he felt the soft full lips of Tammy being pressed up against his neck while her pretty French manicured hands massaged his growing manhood through his jeans. Being caught off guard like that caused Gator to naturally back up and remove her hand away from his crotch area as he put up a slight fight.

"Look Tammy this shit ain't right, we can't do Ma Ma like this," said Gator as his manhood began to grow. Gator didn't have the slightest idea of who he was dealing with, because before he could protest any further Tammy's head was in lap with all eight inches of him in her mouth. Needless to say that sealed the deal for the young hustler from across the tracks.

Tammy took the word blowjob to a whole another level in the eyes of Gator. She didn't just suck on his dick like the average girl from around the way, she made sensual love to it for an entire 45 minutes. Every lick, kiss, and deep throat technique was done with patience and full of passion. She took her time with Gator and gave him a night that he would never forget. Gator woke up the next morning feeling like a new man, but at the same time he was filled with mixed emotions. Part of him felt like everything was genuine between the two of them, while the other part of him felt like Tammy was just trying to set him up to prove to Ma Ma that his loyalty to her was in no comparison of her loyalty to him. Then there was the idea that would she actually take it that far and actually fuck him if all she was trying to do was prove his disloyalty to her sister? Gator didn't know what to think but either way it went he was in too deep now, he had took the bait. As Gator lay in her king size bed laced with Versace sheets Tammy entered the room with a hot plate of fish & grits for him "South Memphis style."

"I told you I would make it worth your while," said Tammy as she sat down beside him in her tee shirt and panties while slowly tracing her fingers across the back of his neck. Yea you definitely a woman of your word, replied Gator as he enjoyed his hot plate of southern hospitality cooking.

So what's on your agenda for today, asked
Tammy. Shit I wouldn't mind laying here kicking it with
you all day but I gotta go check on my spots around the
way, then I gotta go pick up my Lil soulja from the jail.
He been down almost 2 years so you know it's going
down tonight, said Gator as he began to smile while
rubbing his hands together.

"Well if you decide to come back to my place
tonight, just know I got something special lined up for
you," said Tammy as she took a sip from her cold glass
of orange juice. Gator thought about the mind blowing
sex they had last night along with the way she
swallowed him whole and a mischievous grin spread
across his face.

"It wouldn't hurt to have just one more affair"
Gator thought to himself. Picking up on his silence along
with the mischievous grin in his face Tammy asked,
"what's funny you ain't gon' let me in on the joke? Naw
it's a lil inside thang, but to answer your question yea
Ima slide back through here tonight," said Gator as he
gathered his things to take a shower.

After about ten minutes of him being in the
shower Gator was caught off guard as he turned around
and noticed Tammy standing there ass naked. You want
some company? asked Tammy as she stared at him
seductively with her hypnotizing almond shaped dark
green eyes. Gator was so caught up in her trance he
didn't reply, but then again he didn't have to. It was
written all over his face that he wanted her as he thought
to himself, "what's up with this bitch and these strange
shower encounters?"

After Tammy lathered his entire chocolate body
with soap then let the hot water rinse both of their naked
bodied together, she squatted down and began pleasing
him orally. As the shower rain down pellets of hot water
on Gators back she took his dick out of her mouth,

68

looked up in his eyes and told him, "I want you to hit it from the back." Placing both of her hands on the shower rail gripping it tightly, Tammy bent over placing an arch in her back allowing him to slide into her warm fat pussy from behind. The sight alone was enough to make a grown man cry as gator licked his lips while thinking to himself, "I'm bout to punish this bitch." As Gator stroked her with long deep strokes while enjoying the sound of her wet ass cheeks smacking against his thighs, he forgot about Ma Ma for the moment and said to himself, "shit I can get used to this.

CH/7.

~

       Sitting in the Parking lot of the Hampton city jail waiting on T2 to be released, Gators palms began the sweat as he smoked Newport after Newport to calm his nerves. Gator hated the police so this was the last place on earth he wanted to be. Thirty antagonizing minutes later Gator spotted T2 walking through the double doors with his property in a black trash bag bag as his eyes searched the parking lot for Gator. After not seeing the hunter green Cadillac he was looking for he made his way back to the entry of the jail to call Gator but stopped in his tracks when he heard a horn blow.

       Turning around to see who was blowing at him he noticed a smoke grey S550 creeping up alongside of him. "Mane this can't be Gator riding this clean," said T2 as he tried his hardest to see who was behind the tinted window. Finally Gator rolled down the window showing a mouth full of gold teeth, "lil whody what's the word my nig? The two embrace each other then jumped back into the $120,000 car and sped off leaving the memories of hell on earth in the wind behind them.

       T2 was Gator's lil soulja, something like a little brother, where you saw one you saw the other. The two of them together meant trouble. They had been terrorizing the whole city together since they were since they were 14 & 15, but once Gator started getting a lil paper he left the senseless killings behind him making his paper his main priority.

       The only difference between the two was that Gator was a hustler and a killer, while T2 on the other hand was just a killer. No matter how many times Gator threw him a pack to get his money up T2 would always fuck it up. So after several failed attempts at trying to turn him into a hustler, Gator just accepted that T2 was just going to be T2, "a certified body snatcha," nothing more nothing less.

The first place they hit was the Military Circle mall across the water where Gator splurged on his lil soulja getting him out of his jail clothes and putting him in some designer. Feeling refreshed and dressed to impress they hit the interstate and headed to Gators place that he shared with Ma Ma in Virginia Beach. What we doing out this way? "I thought we was going to your spot, said T2." Oh yea I ain't tell you I moved out of moma crib not too long ago after you got locked up, me and Ma Ma got a condo out here now, said Gator as he flicked the ashes from the blunt in the ashtray then passed it to him.

Ma Ma? You talking bout light skin Ma Ma from New Orleans with the light brown eyes? Asked T2 as he began to cough from the potent marijuana that his body had been missing for the past 18 months. Yea that's my old lady now, I done put a baby up in her and errthang, said Gator proudly. T2 felt a slight bit of jealousy overcome him as Gator spoke of his relationship with Ma Ma, but he tried his best not to show it. T2 had a major crush on Ma Ma since they were younger, she was the girl of his dreams but she always showed interest in Gator because he was a hustler while T2 was just a killer. Whenever they would link up she always ended up with Gator while he had to settle for one of her friends but T2 told himself that he would never let her come in between them.

Snapping back into reality as they pulled up in front of Gators condo, T2 looked out the window and noticed Gator still had his STS Cadillac which was one of T2's favorite cars. He always told himself once he got his money up he was going to get him Lac' but before he could achieve his goal he got locked up.

"So what's the plans for tonight?" asked T2 as he sat on the cocaine white leather sofa while surfing through the channels on the 60 in flat screen in front of him. "Liquid Blue my nig," I already got everything set up, all you gotta do his show up, said Gator as he cracked the seal on a pint of codeine and began pouring it in a pineapple fanta. Before I forget, I got something for you too my nig. T2 got up from the sofa and followed Gator to the back room where he typed in a combination to his safe and pulled out ten grand for his lil soulja. Looking over Gator's shoulder T2 noticed all the stacks off money in the safe causing his eyes to grow wide as he admired the hustle of his big dawg. "Welcome home my nig," said Gator as he tossed him the ten grand along with the keys to his Lac', making his first day out as special as ever. Later on that evening Gator and T2 pulled up to club Paradise in his black Escalade on 26 inch rims. It was an all-white event so Gator came dressed to impress rocking an all-white Louis Vuitton collar shirt, white Prada shorts, with a pair of white Louis Vuitton loafers. T2 kept it gutta in a white Polo shirt, white Tru Religion jeans, and a pair of white and blue Jordans, with a white skully to top it off. Once inside the club the two of them received love from everybody who was somebody, half out if respect and the other half out of fear. One thing everybody knew for sure was that the murder rate was about to turn up a notch with T2 back on the scene.

Gator made sure he did it big for his lil soulja's welcome home party. They had their own section in the back of the club and their table was filled bottles of Rosé' Moet' and Hennessy, along with a Gucci knapsack filled with $10,000 in ones.

"So what's up big bruh what's the business that you wanted to talk to me about?" asked T2 as he continued to break down his Kush weed on the table. Gators mind was elsewhere as a new dancer who went by the name Skiddlez, sat on his lap with just a G- string on whispering sweet nothing in his ear. After hearing T2 call his name for the second time he programmed Skidlez number in his phone before smacking her on ass and sending her on her way.

Aight lil bruh this how I'm rocking, you know I ain't fucking the crack no more, I stumbled across a legit connect, now I'm in the heroin business. I got an out of town plug and we got the best shit on the peninsula, me Poncho and Jux already took over the entire city now we working on Newport News, that's where you come into play. Gator looked into his eyes to see how he was taking it all in before he continued. So this is what I'm gon' do, I'ma give you 9 ounces and set you up in a spot I got on 17th St and from there on out you should be able to handle the rest, "so you down or what?" said Gator with a stern look in his eyes. Damn right I'm down you ain't gotta ask me twice, said T2 as the two of them grabbed their own bottle of Rosé and made a toast to their new foundation.

For the next couple of hours the two of them roamed through the club as if they owned the place, dropping thousands of dollars the women who get the nastiest for them. By the end of the night they had four of the rawest bitches from the club seated in the backseat of his Escalade headed to the Marriott where the real party was awaiting them. Checking his cell phone he noticed he had two missed calls from Tammy. He knew she had something special in store for him but after weighing his options the young hustler came to the conclusion that four is always better than just one. The following morning Gator wake up with a slight headache but still managed to make his way down to the Hampton roads regional jail to visit Ma Ma. Even tho he was having a secret affair with her sister he still held he down to the fullest extent. Keeping her commissary account full at all times, keeping money on the phone at all times, and making it his business to visit her once a week faithfully. The way Gator saw it, the more he did for her and held her down, compensated for his infidelities.

A wide smile spread across her face as she spotted the love of her life sitting in the booth waiting on her. In the woman's part of the jail it was rare for them to get visits on the regular or even a constant flow of mail so Ma Ma felt good knowing she had somebody like Gator in her corner who loved and cared for her as deeply as he did. "Baby girl how you been?" said Gator as he placed his hand on the opposite side of the glass while Ma Ma did the same. Even through a three inch thick glass wall their connection still thrived.
I've been okay I can't complain, what about you? Asked Ma Ma. Everything gravy on my end, just taking it one day at a time out here. I linked up with your lawyer a few days ago and gave him the rest of the money so he should be down here to see you Monday morning. There was a long pause as Ma Ma fidgeted with her hands while looking down at the table, Gator sensed something was bothering her so he asked, "what's wrong baby you aight?"

As Ma Ma looked up Gator noticed her hazel eyes were now filled with tears as she began to speak.

"Gator I miss you so much words can't even explain it," said Ma Ma as a steady flow of tears began to cascade down her pretty caramel colored face. Seeing her in that state of mind had Gator emotional and he hated feeling emotional so he did his best to cheer her up and take her mind off of the negative.

"Look baby girl everything gon' be aight," said Gator as he stare back into her puppy dog eyes. I got you and I love you too much to let anything happen to you so all you gotta do is trust me.

"You do trust me don't you?" asked Gator.

"Of course I trust you, what kind of question is that," replied Ma Ma as she wiped away the tears with the back of her hand.

Aight well just ride with me then baby that's all you gotta do, and once all of this shit blow over I'ma fuck you so good I'ma put another baby inside of you, said Gator as he began to undress her with his eyes. A warm smile spread across her face as she began rubbing her stomach while biting down on her bottom lip.

"There go that million dollar smile I was looking for," said Gator feeling good that he could put a smile on his woman's face.
For the next 30 minutes they talked, laughed, flirted back N forth, even reminisced on the day they first met. Interrupting their family affair was the short stubby guard as he yelled out 1 minute!

"Damn baby I gotta go," said Ma Ma as she gave Gator the sad face. Knowing that she had to be separated from the love of her life and return back to her cage had her deep in her feelings.

"Don't look like that baby girl, and make sure you call me tonight so I can hear you moan while you play with that pussy for me," said Gator as he grabbed at his manhood giving Ma Ma a tease. Once again that same warm smile spread across her face as she replied, "I got you baby, just make sure you pick that phone up cause I called you last night and all I got was your voicemail." Yea I was out with T2 last night, you know I threw him a lil welcome home party at Liquid Blue that's probably why I ain't get your call. Ma Ma fell silent for a second, she knew the type of hell that the two of them could cause together and truth be told she didn't really trust T2, he was too much of a live wire. Times up ladies, let's go!

Later on that evening Gator and Poncho met up with T2 out Park Place to hit him off with his dope and discuss how they were going to avenge his mothers' death. T2 was sitting in his Cadillac with a well-known killer from Shell Rd named Smoke when Gator and Poncho pulled up beside them in Pancho's Rang Rover. As they entered the rundown trap spot on Spruce St. Gator dropped the duffle bag of guns on the kitchen table and began to speak as if he were a general directing a small army.

Aight this how it is, out of them four dudes who came through here and pulled that lil stunt, only one of them is still breathing and that's lil Kevin. I just got word from Jux that he been hiding out uptown with his baby moma and their 8 month old son. A wicked grin spread across T2's face and Gator knew what he was thinking so he wasted no time addressing the issue. We gon' hit his spot tonight, but when we hit it the only person who's leaving out of there in a body bag is lil Kevin, "everybody clear on that?" said Gator as he gave T2 a stern look.

T2 was the first one to speak up, I feel what you saying bruh, but mane fuck all that keep the peace, play it by the rules shit, I'm going in there and killing everybody in that muthafucka. They ain't play it by the rules when they killed my moma so fuck em. Everybody who had something to do with her getting killed is gon' feel my pain "EVERYBODY." Poncho caught on to it when he emphasized the word everybody and made a mental note to himself.

Look lil bruh I know how you feel, Ms. Jackie was like my moma too but we gotta play it smart. Between me, Jux and Poncho we done killed four of their men in the past year and we still out here, but I guarantee you if we start killing women and kids the

Feds gon' be crawling all over this shit.

"We getting too much money to be sitting in the pen reading Phat Puff magazines so you need to get that wild shit out of your head because it ain't going down like that," said Gator with great authority behind his words. The room fell silent as they waited to see what T2's response would be. It was no secret he was a certified killer, but Gator was the one who installed it in him so he knew when to calm it down and play his position.

"You got it bruh I ain't gon do no wild shit," said T2 as he scrolled through his phone while taking pulls from his blunt without even making eye contact with Gator. Give me your word, said Gator. T2 looked at him for a few seconds without speaking then replied, "you got my word."

With water under the bridge Gator proceeded to continue. Aight fellas this what we working with. Gator turned around and began pulling the military style guns out of the duffle bag when Poncho noticed T2 staring a hole in the back of Gator's head. "Y'all pick which ones y'all want but this one right here is all me, said Gator as he held on to his fully equipped AR15 with much pride. The four of them jumped onto a burgundy Explorer and made their way to the Aquaduck projects in uptown Newport News.

"Damn this shit jumping out here," said Smoke as they sat in the parking lot across the street watching the heavy flow of traffic fluctuating throughout the building where like Kevin was hiding out at.

"So what's the plan Gator, we just gon' wait until he come out?" asked T2. Gator sat there in silence for a few seconds before responding, "Naw this block too hot for us to be sitting out here waiting with all these guns on us, I got an idea."

Gator rolled down his window and called one of

the dope heads over to the truck. What's up young blood? Look I got a proposition for you, apartment 22, I need you to go inside buy some dope and let me know how many people you see inside, said Gator with a straight face. The dope head looked at Gator strange while examining the other occupants of the truck with guns scattered all throughout the truck, then replied,

"You know young blood ain't nothing in this world free."

"Dope head larceny," said Gator to himself before digging in his pack and weighing out a whole gram for him. Once Gator dropped it in his hand his eyes grew wide and a huge kool aid smile spread across showing his brown stain teeth.

Two minutes later the dope head was back at Gators truck with info like clockwork. Aight young blood it's for dudes in the house, two in the living room and two in the kitchen. What about guns, you see any guns?" asked Gator. Yea the two in the kitchen got guns laying on the table but that's all I saw. By now the dope head was fidgeting as he continuously looked back N forth as if he thought someone was watching him. Gator could tell he was in a hurry to get high so he sent him on his way.

Ten minutes later the four of them crept up on the side of the project building with guns drawn and mask on making it a scary sight for whoever had eyes on them. Once in position Gator gave the signal as Poncho kicked the cheap featherweight door off the hinges with one powerful kick allowing all four men to swarm the house laying everybody face down on the ground. One of the men in the kitchen reached for his .38 on the table and in one quick motion fired a shot at Poncho sending him tumbling to the ground. Before he could get off another shot, three finger length bullets from Gators AR15 ripped through his torso leaving pieces of his

stomach and chest on the wall behind him. T2 tie the rest
of these muthafuckas up if anybody even breath too hard
I want you to knock they muthafuckin head off they
shoulder, barked Gator.

"Now you talking my language," said T2 with an
evil gin on his face as he and Smoke tied up the
remaining three men while Gator went to go check on
Poncho who was bent over his stomach. You aight bruh,
asked Gator as he knelt down beside his right hand man.
Yea I think the vest caught it, that shit just knocked the
wind out of me, said Poncho as he bent over holding his
stomach in pure agony.

I got all of em' tied up but before we kill em' we
might as well take all this shit. T2 was referring to the
two bricks of cocaine on the table and the half pound of
sour diesel sitting in the empty ice cooler in the living
room. While T2 and Smoke were stuffing the pillow
case with the recompressed cocaine and high grade
marijuana, Gator could hear a noise coming from
upstairs. "T2 go check upstairs and make sure it's clear,"
said Gator as he went to assist Smoke. Aight I'm on it,
replied T2 before making his way upstairs with gun in
hand.

Satisfied with the amount of free drugs and
money they had scored, Gator and Poncho lined the
three men up side by side and prepared to take them out
execution style. Mane what the fuck is taking T2 so
long? Asked Poncho as he held his Mac90 to the back of
lil Kevin's head. Feeling like it was now or never lil
Kevin spoke up as the sweat dripped down his forehead.

"My son and my babymama upstairs mane, y'all
can kill me just let them go they ain't got nothing to do
with this shit!" pleaded Kevin.

"Nigga shut the fuck up you ain't in the position
to be making no demands around here," barked Poncho
as he jammed the barrel of his assault rifle into the back

of his head. "I'ma go see what's going on, watch these fools down here and don't start the party without me," said Gator with a wicked grin on his face as he made his way upstairs.

Before Gator could reach the top of the steps he could hear muffled cries coming from the first room to his left so he cautiously entered the room with his gun drawn. What he saw next made him sick to his stomach as T2 held his .44 Magnum to the helpless woman's head and viciously raped her while her 8 month old baby lay on the floor in a pool of blood with his throat slit. Gator quickly snatched T2 off the woman sending him flying back into the closet door. Once she was free from his assault she picked up her babies lifeless body and began to cradle him in her arms as she cried out uncontrollably.

"Bruh what the fuck is wrong with you I told you not to do no wild shit!" barked Gator as he held T2 up against the closet door by the collar of his shirt.

"Shit I was just having a lil fun," replied T2 in a calm collective tone.

"He killed my momma so I killed his baby, even exchange," said T2 as he stare Gator in the eyes right before Gator released him from his tight grip. Standing there staring up at the ceiling while rubbing his hands over his face, Gator contemplated his next move. You know what mane fuck it, clean this shit up and make it quick, we gon' be waiting outside.

As Gator made his way out of the room the young traumatized woman cried out to him in agony for help. Sitting on the floor with her babies lifeless body in her arms she grabbed hold of his shirt and began yelling; please don't leave me here with him! Please don't let him kill me, I swear I won't tell the police nothing! Her cries were useless as T2 grabbed her by the ponytail and threw her back to the ground as Gator walked off leaving T2 to clean up the mess he made.

As Gator closed the door behind him and made his way back down stairs, he was filled with regret, this was the part of the game that he hated the most. Before he could make it to the bottom of the steps two loud shots from T2's .44 Magnum shook the whole apartment letting him know that the job was done. What the fuck going on upstairs? asked Poncho as Gator entered the kitchen. Gator looked at him with a bland look on his face before replying, "Kill these muthafuckas so we can get the fuck outta here. With no further explanation needed Poncho walked down the line of men unloading two shots a piece into the back of their skull leaving a bloody mess of brain fragments all over the kitchen. The twenty minute ride back to Hampton was silent. The only thing that could be heard was the Project Pat album "Getty Green" as it blared through the speakers while each individual was consumed in his own thoughts. Where you wanna park at? Asked Poncho as he pulled across the train tracks entering Park Place.

"Pull up in Chicken Wing's driveway so we can split this dope and money," said Gator with a hint of exhaustion in his voice.

Once the four of them got their share of drugs and money they exited the rundown two bedroom shack and proceeded to go their desperate ways for the night.

"Hold on Gator let me holla at you for a second," said Poncho as the two men stood on the front porch. What's up big bruh? "Come sit in my truck with me, this ain't for everybody to hear," said Poncho as they walked off the raggedy wooden porch. The two of them made their way to Poncho's Rang Rover and began to talk but they never noticed T2 standing in the cut a few houses down watching them like a hawk.

"So what's up Poncho what's on your mind?" asked Gator as he broke down the Kush weed on a $20 bill. Look Gator I'ma cut straight to the chase, I'm getting a bad vibe from T2, and I don't think he can be trusted. Gator screwed his face up the replied, "what you mean he can't be trusted? We been thuggin together for years you know he ain't no rat," said Gator defending his lil soulja's honor.

"I ain't talking about him being a rat," said Poncho.

"Aight so what you talking about then?" asked Gator as he stopped rolling his blunt and made firm eye contact with Poncho.

There was a few seconds of silence as Poncho gathered his thoughts before he continued. Look lil bruh, I could be wrong about this but my gut feeling is telling me I'm right, I think he feel some type of way towards us about his moma getting killed, and I feel like he might try to make a move on us to be honest with you. All of this took Gator by surprise as he took pulls from the Kush filled blunt trying to digest Poncho's words. We family Poncho, is moma was like my moma I don't think he'll play it like that, said Gator not wanting to believe that his lil soulja would have any ill will towards him. Look bruh, I'm just telling you what my gut feeling is telling me, and like I said I could be wrong, just keep an eye on him that's all I'm saying.

Gator had a lot on his mind so after Poncho left he sat in his S550 just sipping syrup while smoking blunt after blunt. The ringing of his cell phone woke him up as he was occasionally nodding off from the potent codeine. Hello, hey baby boy you aight?

"I ain't heard from you in a couple days," said Tammy with a bit of concern in her voice. Just the sound of her soft beautiful voice put Gator at ease. It was moments like this where he needed a beautiful down to earth female to take his mind off the trials and tribulations he was going through, even if it was just momentarily.

Damn it feel good to hear your voice girl, I'm aight though, just sitting around the way getting my mind right.

"After two days of not hearing from you I was beginning to think you forgot about me," said Tammy in a playful tone.

"Me forget about you? yea imagine that, not the way you put that pussy on a young nigga," said Gator with a smile on his face as he reminisced on how good her pussy taste as she sat on his face and rode it like a full time job.

Tammy was overwhelmed with smiles and a warm tingling feeling inside as she thought about how good he felt deep inside of her. With her body yearning is touch she put her pride to the side and asked him, "You coming through here tonight?" Gator looked at his watch which read 12:44am and thought about the hour and half ride to Richmond. As bad as be wanted to chill with her and let her help him ease his mind, he knew he was in no condition to be driving.
I don't know lil moma, I done fucked around and got all hied up fucking with this syrup and pills I might not be able to make that trip tonight," said Gator as his words began to slur a little.

"You sound like you got a lot on your mind you wanna talk about it?" asked Tammy. Gator wasn't the type to talk about what he was going through, he let the codeine and high grade marijuana be his personal therapist, but it was something about Tammy that made him feel comfortable like he could confide in her.

"Yea we can talk but I wanna talk face to face so I can see them pretty eyes," said Gator with a grin on his face.

"Yea I bet you do," replied Tammy.
About an hour and forty five minutes later, Tammy pulled up in front of Gator's trap spot in her pecan brown

Audi A8. Even though it was two in the morning there were still quite a few people outside so Gator motioned for her to come sit in the car with him so all the old heads and young hustlers could get a good look at her exoticness. Stepping out of her $90,000 car in a pair of tight fitting grey Ralph Lauren shorts, a white Chanel tee shirt, and a pair of white Prada sandals, all eyes were on her as her ass jiggled with every step she took to his Benz.

Girl you can't be coming through here on a late night showing them legs off like that, "what if one of these old heads try you?" said Gator in a joking tone.

"Yea they can try me if they want and they gon' meet my lil friend," said Tammy as she reached into her Fendi bag and pulled out her chrome .380. Gator couldn't help but crack a smile, now I see where Ma Ma get it from, "I'm glad y'all on my team," said Gator to himself.

Over the next few hours they talked about everything under the sun over a cup of syrup and blunts of O.G Kush. They learned things about one another that they never would've figured out on their own which ended up bringing them closer while at the same time strengthening their bond. They were so caught up in their conversation before they knew it the sun was coming up so they decided to take it in. Being that they were both floating on cloud 9 from the effects of the codeine they decided to crash at Gator's place which was only about 20 minutes away.

"Wow I like y'all place," said Tammy as she explored their condo looking at pictures of her sister and Gator on the wall. Yea I appreciate it, you know I don't do no decorating Ma Ma decorated the whole spot, replied Gator giving Ma Ma credit for her good taste.

"Yea that's my sister, she did her thang with the coloring," said Tammy as she admired the exotic style and pattern of colors throughout the condo. Gator stood their wondering how she could speak so freely of her sister like she wasn't having an affair with her man, not to mention the fact that she was about to fuck him in her home while she was locked up. Just the mention of Ma Ma's name brought a wave of guilt over him as he looked up at a picture on the wall of them two hugged up and kissing one another.

"Look Tammy I been meaning to holla at you about something that's been on my mind lately," said Gator as he stare off into her beautiful almond shaped green eyes. I'm feeling what we got going on between one another, but we both know this shit ain't right. Ma Ma too loyal to me for me to be sleeping with her sister so as much as I hate to do it, we gon' have to put an end to this. Tammy sat down on the edge of the bed and began getting undressed as if she didn't hear a single word Gator just spoke.

"I feel you and I respect your decision just give me one more night to make love to you," said Tammy as she began slipping out of her laced panties.

Tammy knew the power of her pussy, and she knew if Gator didn't turn her down tonight, then he would never turn her down. Just one more night ugh? Yea just one more night, said Tammy. Gator stood there hard as a rock barely able to contain himself as he watched her slowly insert one finger at a time into her tight slippery pussy. Without another word being said Gator made his way over to the bed and gave her what her body was yearning for.

CH/8.

~

      Ma Ma sat in her cell listening to the Keyshia Cole song "Love" while her cell mate Bianca braided her hair. Bianca was a few years older than Ma Ma and they had both been through similar trials and tribulations growing up so they took a liking to one another giving them a sister like bond over their time spent in the same cell together.

      "When was the last time you talk to your boo?" asked Bianca as she finished up the last braid on her head. Yesterday afternoon, you know how Gator is he so damn protective over me he gotta here my voice at least once a day to make sure me and the baby aight, said Ma Ma as she checked out her new hairdo in the scratched up, cloudy mirror.

      Shit girl you got it made. I wish I had a man who cared for me like that, I been down 15 months and I can't even get a piece of mail from my baby daddy. Niggas ain't shit but it seem like you got a rare one so you better hold on to him, said Bianca as she swept up the loose pieces of hair with an envelope. Ma Ma took a minute to ponder on the words Bianca was speaking to her and after looking at her fellow inmates' situation, she did have a point.

      Her thoughts were interrupted by her friend Candace calling her name.

      "Come catch the news girl, some people got killed uptown last night! Hurry up before you miss it. Ma Ma quickly made her way down to the TV area and caught the breaking news just in time.

      Breaking news from uptown Newport News, around 11pm. last night in the Aquaduck community, four masked men forced their way into the apartment of 23 year old Nicole Harper. Upon entry to the home police found three young men tied up with gunshot wounds to the back of their heads all killed execution style, but what police discovered upstairs made the murders even more horrific and gruesome. 23 year old Nicole Harper was found raped murdered and set on fire, along with her 8 month old son whose head was nearly severed off with a large blade of some sort. Anyone with information pertaining to these brutal homicides please call 187- lock u up. A lump formed in Ma Ma's throat as her gut feeling told her that T2 and Gator were somehow connected to those homicides.

CH/9.

~

       Weeks then months eventually passed by and there were still no arrest made in the uptown murders. Things were looking good for Gator and his team, T2 was making a name for himself in the dope game by running the trap spot on 17th St that Gator had given him, while he, Jux, and Poncho were still flooding the entire Hampton and parts of Newport News with the help of Tammy. Gator had given his smoke grey S550 to his mother and moved her out of the city to a quiet suburb in Williamsburg, while he upgraded to a Porsche truck and a two door Rolls Royce Wraith. Tone was still nowhere to be found and that had Gator stressing big time. Just the fact of knowing that if he shows up to court Ma Ma would never see the streets again gave him a desperate need of action so he decided to pay T2 a visit.

       Later on that evening Gator met up with T2 in the parking lot of the neighborhood corner store "Chicken N Pork," but to his surprise he wasn't alone. He was accompanied by two other well-known killers from downtown Newport News, Big head, and lil Paul which had Gator scratching his head cause Park Place and downtown Newport News has history of bloodshed between one another. Lil bruh what it do my nig? Said Gator as T2 jumped in the passenger seat of Gator's brand new $140,000 maroon colored Porsche truck. What up mane what's so important that you needed me to meet you asap, I got shit to do. Gator looked at him sideways wondering where this attitude was coming from but quickly shook it off.

       Look mane fuck all that, we gotta find this bitch

ass nigga Tone. Ma Ma go to court in a few months and ain't nobody been able to get the drop on him yet.

"I took the bounty off of his head thinking that would ease his mind and bring him out of hiding but that shit ain't working," said Gator with frustration behind his words.

"That's supposed to be your old lady, she facing a life sentence behind you and you can't even protect her," said T2 as he stare out the passenger side window while blowing the purple haze smoke out of his nose. Once again Gator looked at him sideways, bruh what the fuck you tryna say?

"If you got something to say you need to just get it off your chest," barked Gator as he sat up in the driver seat with his fist clinched. T2 smirked as he shook his head from side to side before replying, "I said what I had to say." How much you gon' pay me?

"I can have the job done in a couple weeks," said T2 with a hint of arrogance.
Pay you? What the fuck you mean pay you?

"Since when did we start charging each other to put in work?" asked Gator. Look mane I ain't killing shit for free no more, you was gon' pay the next man so why you can't pay me? Gator sat back thrown off by his lil soulja's comments.

"How the fuck is he gon' charge me after all the shit we done been through, all the shit I done did for this lil nigga," said Gator to himself. With thoughts of Ma Ma and his unborn child racing through his head who he refused to let be born in the penitentiary, Gator put his pride to the side and did what he had to do.

Forty grand, I'll get you twenty now and the other twenty once the job is done, said Gator in an assertive tone.

"Make it sixty and we got a deal," said T2 nonchalantly as he flicked the ashes out the window.

Gator looked at him like he had two heads on his
shoulder as he clinched his fist then took a much needed
sip from his cup of syrup to calm his nerves. Gator knew
if anyone could get the job done in a timely manner it
was T2 so he counted out thirty grand and threw it in his
lap.

Gator had a lot on his mind so he decided to take
the rest of the day off and just gather his thoughts. For
some reason the words that Poncho spoke to him just
kept replaying over and over again in his head, "I'm
getting a bad vibe from T2, I don't think he can be
trusted." Gator and T2 had been thuggin together since
they were 11 and 12 years old. They used to rock the
same cloths and fuck the same hoes, trust was all they
had.

As Gator sat in his Porsche truck backed into the
driveway of one of his trap spots on Childs ave, the
constant vibrating of his cell phone woke him up out of
his slight nod. Poncho, what's the word my nig?

"I ain't doing shit lil bruh, look I need to holla at
you bout some serious shit where you at?" asked
Poncho. I'm across the tracks on Childs.
15 minutes later Poncho pulled up in his Range Rover
then jumped in the passenger seat of Gator's ride. "Got
some good news for you my nig," said Poncho as he
gave his right hand man some dap. You know my lil
shawdy I be fucking without Portsmouth right? Gator sat
there and thought for a few seconds before replying, yea
lil short Shawnda with the fat ass that work at Pure
Pleasure.

"Yea well she just solved all our problems for
us," said Poncho with a wicked grin on his face. Gator
sat there perplexed wondering what the fuck Poncho was
talking about, and how the fuck could a stripper solve
the type of problems he had.

"I'ma need you to be a lil more specific," sad

Gator with an inquiring look on his face. Aight lil bruh check this shit out, come to find out our lil friend Tone been fucking around with Shawnda for the past eight months, not on some relationship shit but on some trick shit. He pay her $500 every time they link up twice a month for her to fulfill all types of wild fetishes and fantasies for him. Long story short she found out who he was then gave me a call to verify it. Once I confirmed it was him she sent me a picture a couple hours later of him laid up in the hotel bed with his throat slit from ear to ear and the word RAT carved in his chest with a box cutter.

A devilish grin spread across Gator's face as he and Poncho made a toast with their Styrofoam cups.

"How much we gotta pay her? asked Gator. We ain't gotta pay her shit, she did that shit off the strength. I changed lil moma life. When I met her she was selling pussy in the bathroom of the Moon Light for $50, but I noticed the ambition and potential in her so I gave her the game. Now she pulling up in foreign whips getting $1000 a pop every time she open them legs, said Poncho with a smile on his face as he and Gator made another toast.

I put her in a position that would change her life for the better now she just showing her loyalty and gratitude. Gator sat there in silence as he thought about T2 and how he showed no loyalty or appreciation ever since he came home. Maybe Poncho was right, maybe he did blame him for his mother's death. Just then Gator snapped out of his deep thought remembering that he had to call T2 and let him know that the job was already taken care of.

As his phone rang T2 stared at the caller ID wondering what Gator wanted. Lil bruh what up? Ain't shit talk to me, said T2 in a dry tone. Yea mane that lil situation got taken care of this morning so everything is

good on that end, you ain't even gotta get your hands
dirty.

"So let me guess, you want me to bring the thirty
grand back?" asked T2 in a sarcastic manner.

"Damn right I want you to bring it back, what
type of question is that?" said Gator with a hit of
hostility in his voice.

T2 sat there in silence as he continued to thumb
through the two large stacks of money Gator had just
given him. He had never in his life made thirty grand so
quick and it was a feeling that he didn't want to abandon.

"You heard what I said right?" asked Gator on
the other end of the phone.

"Yea I heard you," replied T2 nonchalantly.
Aight meet me on, I ain't bringing you back shit, fuck
you nigga get it how you live CLICK!
Gator sat there in shock, disbelief, and full of rage as be
replayed the conversation over and over again in his
head. What up lil bruh you straight? asked Poncho as he
looked over and noticed Gator clinching his fist while
breathing heavily.

"You was right the whole time my nig," said
Gator as he stare out the driver side window with murder
on his mind. Poncho knew exactly what Gator was
talking about so he needed no further explanation.

"Meet me on Spruce St first thing in the morning
and bring Jux and Murdock with you," said Gator in a
calm cool collective manner.

Poncho knew shit was about to hit the fan. Yea
T2 was a stamped killer but at the same time Gator was
the one who installed in in him. T2 thought that since
Gator was on his get money shit it had softened him up,
but he was sadly mistaken. Now he was about to feel the
wrath of a Tru Stone Cold Killer.

Gator hopped on interstate 64 and headed north
to Richmond. He had a lot weighing on his 20 year old

mind on top of pinned up aggression so a stress reliever was what he needed and he knew the perfect person for the job. As his fingers dialed up her number she picked up on the third ring.

Lil daddy what's going on? "I can't call mane, shit crazy right now, where you at?" asked Gator as he maneuvered his Porsche truck through the heavy 6:00 traffic. I'm at the salon ready to close up, what's the business? I'm leaving Hampton now, I'll be at your spot in a lil over an hour, and I need you to meet me there. Aight baby, say no more.

Tammy pulled out of the parking lot of her salon with a smirk on his face. It had been a little over a week since she last put the pussy on him so she knew exactly what he wanted and she didn't have a problem in the world giving it to him. Over the last few months Tammy had begun to fall for Gator in a way that was hard for her to contain her emotions, but deep down inside she knew that his heart belonged to Ma Ma, she was just keeping him occupied while she was away.

As she pulled her candy apple red G- Wagon Benz truck into the driveway she checked her watch which read 6:54pm. She had about 45 minutes before Gator got there so she decided to set the mood then fuck and suck him so good he would forget Ma Ma's name. Stepping out of the tub her naked body glistened as she gently massaged her entire body in baby oil while listening to smooth sound of Xscape's throwback song, "Tonight."

You need some help with that? Asked Gator startling her a bit as he stood behind her placing his hands around her waist while planting soft kisses all over her back and neck. Just the way he touched her sent chills all through her body along with the aroma of his Ferragamo cologne was enough to have her pussy dripping wet. She tried to contain herself but it had very

93

little effect as Gator's hands found their way to her neatly trimmed, juicy pussy.

As Gator massaged her clit, while kissing on her neck, the anticipation was driving her off the wall. Yearning for his thickness inside of her and no longer able to withstand the foreplay, Tammy bent over placing her hands on the top of the mahogany oak wood dresser so Gator could dick her down from the back. The sight of her beautiful phat butterscotch ass bent over in front of him like that with her phat pussy lips poking out had Gator hard as a rock as he knelt down and began eating her pussy from the back.

After a few minutes of him tasting her sweetness, he stood up and slowly entered her from the back causing her to bite down on her bottom lip as she look back at him. With each long deep stroke her pussy got wetter & wetter as she threw her as back with her own special rhythm while talking shit and rubbing his nuts at the same time. All of this veteran fucking was driving Gator crazy! Along with the sight of her pussy swallowing his dick every time she threw her as back put him over the edge.

Stick your thumb in my ass, ordered Tammy as she continued to throw her ass back. Her asshole was already wet from the juices spilling out of her pussy so there was no need for using spit. Gator rubbed his thumb in her pussy juice then began massaging her asshole with his thumb before gently inserting his thumb inside. Having her asshole finger fucked in a slow circular motion while getting dicked down from the back had Tammy feeling some type of way and before she knew it she was cummin uncontrollably as her thick white cream covered his manhood leaving it with a glistening glaze. Gator had never ran across a creamer until he met Tammy and the young hustler from across the tracks was loving every second of it.

After covering his thick manhood in her sweet juices she turned around pushed him on the bed and swallowed him whole. Tammy made love to his dick and balls for almost a full hour treating it as if it were the only ice cream cone in a scorching hot desert. Before Gator could bust his second nut she straddled his lap and rode his dick like a Rolls Royce Phantom. With every deep, slow, passionate, grind, she felt his dick growing bigger inside of her by the second. Knowing he was on the verge of cumin, she pulled a little trick her best friend taught her back in Memphis and tightened up her pussy muscles causing him to explode deep inside of her.

As they both lay there naked, with their bodies glistening is sweat, trying to catch their breath, Tammy climbed off of his semi hard cum soaked dick and began to clean him up with her mouth. She sucked, kissed, and licked, every square inch of his manhood before making her way to the tip and sucking every last juicy drop of cum out of his dick head that his body had to offer. Gator lay there in pure ecstasy lost for words as he stare at the ceiling wondering what the fuck just happened. Tammy took him to a whole nother level, no woman had ever made him feel the way she did sexually, but deep down inside he knew he was dead wrong. How could something so wrong feel so right, is what gator asked himself as he closed his eyes and drifted off to sleep.

The following morning Gator lay in Tammy's bed consumed in his own thoughts as he inhaled the Kush smoke while she lay her head on his chest, softly rubbing the hairs on his chin. You been quiet all morning you okay? asked Tammy. Yea I'm good, just got some shit on my mind right now that's all, replied Gator without even making eye contact. There was a wave of silence in the air before Tammy replied, "let me guess, you must be thinking bout Ma Ma." How you

95

figure that? "Boy it's written all over your face," said
Tammy as she sat up in the bed.

Look Gator I'ma keep it solid with you. Yea Ma
Ma that's my sister, she Trill, and she'll ride with you till
the wheels fall off, but at the end of the day she a little
ass girl who can't do shit for you. That shit she pulled on
Angel and Tone was dumb and reckless and could've got
you sent to prison right along with her, a real woman
would've never handled a situation like that in the
manner of which she did. Every boss nigga need a boss
bitch by his side and if you ever fall I can't be your
crutch. I ain't telling you to say fuck Ma Ma I would
never do that, just look at the bigger picture that's all I'm
saying.

Gator sat there in silence digesting everything
Tammy had just laid on him. What they had going on
between one another was a "secret affair." There was no
way in hell he could leave Ma Ma for Tammy even if he
wanted to. As soon as Ma Ma came home his secret love
affair with Tammy would be a thing of the past, but from
the sound of things, it looked as if she had different
intentions.

Before he could finish is conversation with her
his phone began to ring, it was Poncho. Remembering
that he had to meet him around the way he cut their
conversation short. Just the thought of T2 disrespecting
him the way he did left a bitter taste in his mouth as he
fantasized Jamming his .44 bulldog down his throat and
squeezing the trigger. "Look Tammy I got some shit to
handle we gon' have to finish this conversation another
time," said Gator as he began to get dressed. Tammy
wanted to protest him leaving so quickly but she decided
against it, nagging and. complaining is something that a
woman of her caliber doesn't indulge in.

Gator pulled up across the tracks around 9:40 in
the morning, but the hood was already jumping like it

was a Friday evening. Fiends could be spotted coming back N forth out of the cuts getting served while the two trap houses that he had on Childs ave were both flooded with traffic like Walmart on the first of the month. Once he got to the end of Childs ave he bust a right and made his way down Spruce St. where Jux, Poncho, and Murdock were sitting in a dark green Suburban parked in Chicken wing's driveway already waiting on him. Murdock was one of Gators most trusted henchmen. He and Gator were similar in certain ways, young, flashy, and a fool with the pistol play. Ever since Murdock got acquitted of his double murder charge a year ago he had been ducked off playing the cut. The only person from around the way who saw him on a regular was Gator, and that was once a week when he would drop off his normal three ounces of heroin to him.

      The four of them embraced one another before making their way into the rundown two bedroom shack. As they sat at the small wooden table in the kitchen like the Mobb, Gator was the first one to speak. So this what it is fellas, we got a problem on our hands and it must be taken care of. This problem is like a tumor, "if we don't get rid of it and kill it now, it's gonna grow and become 10 times worse," said Gator in a calm but assertive tone.

      "Aight so who is it?" asked Murdock as he split open the Vanilla Dutch and filled it with purple haze. Gator took a sip from his cup of syrup then blew the Kush smoke out his nose before replying, "It's T2." Jux an Murdock both looked at each other as if they heard wrong. T2? "He family, that's your lil soulja, why you wanna kill him?" asked Murdock with great curiosity in his voice.

      "Shit I don't want to kill him, I have to kill him," said Gator with a straight face.

      Ever since he came home he been acting real strange. I tried giving him the benefit of doubt and brush

it off being that he just lost his moma but his level of
disloyalty and blatant disrespect just kept increasing.
That lil stunt he pulled yesterday was the last straw,
"disrespect will not be tolerated by any nigga, or bitch,"
said Gator as he made firm eye contact with his
comrades. It hurt Gator to the core that he had to declare
war on his lil soulja, but at the end of the day T2 was a
threat, and real men don't play around with threats, you
put an end to them.

For the next few days Jux, Murdock, and
Poncho, did surveillance on T2's trap spot in downtown
Newport News trying to figure out his routine so they
could strike at the perfect time. The only problem was
that he didn't have a routine and he was never alone. On
the third day of them doing their surveillance Jux
noticed a pecan brown Audi A8 dropping him off while
thinking to himself, "Mane that Audi look real familiar."
This was the first time T2 was spotted by himself so they
decided it was the perfect time to strike. They were
given orders to call Gator as soon as they got the drop on
him but it had took them so long to catch him without
his shooters around him, they didn't want to miss their
opportunity. Strapped up like the Navy Seal they slowly
crept up on the side of his building with murder on their
mind. Once in position, Jux gave the signal for Poncho
to kick the door in but to his surprise, it didn't budge. T2
had a burglar proof door built specifically for occasions
like this. After several failed attempts, Ponch aimed his
sawed off shotgun at the door knob and pulled the
trigger leaving a hole in the door the size of a small
watermelon.

Once inside they were thrown off guard and felt
as if they walking into a trap. The apartment was pitch
black, quiet as a mouse, with T2 nowhere in sight. All of
that excessive noise they had made upon entry to the
apartment had alerted T2, now he was in guerilla warfare

mode.

Lurking in the dark shadows of his apartment, T2 clutched his Calico tightly and waited patiently for the first intruder to bend the corner. As Poncho entered the dark kitchen with his twin sawed of shotgun drawn, he heard a noise coming from the closet so he went to go check it out. T2's plan had worked. He threw something by the closet to distract Poncho, "a tactic that Gator had taught him," now he had him right in his sight.

As Poncho went to turn the knob on the closet door, T2 emerged from the shadows of the darkness and let him have it. Huge blue flames from his Calico lit up dark apartment as he fired shot after shot hitting Poncho a total of 6 times before ducking off and sliding out the back door into the night. As soon as they heard the gunshots Jux and Murdock ran downstairs but it was too late. Poncho lay on the concrete floor in a pool of dark thick blood trying his hardest to stay alive as he choked on his own blood with every breath he took. Jux knew they didn't have enough time to wait on an ambulance, so he and Murdock quickly stuffed him in the back of the suburban and sped off to the nearest hospital.

With Poncho laid up in the hospital on life support Gator turned into a madman. Every spot T2 ever hung out at, every bitch he ever dealt with, and every close associate he ever had, was met with a barrage of gunfire for an entire two weeks straight until T2 came out of hiding. So many lives were lost over that two week period that the mayor put the city on curfew and was even considering declaring a state of emergency.

Gator couldn't stand the sight of seeing his right hand man laid up in the hospital like that with a million tubes running in & out of his body so after the first time he and Jux visited him he never returned again. The only way he knew how to cope with the pain was to murder and get high which he was doing plenty of. He was so

caught up in causing hell throughout the city that he
never even realized it had been over two weeks since he
last heard from Ma Ma, which was out of the normal
because she always called him at least once a day.
The next morning Gator took some time off from
hunting down T2 and went to go visit Ma Ma. Just the
sound of her soft voice, along with the sight of her
beautiful innocent looking face was enough to put his
mind at ease and that's exactly what he needed. She was
the only thing that could put some balance in his life at a
time like this, it was as if she were a breath of fresh air
for him while he was drowning in the Atlantic Ocean
fighting to stay alive.

"I'm here to see Mercedes Fuller," said Gator as
he signed his name on the visitors list. Looking at the
computer screen in front of her for what seemed like an
eternity the tall dark skin woman from behind the desk
finally replied, I'm sorry sir, Mercedes Fuller is unable to
receive any visitors at this moment.

"Hold on you sure you typed in the right name?"
asked Gator as he leaned on the counter trying to get
glimpse at the computer screen. Yes sir, Mercedes Fuller
inmate number 0036685 was placed in segregation 16
days ago.

Gator stood there perplexed wondering why she
was in the hole, she was five months pregnant so he
knew she wasn't involved in a fight.

"Look ma'am, that's the mother of my child,
she's five months pregnant I need to make sure she's
okay, could you please tell me why she's in the hole?"
asked a concerned Gator.

"I'm sorry sir were not allowed to give out that
type of information," said the lady behind the desk
without even looking at him as she continued browsing
the internet. Gator knew just how to deal with her type
as he peeled off five crisp $100 bills from his knot, then

discreetly slid it in from of her. Looking at the money then looking back at him, she nonchalantly placed her notebook over the money and continued to search through the computer.

Okay sir here it is, said the woman from behind the desk as she put on her reading glasses to make sure she had the correct information. After a few clicks and passwords typed in she printed out a piece of paper and discreetly handed it to him. This is the incident report.

"Everything you need to know is documented in this report, but don't read it until you get outside and if anyone asks you didn't get it from me," said the woman from behind the desk in a whisper like tone so no one else could hear their conversation.

Once outside Gator sat in his Porsche truck, reclined the seat and began to read the incident report. On December 22nd, 2008 at approximately 2:43pm. Officer Hill observed inmate M. Fuller in a physical altercation with four other inmates in unit 2C. Officer Hill gave several commands for the inmates to stop fighting however, they did not comply therefore pepper spray and physical force was used to break up the fight. Upon breaking up the fight officer Hill noticed inmate C. Towns, and S. Thomas, both had severe lacerations to their face and upper body which looked to be the cause of a homemade weapon. Upon further investigation, the camera was reviewed by Sergeant Duncan who observed inmate M. Fuller with a homemade weapon in her hand attacking other inmates involved in the altercation, leading her to be charged with offense code 105 aggravated assault.

Gator sat back in his buttercream leather seat and rubbed his hands over is face before punching the steering wheel. Part of him was proud of her for handling her business the way she did, while the other part of him wanted to smack the shit out of him for putting their unborn child at risk. If it ain't one thing it a muthafucking nother, said Gator as he slowly pulled off.

CH/10.

~

       Over the course of the next few days Gator was persistent as he continuously called down to the jail trying to get an update on Ma Ma but every time he called he ended up with the same response, "we can't give you any information, and she'll contact you once she's released from segregation." He was hoping that he would at least get a piece of mail from her informing him that she was okay but he got nothing. All Gator could do was wait it out and try to think positive but the uneasy feeling of not knowing whether or not is unborn child was safe, had him stressing like never before. With her court date scheduled in just three weeks, Gator hit the streets and continued on his rampage while praying for the best. He had been so caught up in searching for blood that he never even got a chance to tell Ma Ma that Tone had been taken care of. With the prosecutor's star witness dead, along with no physical evidence, Ma Ma was sure to walk out of court a free woman.

       What's on your mind bruh, you aight? asked Jux as he navigated the rented Ford Taurus through the slums of downtown Newport News. Gator had been silent in his own world ever since Jux picked him up so he knew something was bothering him. I'm good bruh, just thinking bout Ma Ma and the baby.

       "You know them muthafuckas wouldn't even tell me if she was okay or not after she just got into a brawl with four other bitches while she five months pregnant," said Gator with disbelief and rage in his voice. Ma Ma a soulja she straight, I think you just over thinking it, and besides, she's the one who pulled out the blade and started slicing bitches like Michael Myers, she aight, said Jux as the two shared a much needed laugh. After four straight hours of them being on the hunt with no sign of T2 or any of his comrades, they decided to stop a Chic a Sea on Jefferson ave to grab a bite to eat. Chic a Sea was famous for their Big Chick sandwiches and cherry soda, just the aroma of it lingering in the air had Gator's stomach talking to him. In the middle of Gator placing his order at the drive through, Jux suddenly pulled off leaving the lady on the intercom talking to herself. Bruh what the fuck you doing?

"I ain't even finish ordering my food," said Gator with a look of confusion on his face. Jux didn't reply he just nodded in the direction of the stop light across the streets and Christmas must've came early because there was T2 with three of his comrades chilling in a brand new cranberry Lexus LS430 like he didn't have a care in the world.

Pulling out of the Chick a Sea parking lot, Jux and Gator lurked in the distance three cars behind stalking their prey. Jefferson ave was a busy street, so instead of giving them the business right there on sight like Gator eagerly wanted to, Jux suggested that they follow them until they got on a side street, where there would be less witnesses. Four stop lights and two left turns later, T2 was pulling down Oak ave oblivious to the fact that the devil himself was right beside him until it was too late.

Shots from Gators AR15 lit up the quiet side street as he hung out the passenger side window sending shot after shot into the brand new shiny Lexus trying to kill everything breathing inside of it. Shattered glass and hot metal exploded everywhere as the first two bullets struck T2 in the arm while the third one grazed his forehead causing him to duck and mash the gas. Refusing to let their prey get away, Jux coasted the

104

rental car right alongside of the Lexus as they tried to flee, allowing Gator to finish his vicious attack until the 50 round magazine on his AR15 was as empty as his soul. In dire panic and unable to see the road , T2 crashed into a parked car about a half block down as Jux and Gator fled the scene laughing.

"We finally got that bitch ass nigga!" said Gator excitedly as they pulled across the train tracks entering Park Place.

"Mane you should've seen his face when I let that muthafucka rip, I think I hit him in the head too," said Gator with a devilish grin on his face. The constant ringing of his cell phone interrupted their celebration as he took the call.

"You have a pre-paid call from, Ma Ma, to accept this call press 1." Gator quickly pressed one accepting the call, it had been almost a full month since he last heard from her so knowing she and the baby were okay was exactly what he needed to hear to calm his nerves.

Baby girl I been missing you, you aight? asked a concerned Gator but to his surprise there was nothing but silence in the other end of the receiver. He knew that she was still on the phone because he could hear the sounds of women talking and dominoes being slammed on the metal tables in the background. Hello? Ma Ma! A muffled cry crept through the other end of the receiver as Ma Ma broke down crying without saying a single word. Their connection was so strong Gator didn't need words or an explanation to decipher what she was trying to tell him. She had lost the baby.

Gator spent the next few weeks ducked off at Tammy's place. He was so distraught about Ma Ma losing the baby that he almost overdosed a couple times off percocets and codeine just trying to cope with the pain. Poncho was still in the hospital and word had got back to him that T2 had survived the shooting but was in the hospital in critical condition, while the other three men died from their injuries on the scene. Gator knew there was a good chance if T2 survived there would be an all-out war, but he had made such a fierce and bold statement over the last month that he wasn't even worried about any retaliation any time soon.

Laying in the bed next to Tammy Gator rolled over and looked at the clock which read 7:12am. Ma Ma was to appear in front of the judge at 9:30 and the last thing he wanted to do was be late.

"Where you going so early baby?" asked Tammy as she rolled over and noticed Gator getting dressed in a pair of black Ferragamo slacks, white silk Armani shirt, with a pair of black Gucci loafers, and his Cartier Frames. Gator didn't reply right away. He took a sip from his cup of syrup thinking to himself, "This bitch is getting too attached."

You already know where in going, it's February 11th, Ma Ma's court date. I been waiting on this day for the past seven months, baby girl coming home today, said Gator as he smiled from ear to ear while buttoning up his shirt. Just the thought of him being able to hold her in his arms again was enough to shed some light into his dark gloomy life despite everything he was battling.

If Gator thought Tammy was going to be ecstatic about her younger sister coming home he was sadly mistaken. As gator looked up and the two locked eyes for a brief moment Tammy had a look of disgust written all over her face while trying to disguise it with a phony smile. Gator didn't pay it any mind, he figured she would eventually get over it, and once Ma Ma came home everything would go back to normal between the two.

As Gator sat in the back of the courtroom he watched in agony as the two heavy set deputies escorted

Ma Ma from the back in handcuffs and shackles. He hated seeing her like that but some things are just inevitable in the wicked life they live. With everything that she was going through she still managed to looks beautiful as ever with her thick wavy honey colored hair braided in two long corn rolls complimenting her dark blue jumper as it hugged every curve on her 5'6 frame perfectly. Sitting in the chair next to her defense team she casually turned around to scan the crowd for Gator. Once she spotted him they both locked eyes then she blew him a kiss right before throwing up the Mobb sign that the two of them shared.

Mercedes Fuller VS. Commonwealth of Virginia, prosecution may you please present your case.

"Your honor I would like to ask for a continuance due to the fact that my star witness is unable to be with us today," said the district attorney.

"And why is that sir?" asked the judge as he tilted his head and looked at him over the brim of his glasses.

Well your honor, our star witness Tony Riddick was found deceased in a hotel room a few months ago and we have reasonable doubt to believe that Ms. Fuller had a hand in it, we just need more time to investigate.

"Your honor I object," stated Ma Ma's attorney as he rose from his chair. My client was incarcerated during the time period that the witness was murdered, there's no way possible she could've had anything to do with his murder, not to mention while she was incarcerated for a crime she didn't commit she was brutally assaulted by a gang of women while five months pregnant, causing her to lose her unborn child. My client has suffered enough your honor.

The judge looked at Ma Ma for what seemed like an eternity then asked the prosecutor, "Do you have any physical evidence linking the defendant to the homicide?" Fumbling through his paperwork as a substantial amount began to fall to the ground he replied, "no your honor not at this moment, but if you give us a few more months I can assure you that we will have all the evidence we need to convict her. Don't allow the innocent look to deceive you your honor, Ms. Fuller is extremely violent and a menace to our society. If she is released back into the community it won't be a question of "if" she will kill again but "when" will she kill again?" stated the prosecutor in a stern assertive tone.

Once again the judge gave Ma Ma that same piercing stare like he was looking right through her soul. Gator had no clue what the judge was thinking but it had him nervous as hell as he sat in the back row tapping in foot on the hardwood floor. After an intense five minute stare down the judge finally spoke, " no witnesses, no physical evidence, no case, your case is dismissed. A huge smile spread across her face as she turned around, locked eyes with Gator then mouthed the words "I love you," before being escorted back the jail to be processed and released.

Gator sat in the parking lot in his maroon colored Porsche truck patiently waiting for the love of his life to walk through the heavy metal doors and into his arms. So many things were running through his mind as he sat there in deep thought, he never noticed her walk up on his truck until she tapped on the window startling him a bit. You gon' let me in? asked Ma Ma as she stood in front of him looking like a young Lauren London from the movie ATL. From the looks of things those seven months in the can did her some justice. She was already a 10 in the face now she had the body to match causing Gator to lick his lips as he examined her ripe body that was now thick in all the right places. Smiling from ear to ear showing is full set of shiny gold teeth, Gator put his cup of syrup down and stepped out of the car to properly greet his woman. The two of them hugged and kissed for what seemed like forever. Her soft warm body felt so good in his arms he didn't want to let her go, he wanted that moment to last forever, and she must've felt the same because when he went to let her go she tightened up her grip pulling him in closer to her chest as a single tear slid down her cheek.

The conversation about her losing the baby was never brought up by either one of them. Bringing it up would've been the same as pouring salt on an old wound so they both stayed clear of it and left it in the past. Gator had managed to obtain the names and addresses of all four woman involved in her attack so that was justice enough. Once the time presented itself he planned to avenge the death of his unborn child with so much fury and mayhem one would think he was Satan himself reborn again, but for the time being it was time to hit D.C. and get his queen fresh.

After a well-deserved shopping spree dropping over 10,000 on her favorite designers, Fendi Chanel, & Jimmy Choo, they made their way to a famous soul restaurant in the city called "Moe's Spot," and got their grub on. It had been seven long months since Ma Ma enjoyed a decent meal so she wasted no time digging into her hot plate of baked turkey wings smothered in BBQ sauce, homemade Mac N Cheese, deep fried cornbread, and some of the best sweet potato pie she had ever ran across in her entire life. Its small things like this that we take for granted while were in the free world, but the second our freedom gets snatched up, we cherish and appreciate it like never before.

So what's been going on baby? I've been hearing a lot behind those walls.

"Believe it or not, you Jux and Poncho are hot topics in the daily jail gossip," said Ma Ma with a grin on her face. Gator sat there trying to see where she was going with this before he replied. There was a slew of things she could've heard about him but only one really mattered. If she did hear he was fucking Tammy she had one hell of a poker face.

Yea baby girl a lot has transpired since you been away, good and bad, that's why I wanted to sit down and have this conversation with you. As far as finances we looking good, "I mean real good," said Gator with a grin on his face. Tammy kept her word and her people have been consistent since day one. Shit I'm bringing in anywhere from 90 to 120 grand a month in profit alone so we straight, said Gator as he bit into his fried pork chop smothered in BBQ sauce.

Ma Ma couldn't help but crack a smile as she admired her man's hustle and ambition. Not to mention the way he was eating that pork chop while licking the BBQ sauce of his fingers was beginning to get her moist as she reminisced on his he would eat her pussy early in the morning giving her orgasm after orgasm, drowning him in her sweet juices. Ma Ma had seven months of backed up pressure that needed to be released and from the looks of things Gator's face and soft full lips were screaming for her sweet juices.

"So how's Poncho, is he still in the hospital?" asked Ma Ma snapping out of her lustful daydream. Gator took a sip from his ice tea then wiped his mouth with a napkin before replying, "yea he still in the hospital, but they did take him off life support so that's a plus." Now we just gotta wait it out and hope he make a full recovery. Ma Ma could tell he was truly hurt behind Poncho getting shot up the way he did, she could see it in his eyes and hear it in his voice. She had also hears about all of the retaliation killings that had took over the city in the last month. One thing for sure she knew about Gator was that, if you crossed him or his people he had no limitations on how far he would take it to even the score.

"So let me guess, you must've already heard about the lil drama brewing between me and T2," said Gator looking into her eyes with a slight smirk on his face.

"Lil drama?" um baby let me enlighten you on something, 19 homicides and 14 wounded in less than thirty days isn't what you would consider "lil drama.

"Yea you got a point," said Gator as he stroked the hair on his chin while secretly admiring his path of death and destruction he had caused.

To be perfectly honest with you, it was always something about T2 that rubbed me the wrong way, something that gave off a vibe that he couldn't be trusted. It's like he was always envious of you, said Ma Ma as she cut into her sweet potato pie. Envy? Shit I always broke bread and made a way for him. When he came home I shot him ten grand, gave him the keys to ma Lac', and set him up with his own trap spot. "It ain't no way in hell a muthafucka can envy you when you putting them in a position that can change their life for the better," said Gator as he looked into her eyes trying to detect if she felt where he was coming from.
Ma Ma definitely felt where he was coming from but it was a little more to it than just that, now she was contemplating on whether or not she wanted to open that door. Her silence caught Gator's attention and he could sense something was on her mind. "What's going on baby girl, you aight?" asked Gator as he grabbed a soft buttery roll from the small basket in the middle of the table. Ma Ma continued to eat her food while trying to avoid eye contact, she knew if they locked eyes would see right through her.

Taking a deep breath while staring out the window of the diner, Ma Ma replied, "Look baby it's a lil deeper than what you think. When I said T2 always

showed envy towards you I wasn't just referring to
materialistic things, I was referring to me as well. Back
when we were in the 9th grade he had the biggest crush
on me ever. I mean he would get his friends to pass me
notes and poems telling me how much he liked me and
how beautiful I was but I was feeling you so I always
shot him down and I think that really hurt his pride.
I feel what you saying baby but I don't think, naw Gator
I'm not done let me finish, said Ma Ma cutting him off in
mid-sentence. Ma Ma tried to look away as she felt the
tears began to well up in her eyes but it was no turning
around now.

      "What's wrong baby talk to me," said Gator as
he leaned over and wiped away the single tear as it
cascaded down her soft, pretty face. I should've been
told you about this, I've been holding it in for so long I'm
sorry baby, I'm sorry. Now she had his mind racing
100mph as he held on to her hand trying to console her.

      Back when we were 15 and you got sent upstate,
I fucked up. "I did something that I should've never done
and I will forever regret it," said Ma Ma as she padded
her eyes with the napkin while staring out the window.
There was a few seconds of silence before she continued
then she released what her heart had been holding in for
so long, "I started fucking T2."
Gator sat back in his chair and looked at her as if she
were joking.

      "You bullshittin right?" said Gator as he took a
sip from his drink waiting for the joke to be over. No
Gator, I wish I was but I'm dead serious, I'm telling you
this because you need to know, but that's not all. By now
the tears were flowing down her face uncontrollably as
she used the back of her hand to wipe away the river of
tears.
After the second time we slept together I ended up
getting pregnant. He was so happy and wanted to have a

family with me but when I told him that what we were doing was a mistake and that I was in love with you it really hurt him and put a dent in his pride and ego. Two weeks later I got an abortion without him knowing and I guess he sensed it because he never spoke another word of it since that day.

Gator sat there in silence consumed in his own thoughts trying to make sense of what she had just revealed to him. Truth be told he didn't know who the woman was sitting across from him. The whole time he was thinking T2's transgression towards him was behind the fact that his mother was killed on Gator's watch but in all actuality what really fueled his hate and envy was a piece of pussy.

The three hour ride back to their condo in Virginia Beach was tense and silent. The only thing that could be heard was the smooth voice of Anita Baker floating through the Alpine speakers, along with the occasionally sniffing from Ma Ma as she silently cried the entire ride back. As they pulled up in front of their condo Ma Ma waited for him to get out of the car and come inside with her but Gator had way too much on his mind and the last thing he wanted to do was lay-up with her after hearing what he just heard.

So what you just gon' drop me off? "You not even gon' come lay with me?" asked Ma Ma as she looked at him through her puffy red eyes.

"After everything you just told me you think I wanna come lay with you?" said Gator as he shot her a "bitch are you serious" look. Bitch you was fucking my lil Soulja while I was locked up, then you had the nerve to keep it a secret from me for damn near five years! Bitch get the fuck out my car. Gator leaned over opened the passenger side door and pushed her as hard as he could causing her to fall out of the car and hit the pavement with a thud before backing out of the driveway

113

and speeding off into the night.

Ma Ma lay in her driveway crying her heart out once again. As she began to sit up and wipe the blood away from her elbow she thought to herself, "how could the one person she loved more than life itself, crush her heart so bad. This was definitely not how she expected her first day home would turn out.

CH/11.

~

Over the next few days Gator was ducked off at Tammy's place, getting his mind right, while at the same time being treated like the young boss he was. Gator would wake up to a blowjob and go to sleep to a blowjob like clockwork. He was even getting his dick sucked while sitting on her plush velvet sofa playing Madden as he inhaled some of the best purple haze on the east coast. As Tammy slowly pulled his throbbing wet dick out of her mouth she looked up at him with those almond shape dark green eyes and gave his dick one last kiss before getting off her knees and snuggling on the couch with him. It had been three days since he left Ma Ma crying on the ground in their driveway, and to be honest it was eating him up inside but his pride was standing in the way of him making things right with her. You aight lil daddy? You been quiet all day and you got that look in your eyes, what's on your mind? asked Tammy as she caressed the side of his face with her French manicured nails. Looking at her through his blood shot half closed eyes it was no secret he was feeling the effects of the xanez, percocets, and high grade marijuana.

Shit so crazy right now Tammy I don't even know where to start. From Poncho being laid up in the hospital, to going to war with somebody who I used to love like a lil brother, to stepping on Ma Ma's heart like a door mat after she just lost the baby, I'm all fucked up. Gator looked up at Tammy waiting for some type of response but was met with that same look of disgust on her face as she had when he told her he was going to Ma Ma's court hearing. Every time he mentioned her name

115

around Tammy he got that same look and vibe from her, it was a vibe of envy and hate. Right then and there a light bulb clicked in his head and he knew he was laid up with the wrong woman.

Later on that evening Gator left Tammy's place and went to go make things right with Ma Ma. He told himself he was done fucking with Tammy. If she would double cross her own sister he could only imagine what she would do to him.

Making his way into his condo, the sweet scent of mango candles drifted through the air while the soulful voice of Aretha Franklin played softly in the background. As he made his way to the living room he could hear Ma Ma singing along to the sad love song, "It hurts like hell." Sitting in the oversized plush sofa with the lights dim, TV off, and candles burning, Ma Ma looked beautiful as ever with a snug fit yellow tank top on, a pair of lavender boy shorts hugging her smooth thick caramel thighs, with her golden brown hair tied up in a bun.

Before making his presence known Gator just stood there admiring her beauty while thinking to himself how much he had fucked up. The things he had done to her she didn't deserve. Yea she kept a big secret from him, but at the same time, she and Gator weren't even together when she fucked T2. It was more so of just the thought that someone he was at war with, had one up on him because he had fucked his old lady, it was an ego thing. She had killed Angel for him, introduced him to a plug that change his life, did time for him, I mean the list goes on. Not to mention, he had double crossed her by having an affair with her sister while she was locked up. After getting his thoughts together, Gator walked into the living room and cleared his throat startling her a bit as she pour herself a glass of Hennessey on the rocks.

"Damn baby it's just me, I ain't gon' hurt you,"

said Gator as he sat down beside her on the sofa. Ma Ma shot him a look so fierce and cold that it caused him to slide back a bit and create some space between the two. You know what, fuck you Gator. I ain't just some random toy that you pick up and play with then toss it back on the ground when you're done with it. You treat the rest of them bitches like that, not the bitch that's gon' put her life on the line for you and ride with you to hell and back. Ma Ma spoke in a calm assertive tone meaning every word that rolled off of her tongue as she stared into his soul with her puppy dog light brown eyes that now had a red tint to them from the Hennessey and O.G Kush.

You right baby, you right, that's why I'm here to make it up to you and get things back right between us, said Gator as he placed his hand on her thigh while staring into her eyes trying to find the slightest bit of forgiveness. Over the last few days I realized that your love is what keeps my heart pumping, we got something special I love you girl. As Gator's hand crept up her thigh while he leaned in for a kiss, Ma Ma stopped him in his tracks as she backed up and smacked his hand away from her thigh with tears in her eyes.
Unfazed by her resentment, Gator pinned her down on the couch and began kissing on her neck while massaging her pussy through her shorts. Slowly pulling off her laced boy shorts he began planting soft kisses on her pretty feet then worked his way up to her inner thighs kissing and slowly licking while massaging her clit. The anticipation was causing her to get moist as she thought about grabbing the back of his neck and smothering his face in her pussy but she was still mad at him so she put up the resentment act as long as she could. As Gator glanced up at her noticed her rubbing her nipples while biting down on her bottom lip, "all that tough girl shit gone out the window, I got her ass now,"

said Gator to himself with a smirk on his face. Leaving a trail of kisses from her feet to her love box, Gator tongue finally made its way to her warm pussy which was now dripping wet as her body yearned for his soft lips to devour her and take her to another planet.

For the next 45 minutes Gator ate her pussy with so much passion, patience, and love, it caused her to have multiple orgasms as she lay back on the couch with tears in her eyes. Gator didn't just stick to her pussy he paid attention to every part of her body even licking her asshole in a slow circular motion sending chills all through her body causing her to fall even deeper in love with him. Unable to withstand the first class head treatment her body was receiving, she wiped off his face then took his hand and led him upstairs to their bedroom where the two of them made sweet love until the sun rose. Needless to say, that ill will she was harboring towards him was nowhere to be found.

Waking up next to the love of his life Gator watched her sleep peacefully as he took pulls from the Kush filled blunt that he left in the ashtray the night before. Snapping out of his daydream he remembered that he still hadn't given her the welcome home/ birthday gift he had for her. Since her 20th birthday was only a week after she was released he figured they would celebrate it all as one. After that little situation took place between the two of them a few days ago he had totally forgot about it.

Dialing up Jux, Gator walked into the bathroom so she couldn't hear his conversation. My nig, what's the word? I ain't making nig noise mane, on my way across the tracks, said Jux as he navigated his new Escalade through the early morning traffic.

"At 7:12 in the morning?" asked Gator.

"Damn right, early bird get the worm, I got to get it," said Jux as they both shared a laugh thinking

118

about Poncho who was famous for that saying.

"Look I'm at the crib, I need you to bring that gift to me when you get a chance," said Gator as he spoke in a tone low enough so only Jux could hear him. I got you, say no more, said Jux as the two ended the call.

"What you doing in here?" asked Ma Ma as she walked up behind him wrapping her arms around his waist while pressing her fully nude body up against his warm flesh.

"Shit I'm bout to be doing you if you keep this up," said Gator as he turned around mesmerized by her fully nude beautiful body as she stood in front of him with enough confidence for the both of them.

"Well what's stopping you?" asked Ma Ma as she began massaging his growing manhood through his boxers while staring into his dark brown eyes. Taking his hand and leading him into the double door walk in shower, they let the shower rain down pellets of hot water on their naked bodies as they stood under the massaging water and just held one another. For the next half hour they passionately bathed one another while planting soft kisses up and down each other's body. Gator was so caught up in the moment, sex wasn't even a priority for him at that moment, this was something new to the young hustler, and he was truly in love.

The constant vibrating of his cell phone on the sink brought his escape to paradise to a halt. My nig what's the word? Yea I'm outside bruh, said Jux as a pulled up beside Gators new Wraith. Aight she'll be down in about ten minutes, said Gator before hanging up.

"Who was that baby?" asked Ma Ma as she stepped out of the shower behind him with a towel in hand. Oh yea I ordered us some Chinese food, "I know you probably ain't feel like cooking so I did both of us a favor," said Gator with a grin on his face as he gave her a kiss in the lips. Aww look at you, being so thoughtful.

"Hand me my purse so I can go pay them," said Ma Ma as she began drying off before throwing on a pair of Ralph Lauren sweat pants with a snug fit V- neck white tee shirt. Ma Ma opened the door and looked confused, there was no delivery man at her doorstep, but what she saw next made her jaw drop. A white on white big body Mercedes Benz S560 with a big red ribbon in the front.

"Oh my God I know he didn't," said Ma Ma as the tears began to well up in her eyes. Slowly walking over to the $150,000 luxury car to examine it, her heart skipped a beat as she as she sat on the soft white leather that felt like velvet rose pedals to her warm skin. She was so caught up in the moment she didn't even notice Gator standing outside of the passenger door until he tapped on the window. Fumbling with the buttons, she finally got the door unlocked and before he could get his entire body inside she was all over him with hugs and kisses.

Baby I love you sooo much, when you said you had a surprise for me I was thinking a new bag or some jewelry, but a fucking Benz!

"I told you I got you girl," said Gator nonchalantly.

"Look inside the glovebox I got you something else too," said Gator with a grin on his face. Ma Ma looked at him with a look of curiosity on her face before opening the glove box and what she found inside lit up her face like a Christmas tree.

A compact Glock 26 with a pink rubber grip, and the words Murder Moma engraved on the side. A huge smile spread across her face as she clutched her new pistol while licking her lips.

"Oh yea before I forget, here read this," said Gator as he dug in his pocket and pulled out a small folded up piece of paper. Once again, Ma Ma had a puzzled look on her face as she began to unfold the paper. Baby what's this? That's the names and addresses of every one of them bitches who jumped you, "I told you I got you," said Gator with a wicked grin on his face.

CH/12.

~

Over the next few days things were going smooth for the young hustler. Business was doing big numbers, and he and Ma Ma couldn't get enough of each other. It had been about a week since he last saw Tammy, she had called him a couple times but he ignored her calls on the strength of him trying to make things right with Ma Ma. He knew the power that Tammy could possess over him if he were in her presence, so he tried to play her from a distance.

It had been a little over a week since Ma Ma was released and tonight was her 20th birthday. Gator was throwing her a party at a club on Granby St in Norfolk that he had rented out for the evening and it was definitely going to be a Ghetto Fabulous event. Gator told himself that he would celebrate the birth of his queen tonight, while tomorrow he would be avenging the death of his unborn child.

Pulling up to the club in her pearl white S600 Ma Ma killed the parking lot and was definitely making a statement. All eyes were on the couple as they stepped out of the luxury spaceship looking like Beyoncé' and Jay Z of the Ghetto. Gator was sharper than a #2 pencil rocking a brown Louis Vuitton sweater, white Ferragamo jeans, with a pair of brown Louis Vuitton boots, and a pair of $1500 Cartier frames with the brown lens. Ma Ma was on her elegant shit tonight draped in an all-white Versace two piece skirt and jacket suit, white Jimmy Choo stilettos, with a pair of clear frame gold Versace glasses. Her hair was braided in box braids that she had tied up in a bun exposing her smooth caramel colored neck that was laced in over $40,000 worth of gold and diamonds.

Walking into the club the sound of Pastor Troy's hit song "No mo play in GA," was blaring through the speakers as the two of them were greeted with daps and hugs from everybody who was somebody. The entire city came out to show Ma Ma love. She had did a bid for her man without snitching while facing a life sentence, along with the way she gunned down Tone and Angel in broad day was getting her plenty of recognition. She was respected by many and feared by more, little did she know she was beginning to earn the same reputation as her man.

The entire Park Place was in the VIP section. Gator didn't believe in leaving anybody behind when it came to having a good time, he had even brought along a couple of the old heads from around the way. Ma Ma knew how he felt about his people from across the tracks so she put up no argument when she noticed the two old school alcoholics cleaned up and draped in Versace that Gator had given them. Truth be told it actually put a slight smile on her face when she noticed them partying with the rest of the hood, that was just a reminder of how big her man heart was.

Bottles of Hennessey, Remy Martin, and Rosé flooded their tables as blunts of almost every exotic batch of weed rotated through the air the entire night. As Ma Ma sat in Gator's lap with a bottle of Rosé in her hand, a beautiful chocolate woman approached their table, one could've mistaken her for the female rapper Remy Ma. Gator had never seen this woman before so he was a bit confused when Ma Ma got up and excitedly embraced her as if she had known her, her entire life. Damn you looking good girl when you get out? Asked Ma Ma as she stepped back and took a look at her friend.

"Two days ago, I heard they were throwing you a birthday party here tonight so I had to come show you some love," said the beautiful chocolate woman with a New York accent. Oh girl let me introduce you to my man, Bianca this is Gator, Gator this is Bianca.

"Me and Bianca were cell mates, this is the girl I was telling you about," said Ma Ma as she wrapped her arm around Bianca's shoulder.
Gator stood up and greeted Bianca with a warm, welcoming, hug. Her body felt as soft as cotton candy, while her smooth chocolate skin gave off an alluring scent of sweet mango.

"Any friend of Ma Ma is a friend of mine," said Gator as gave her a head nod of approval.

"We got plenty food, plant liquor, and plenty weed, so enjoy yourself," said Gator as he pour her glass of Hennessey.

The VIP section was lit up. Gator and Jux had orchestrated a twerk contest rewarding the winner with a $2,500 prize so when the DJ played Juvenile song "Back that ass up," shit got too live for TV as almost every girl went crazy twerking and pussy popping. Ma Ma even joined in on the action giving the crowd a taste of her "New Orleans bounce," as she squatted down and began popping her pussy to the rhythm of the beat with her bottle of Rosé still in hand. Sitting back on the plush sofa smoking a 5 gram blunt of sour diesel with his whole hood surrounding him having the time if their lives, Gator thought to himself, "damn I done came a long way."

Cushing up the ecstasy pills on the table while preparing to spike the bottle of Rosé he and Ma Ma were sipping on, Gator just happened to look up and what he saw next had him like a deer caught in headlights. Looking like a Goddess with every seductive step she took Tammy casually made her way up the steps to the VIP section. Dressed in a turquoise Chanel cat suit with a matching pair of Christian Louboutins. Gator hated to admit it but she had stole the spotlight from his beautiful birthday girl.

"You finally made it," said Ma Ma as she stood up to give her sister a hug. Gator was thrown off a bit because he didn't even know she invited her. The entire time she was locked up she only received one visit from Tammy and that was on the strength of Gator, so seeing her here at a moment like this was unexpected to him. Girl you know I wouldn't miss your celebration, said Tammy as she hugged Ma Ma while cutting her eyes at Gator. Oh yea before I forget, I got you something special for your birthday. Reaching into her red Fendi bag Tammy pulled out two small gifts wrapped in wrapping paper then handed them to the couple. As Ma Ma opened her gift a huge smile spread across her face as she pulled out a gold plated $30,000 Rolex flooded with yellow diamonds. Now that's what the fuck I'm talkin' bout, said Ma Ma as she put the Rolex on her wrist and flexed in the mirror before giving Tammy a big hug.

Gator on the other hand was a bit skeptical about opening his gift. It wasn't his birthday, not to mention, he had been ignoring her calls first the past week so why would she be giving him a gift? Curiosity got the best of him as he went to open the gift she had given him, but before he could even get it halfway out of the wrapper he quickly stuffed it into his pocket realizing what it was.

"What's wrong baby, you good?" asked Ma Ma as she walked up behind him wrapping her arms around him. Yea I'm good baby, all that Rosé and Hennessey starting to run through me, I gotta go piss I'll be right back.

As Gator made his way to the men's room he pulled the gift out of his pocket to further examine it and it was exactly what he thought it was; a fucking pregnancy test. Before he flushed it down the toilet something inside of him told him to check the results on the middle of the stick. With butterflies in is stomach and sweaty palms gripping the stick, Gator said a prayer before reading the results and got lightheaded when he read the word POSITIVE.

All Gator could do was put his head down and run his hand over his freshly cut fade while thinking about how bad he had fucked up. Thinking back to all the times he had fucked Tammy raw and nutted deep inside her pussy, he just shook his head wondering his the fuck could he be so stupid. With everything he had going on this was the last thing on earth he wanted to deal with.

Interrupting his thoughts were the sound of expensive heels clicking on the marble floor. With the smell of Dolce` & Gabbana perfume in the air he looked up and there stood Tammy right there in front of him with a wicked grin on her face. Damn lil daddy why the long face? "You just get the best news of your life, we having a baby," said Tammy as she caressed the side of his face then planted a soft kiss on his lips.

Tammy what the fuck is wrong with you? "You trippin, you know we can't have no fucking baby," said Gator as he pushed her hand from his face then took a step back. You know what Gator I'm getting tired of you putting my feelings on the back burner like I'm some bum ass bitch.

"You laid up in my bed and fucked me damn near every night for the past seven months and now just cause this lil bitch out of jail I'm supposed to act like nothing ever happened between us?" said Tammy with a great deal of emotion behind her words.

"You damn right, what we had going on was a secret affair, key word, SECRET, nothing more nothing less," said Gator in a stern tone. There was a few seconds of silence between the two before Tammy replied, "look me in my eyes and tell me you don't love me."

"If you tell me you don't love me I'll walk out of your life right now as we speak and you'll never have to worry about me again," said Tammy as she stare into his soul with those hypnotic almond shape dark green eyes while holding on to his hand.

Gator was lost for words. It was like those enticing, beautiful eyes of hers had him hypnotized as he thought back to all the sweet love they had made, and how she took him places sexually no other woman has ever taken him. Before he could respond, Tammy was squatted down in front of him unbuckling his Fendi belt. Wrestling his thick manhood out of his boxers, she slowly stroked him while licking circles around the tip. In less than ten seconds his entire dick was down her slippery throat and the thought of telling her that he didn't love her was out the window.

As her head slowly bobbed back & forth on his dripping wet manhood she placed both hands at the base of his dick and applied a twisting motion that matched the rhythm of her sucking.

"Spit in my mouth," said Tammy as she popped his dick out of her mouth then stuck her long tongue out showing her royal blue tongue ring. Doing as he was told Gator aimed for the blue tongue ring and spit in her mouth, then watched in amazement as she mixed his spit with hers then spit it all back on his dick making a sloppy mess. Five minutes later Gator exploded in her mouth causing his knees to tremble as he leaned up against the sink looking down into her eyes as she sucked every last drop of cum out of him.

"I wander wants taking him so long?" asked Ma Ma as she passed Bianca the blunt while scanning the crowd for her man.

"Girl you know how those bathroom lines in the

club be," said Bianca. Naw Bianca you see that's the thing, Gator a made man he don't wait in no lines, I'll be right back.

Ma Ma grabbed her purse and made her way through the crown in search for Gator. With him and T2 at war she knew they had to be on point at all times so her hand clutched her Glock tightly as it rest in her Louis Vuitton hand bag. Approaching the men's bathroom she spotted Gator walking towards her while Tammy was headed in the opposite direction leaving the club.

"Where Tammy going? She just got here," said Ma Ma with a puzzled look on her face.

"Shit I don't know, she said something about some business she had to handle," replied Gator hoping she wouldn't put two and two together and start connecting the dots. There was a brief moment of silence in the air between the two of them before Gator picked it back up. Look let's go back upstairs and finish this celebration, it's all about you tonight baby girl, said Gator as he grabbed hold of her hand and led the way back upstairs to the VIP section.

Gator and his entire squad tore the club down and partied like rock stars for the next three hours straight. Popping bottle after bottle, smoking blunt after blunt, while popping double stack after double stack like they were skittles. It was a family affair and Ma Ma was definitely being shown the love and respect she deserved. Throughout all of the fun he was having one thing remained in the back of his mind the entire night; that damn pregnancy test.

The clock on the dashboard of her brand new Benz read 4:08am as she and Gator pulled into the driveway of their condo. The mixture liquor and ecstasy had them both feeling extremely sexual, so they made it their business to give one another a night filled with erotic pleasure that would be sure to go down in history.

Making their way through the front door it was as if they couldn't get inside fast enough because they wasted no time stripping one another of their clothing as Gator picked her up and placed her half naked body on the kitchen table while taking his free hand and knocking everything that was in his way off the table onto the floor. With her caramel thighs spread wide open exposing her neatly trimmed fat cat, Gator put his head in between her legs and began kissing on her inner thighs while massaging her clit.

Feeling how wet her pussy was and from the sound of her moaning Gator could tell that she was ready for him. "That's enough baby, fuck that foreplay I want your face in my pussy," said Ma Ma as her words were blended with her moaning. Before Gator could get a good rhythm going with his tongue, Ma Ma had grabbed the back of his neck and began gyrating her hips to her own special rhythm giving Gator a mouth full of her sweetness.

The sound of the doorbell ringing took him out of his trance as he jumped up and snatched his Glock off the table. Headed towards the front door half naked with pistol in hand, Gator wondered who the fuck could be knocking at his door at 4 in the morning. Who is it? Barked Gator as he stood behind the door with his Glock drawn. A female voice could be heard on the opposite side of the door but he couldn't make out a name so he looked through the peep hole what he saw next made him scratch his head.

"Bianca?" gator turned around with his face screwed up looking at Ma Ma for an answer.

"Well open the door, don't be rude to our guest," said Ma Ma nonchalantly.

As Gator opened the door he was lost for words as Bianca stood in front of him in a burgundy trench coat with the top buttons undone exposing the top half of her perfectly snapped breast. Gator thought the ecstasy had him tripping. Not knowing how to react, he backed up and bumped into Ma Ma as she stood right behind him while wrapping her arms around his waist and kissing him softly on his neck.

"Just like how you had a surprise for me, I got a surprise for you too baby," said Ma Ma as she motioned for Bianca to come in.

As Bianca made her way through the double doors she let her trench coat drop to the floor exposing her fully nude body with Hershey color nipples. Dressed in nothing but a pair of shiny black Christian Loubiton high heels, Gator's heart skipped a beat as she walked up on him and began passionately tongue kissing him while stroking his semi hard manhood through his boxers. It was Ma Ma's birthday but she was treating him as if it was his and he damn sure wasn't complaining.
Once upstairs the real party began as Gator took control and ordered both women on the bed doggy style. The two of them did as they were told and positioned themselves on the edge of the bed side by side face down ass up. Y'all hold tight for one second, "I got a lil surprise for y'all," said Gator as he ran downstairs to grab his pants.

Waiting on Gator to enter her warm, tight, pussy from behind, Ma Ma began massaging her clit until she felt her juices dripping on her fingers. About thirty seconds later Gator returned to the room with a party pack of ecstasy pills and a wicked grin on his face. Bianca noticed him with the pills and motioned for him to come put a couple on her tongue.

"Hold on lil moma, I'ma show you how we do it cross the tracks," said Gator with that same wicked grin on his face.

As Gator knelt down behind both of their big round asses he began eating Ma Ma's pussy from the back while fingering Bianca. Gator's tongue slow danced up and down her pussy as she reached her arm around placing her hand on the back of his head. As her breathing pattern began to pick up pace, and he could taste the sweet nectar her pussy released, he gently inserted two ecstasy pills into her slippery wet asshole giving her entire body a warm tingling sensation. After bringing Ma Ma to an elite orgasm, he then slid over to Bianca and gave her the same treatment, leaving her pussy dripping wet as her body began to feel the effect of the ecstasy.

Satisfied with the amount of juices flowing from her wet pussy Gator began to dick her down with long deep strokes from the back while her pussy talked back to him making all sorts of erotic noises. If he thought Ma Ma was going to be fazed by him blowing Bianca's back out like he was in a scene out of "Booty talk 68," he was sadly mistaken. Taking his eyes off of Bianca's phat Hershey colored ass bouncing wildly all over his cream covered manhood, Gator looked up and a huge smile spread across his face as Ma Ma gripped the back of Bianca's neck burying her face into her cum soaked pussy as Gator dicked her down from the back.

The following day Gator woke up around two in the afternoon still feeling the effects of all the drugs and liquor he consumed the night before. Just the sight of Ma Ma and Bianca's naked bodies lying on side of him made his dick grow a few more inches as he contemplated on stirring up another round of Thug Passion but decided against it. Jux had texted him the Intel that he needed on the four women involved in Ma Ma's assault so today was his day of reckoning.

The Intel that Jux had dug up for him was more than helpful. Come to find out, the women involved were all related, they were part of a large family spread throughout the city of Portsmouth known as the infamous "Franks." They were well known for mob assaults, murder, and extortion, so Gator knew he had his hands full but he was the least bit worried. The one thing that weighed heavy on his brain and had him scratching his head, was how and why they had crossed paths with Ma Ma in the first place. The women who assaulted her weren't even assigned to the same housing unit as her, and from what Ma Ma had told him, she had never dealt with, spoke to, or even acknowledged the women, so in the back of his mind he felt it was something more to it.

After showering and getting dressed, Gator sat at the kitchen table loading the magazine to his AR15. The sound of footsteps coming down the hallway alerted him so he quickly threw a towel over the assault rifle trying to conceal it just in case it was Bianca. She was cool people but he didn't know her well enough to have her all in his business.

My love, good morning baby, said Ma Ma as she walked into the kitchen and wrapped her arms around him before planting a soft kiss on his lips. With her head resting up against his chest Gator inhaled her sweet fragrance while admiring her natural beauty. Fresh out of bed without an ounce of makeup on she was still beautiful as ever.

"Why you got that grin on your face?" asked Ma Ma as she sat on his lap while tracing her finger along the deep waves in his hair. Gator didn't reply, he just caressed her smooth caramel thighs and kissed her softly on the shoulder
Ma Ma couldn't help but notice the high powered assault rifle bulging from under the towel on the floor as she sat on his lap so she asked, "Gator what you got going on?" Gator shot her a look like he didn't know what she was talking about as he continued to scroll through the messages in his phone.

"So that's what we doing, we keeping secrets now?" asked Ma Ma. Gator knew he couldn't keep anything from her, their bond was too surreal, well except for the fact that he was having an affair with her sister of course.

Knowing she was bound to find out sooner or later, Gator went on and let her in on what was happening.

"Me and Jux about to go handle that lil situation for you," said Gator as he texted Jux the location to meet him at. There was a brief moment of silence in the air before Ma Ma causally replied, "take me with you." You sure? Asked Gator with a look of uncertainty on his face. "Positive," said Ma Ma with a stern look on her face as she stare into his dark brown eyes.

Pulling up to the Kroger food market in downtown Portsmouth, Gator and Ma Ma parked next to Jux then jumped in the minivan with him. Gator was reluctant at first about bringing Ma Ma along on the mission, but the moment he looked into her eyes he saw nothing but fire and pain staring back at him, and right then and there he knew he was making the right decision and would be able to live with whatever the outcome would be. If letting her pull the trigger herself was what it would take to free her of her pain then he was all for it. The three of them sat across the street parked in the two tone MPV van observing the activities that were taking place in the Lincoln Park projects. It was a warm spring afternoon that brought everyone out to enjoy the fruits of the hood. Kids ran up and down the sidewalk playing with water guns, hustlers laughed and talked shit while playing dominoes, old heads cooking on the grill while drinking forties of Old English, and women of all shapes and sizes stood around half naked trying to seize the attention of all the ballers from around the way. It was a beautiful day in the projects but there was a storm headed their way so fierce, God himself wouldn't be able to save them.

"Look like they having a block party out here," said MA Ma as she noticed the DJ booth set up in the middle of the field playing reggae music.

"Yea, I hate to be the one to rain down on their parade but this might be our only shot at catching all of them together," said Gator as he handed Ma Ma her AP9tech and Jux a Mini14.

"Gator it's at least 75 people out here, our faces will be all over the six o'clock news if we just hop out and start shooting people," said Ma Ma as she scanned the large crowd. No need to worry about that, I got you covered, said Jux as he reached into his camouflage book bag and pulled out three scream mask along with three blond wigs. Ma Ma looked at Jux then looked at Gator who seemed to be unfazed by the attire while thinking to herself, "these niggas crazy foreal."

After about forty five minutes of scoping the scene with no sight of their target Gator began to get restless. Got damn Jux we done been out here damn near a whole hour and we ain't spotted them bitches yet, "you sure your source gave you the right intel?" asked Gator. Jux didn't reply, he just slowly nodded his head up and down and continued to scope the scene.

Another thirty minutes passed by with no sight of the women and Jux began to consider maybe Gator was right. As soon as he put the van in drive ready to abandon the mission and try again another day, he spotted a group of females coming out of one of the buildings who fit the description of the women they were on the hunt for. As they sat down on the stoop drinking liquor out of red plastic cups while enjoying the music that the DJ played, he nudged Gator on his shoulder then pointed in their direction. Okay we finally got action, said Gator as he sat up in his seat and cocked back his AR15 slamming a bullet in the chamber. Not wanting to have a case of mistaken identity Jux checked the pictures in his phone that his source sent him, then got Ma Ma to confirm it before putting their play into action.

Slowly pulling up in front of the stoop where their targets were seated along with about four or five young hustlers, all hell broke loose as the MPV van came to an abrupt halt and the sliding doors swung open. Jumping out with mask and wigs on it was like a scene out of a horror movie as the trio went berserk chopping down their prey and whoever else got in their way. Scrambling trying to escape the line of fire, a few of the young men managed to draw their weapons and fire back but their mediocre handguns were no match for the high powered assault rifles. .223 and 7.62 caliber bullets repeatedly ripped through their victims' bodies knocking chunks of their stomach and chest through their backs. In less than 12 seconds, Gator, Ma Ma and Jux had turned a beautiful spring day into a cold unforgettable nightmare as piercing cries and screams filled the air while six bullet riddled bodies lay dead on the front stoop covered in blood resembling the infamous "Valentine's day massacre."

CH/13.

~

For the next few days Gator and Ma Ma hid out
at their duck off spot in Suffolk. It was a small two
bedroom brick house deep in the rural part of the county
which they considered their safe haven because they
were the only two who knew about it. Gator assumed
that the brutal murders would have a slight impact on
Ma Ma but to his surprise the violence and bloodshed
actually turned her on, giving her pussy a warm tingling
sensation. Murdering the people responsible for the
death of her unborn child wouldn't bring her baby back,
but the sight alone of her victims taking their last breath
while choking on their own blood as she chopped them
down with her AP9Tech was enough to ease her mind
and put a slight smile in her face for the time being.
    As the streets died down a bit and Gator was
informed that there were still no leads or suspects in the
Portsmouth homicides, he met up with Jux at the Shell
gas station on Mercury Blvd. to chop it up.
    "What's the word my nig?" said Gator as he
jumped in the passenger seat of Jux's midnight blue
Escalade. Coolin lil bruh, "I got some good news and
some not so good news, which one you want first?"
asked Jux as he passed Gator the blunt. Taking a deep
pull from the purple Kush blunt, Gator blew the smoke
out his nose while staring out the window then replied,
right about now bruh it don't even matter.
Jux could tell Gator had a lot on his mind and was
dealing with even more. With Poncho getting shot up,
Tammy being pregnant, and going to war with T2 while
trying to duck the penitentiary, Gator was dealing with

enough drama for two people. Not to mention Ma Ma had recently lost the baby so he could only imagine what his childhood friend was going through.

Aight lil bruh this what the business is, Poncho doing better, they released him from the hospital but as soon as his old lady came to sign him out the detectives arrested him. Arrested him for what? Asked Gator with a puzzled look on his face. Shit your guess is as good as mine, his old lady tried getting some answers about his arrest but they told her nothing. They threatened to lock her up on conspiracy charges if she kept snooping around for information, that's when she called me. Conspiracy? Shit I hope it ain't no murder charge, said Gator as he stoked the hair under his chin. I'm just glad he aight and made it up out of that hospital, whatever he got arrested for money can handle that situation, said Gator as he flicked the ashes in the ashtray then passed the blunt back to Jux. That must be the good news, so what's the bad news? Asked Gator. Jux took a pull from the blunt then smirked as he slowly shook his head from side to side before replying, "T2."

It's like that muthafuckas just won't die. They switched his status from critical to stable this morning and they say he's expected to make a full recovery.

"Now we gotta worry about if he gon' cooperate with the people or not," said Jux as he made firm eye contact with Gator.

Gator sat there in silence for a few seconds pondering on the information Jux had just shared with him. He had known T2 since the sandbox days, and if there was one thing he knew about him, he knew he was no rat. I don't know about that bruh, T2 might be a lot of things but he ain't no rat. "If anything, we gon' have to worry about retaliation but I'm well equipped for that," said Gator with a devilish grin on his face.

Taking Jux's advice, Gator switched it up and

played the cut for the next couple of months. When put in certain situations under certain circumstances, you never truly know how the next man will act under pressure so Gator played it safe. However, money still had to be made so he put Ma Ma in charge of his operation for the time being. She would deliver the heroin to his three main locations throughout the city, then pick up the money from his stash house on Spruce St once a week like clockwork.

Over those couple of months things were beginning to get back to normal for Gator. Money was fluctuating the way it was supposed to, the murder rate had drastically slowed down, and Tammy hadn't mentioned one word to him about her pregnancy. In fact, things seemed to be a bit too quiet and running a bit too smooth. Just like the old saying goes, it's always quiet and calm before the storm.

Once T2 made it out of the hospital he decided to pay Tammy a visit. Laid up in the hospital bed for two long dreadful months gave him ample enough time to think so he figured he might as well kill two birds with one stone. Tammy had brought this proposition to his attention a couple times before but he never took the bait because in all actuality he didn't trust her. However, now that his back was against the wall and he had nothing to lose, he was all in.

The two of them met up at a local bar on Pembroke ave to discuss their affairs. Once Tammy entered the bar she scanned the crowed looking for him. After two or three minutes of him nowhere in sight, she began to get weary thinking he was trying to set her up so she quickly turned around and headed for the exit but was stopped in her tracks when a raspy voice called her name. T2?

"Yea it's me, come sit down," said T2 in an irritated tone.

She looked at him in disbelief as she sat down
across from him barely recognizing him. He had lost
about 40 pounds, his head full of dreads was now bald
with a huge scar going across the top of his head from
the staples, and he was wearing a eye patch over his left
eye due to the fact that he was now blind in one eye from
pieces of shattered metal and bullet fragments.

"Damn baby boy, look like you finally met your
match," said Tammy without a bit of remorse or
common courtesy for the wounded man. T2 didn't reply,
he just shot her a cold stare so fierce with his one eye
causing her to look away.

You sure you gon' be able to handle this? I mean
you look like you need some more time to get yourself
together, said Tammy with a look of uncertainty on her
face. Look bitch let me tell you something, if I couldn't
be here, then I wouldn't be here.

"Now you came to me with this proposition so
let's get to it," barked T2 in a calm assertive tone.
Tammy clutched her .380 pistol as it rested on her lap
under the table and locked eyes with him. The same
blood that ran through Ma Ma ran through her as well,
however, she was a little more cold and calculated with
hers.

Aight lil daddy you wanna get to it, let's cut the
shit and get straight to it.

"You get rid of Ma Ma and I'll plug you in with
my connect," said Tammy as she shot him a stare so
fierce it would make a grown man look the other way.
What about Gator? There was a brief moment of silence
before Tammy replied, "I want him dead too. Just not
right now, he's bringing in too much money to get rid of
just yet. When I get tired of him and he's no longer
beneficial to me I'll give you the green light.
T2 looked at her with a look of uncertainty on his face.
He knew if he killed Ma Ma he would have to kill Gator

as well, and in a timely manner. There was no way in hell he would survive on the streets for more than a couple weeks after killing Ma Ma if Gator was still breathing. And besides, he was far from stupid. Something deep down inside of him told him Tammy didn't really want Gator dead she just wanted Ma Ma out of the picture.

Look Tammy that muthafucka just tried to kill me and my whole squad.

"Had me laid up in the hospital for two whole months and you expect me to play nice and give him a pass just so you can keep fucking him while getting your pockets fat?" said T2 as images of his comrade lying dead in the passenger seat next to him with a chunk of his head missing, kept surfacing in his head.

"Either I kill both of them together at the same time or the deal is off," said T2 as he sat back in his seat with his arms folded across his chest like he was calling the shots.

"Look T2 this is business so ima need you to get your emotions in check," said Tammy with an assertive tone. I'm offering you a connect that will change your life and I'm giving you 50 grand once the job is complete. Now as far as Gator I'll talk to him and convince him to stop gunning for you. "Once I break it down to him how it's bad for business and put this pussy on him he'll see things my way," said Tammy with a devilish grin on her face.

T2 sat there and weighed his options. With Gator and his squad trying to kill him every chance they got, along with his money being fucked up he had no choice. In all actuality he didn't want to kill Ma Ma, he still had feelings for her, but due to the situation he was in and the circumstances he was under he had to think with his brain and not his heart, that meant Ma Ma ass had to go. Aight Tammy you got a deal, said T2 as he reached over shook hands with Tammy. Little did he know he had just made a deal with the devil himself.

Tammy came to the conclusion that the only way she would truly have Gator to herself was if Ma Ma was permanently out if the picture. She had no intentions on killing Gator, she just threw that out there to bait T2 in. Little did he know she had a bullet with his name on it as soon as he came to collect the 50 grand for killing Ma Ma.

Lurking through the city his low key Impala, T2 contemplated on the deal he had just made with the devil. He couldn't believe she wanted her own sister dead just so she could have Gator to herself. It was still something about her that he didn't fully trust but that 50 grand outweighed all of his uncertainties.

"That's one evil ass conniving ass bitch," said T2 as he looked over at Smoke who was in his own world as he continued to text back & forth. Whoever he was texting it had to be important because it had his full undivided attention the entire ride.

"You heard me bruh?" asked T2. Yea, yea I heard you, you definitely right though, she is a conniving ass bitch you gotta be careful when you dealing with her.

"If she'll put a hit on her own sister I can just imagine what she'll do to someone who ain't her blood," said Smoke as he continued to text. T2 didn't know it, but Smoke had a trick up his sleeve that he had been working on for the past few months.

CH/14.

~

Ma Ma navigated her S560 through the streets of Hampton with Bianca in the passenger seat taking care of Gators affairs as instructed. Ever since Bianca came home and was reunited with her old cell mate it seemed as if the two were inseparable. They had even shared moments of intimacy alone without Gator and Ma Ma would never admit it, but Bianca was beginning to fill the void in her life of Gator not being around as much as he should.

Pulling up across the tracks in Park Pace Ma Ma parked in the driveway of one of Gator's trap spots right next door the Angel's old house. Just the sight of Angel's house gave Bianca an uneasy feeling in her gut so she mustered up the strength to asked Ma Ma what she had been meaning to ask her for the past few weeks. Either she was going to give her a truthful response or shoot her some bullshit, either way it wouldn't hurt for Bianca to ask.

So what really happened between you and Angel? Asked Bianca as they sat parked in the rundown driveway waiting on a sale to pull up. Ma Ma was caught off guard by the bizarre question as she scrunched up her face and repeated the question as if she heard wrong.

"Yea what happened?" asked Bianca as she turned sideways in the passenger seat positioning herself the face Ma Ma. Damn bitch what you think I'm the law? I just been hearing so many stories I just wanna know which one is true, said Bianca in a convincing tone. Ma Ma sat there contemplating on whether or not to be

142

truthful with her friend. She was a true friend to her
behind bars and true friend to her on the streets, even
true enough to be welcomed into the bedroom with Ma
Ma and the love of her life. Just the thought of Gator
brought her back to reality and reminded her of the
words he installed into her, "you never discuss murders
with ANYONE, and even if you think you can trust
them."

"Naw baby we ain't even going there," said Ma
Ma dismissing the subject leaving herself no room for
error, and just like that another word about Angel was
never spoken again.
After a long day of trappin through the city the two of
them made their way back to the condo where they
planned on having a night filled with girl on girl pleasure
and passion. Gator was still ducked off playing the cut.

As far as Ma Ma knew, he was down in
Mississippi with his people, but in all actuality he was
only 90 minutes away in Richmond at Tammy's place.
As much as he tried, he just couldn't shake that green
eyed devil.

As Ma Ma went to unlock the front door to her
surprise it was already unlocked. What the fuck? Ma Ma
paused as a million thoughts ran through her head.
What's wrong girl?

"Look like you just seen a ghost," said Bianca as
she noticed the uneasy cautious look in her friend eyes.

"Naw something ain't right, this door should be
locked, I never leave it unlocked," said Ma Ma as she
took a step back and looked at front door as if it were
possessed. "Girl you trippin, maybe you just forgot this
time," said Bianca trying to assure her friend that there
was nothing to worry about.

Ma Ma hesitated before reaching into her Chanel
bag and retrieving her compact Glock 26 that Gator had
given her for her birthday. Cautiously entering the house

with her weapon drawn, Ma Ma did a quick scan of the vicinity and was relieved to find no sign of an intruder. It was times like this when she wished she had Gator by her side but unfortunately that wasn't the case. I told you girl you was trippin. Let's count this money up then I'ma run us a warm bubble bath I got plans for us tonight.

"You being all brave and pulling out that pistol like that got my pussy wet," said Bianca as she seductively licked her lips while gently caressing the side of Ma Ma's face.

The two of them sat at the kitchen table counting up Gator's profit for the day which amounted to $27,000. After separating the money into individual stacks of 5 grand a piece, she then wrapped them up in rubber bands and tossed them into the safe. Now all she had to do was call Gator and let him know what the business was, then she could kick back and enjoy some fire ass head over a glass of Hennessey.

"Hey baby what you doing?" asked Ma Ma as she stocked a few grocery items in the cabinet while on the phone with Gator.

"I can't call it, sitting here thinking about you, I was wondering when you were go'n call," said Gator. Yea we were running a lil late, I had to stop and get some things for the house. We?

"Who is we?" asked Gator with a hint of aggression behind his words.

"Damn baby calm down it ain't nobody but Bianca," said Ma Ma with a slight smile on her face amused at her man's jealousy.

You still running around with that girl? I thought that was just a one-time fling. Look Gator the world don't just revolve around you, I gotta have a life too. Shit you been gone for the past few weeks so she's been keeping me company, "I don't see what the issue is," said Ma Ma with a bit of an attitude. Gator took a deep breath

144

and tried to calm himself down before he snapped on her. He felt she was trying to challenge his authority but this wasn't the time to be arguing with her, especially since she was the one handling his money for him.

Yea I hear you, just be careful I don't want that bitch all in my business.

"We got too much shit going on right now to have any loose ends," said Gator with authority in his tone. There was a slight pause on the other end before Ma Ma asked, so how's the fam? They aight, said Gator as he removed Tammy's hand from his inner thigh while she tried to be funny and seduce him knowing he was on the phone with Ma Ma.

"Yea, well love you call me in the morning when you get up," said Ma Ma.

"Aight baby girl, I love you too," said Gator before ending the call.

"Aww ain't that so sweet," said Bianca as she walked up behind Ma Ma and wrapped her arms around her waist while planting soft kisses across the back of her neck.

"You so worried about Gator, you need to be worried about me," said Bianca with a smirk on her face. You're always looking after people and taking care of everything, it's time for somebody to return the favor and take care of you for a change.

"The hot tub is waiting on you, go upstairs and slip into something a little more comfortable while I make us some drinks," said Bianca as she undressed Ma Ma with her eyes before walking off to go prepare their drinks. Ma Ma sat there with a slight smile in her face thinking to herself, "Gator you better tighten up."
The mood upstairs was set to a tee. Bianca had scented candles lit around the hot tub as the very sensual Xscape song "Do you want to" floated through the surround sound speakers. Once undresses Ma Ma stepped into the

hot tub and let the warm bubbly water relax her body. She had a long day and right about now a fat blunt, cold glass of Henny, and some grade a head was exactly what she needed.

Just like clockwork Bianca entered the room with two glasses of Hennessey on the rocks mixed with Alize` along with an oversized blunt filled with purple Kush. Dressed in nothing but a pair of purple Jimmy Choo pumps with a diamond necklace around her neck, Bianca looked like a Chocolate Goddess as she sat on the edge of the tub and passed Ma Ma the blunt. Eyes red and cloudy from the effects of the purple Kush, Bianca slipped out of her $700 heels and into the open arms of Ma Ma.

While getting her Pussy fingered and nipples gently sucked on at the same time, Ma Ma leaned her head back, closed her eyes and took a few sips from her drink as she cleared her mind of all her worries. When she opened her eyes she thought she was dreaming as she stare down the barrel of a double barrel sawed off shotgun but she wasn't. Thinking fast, she went to reach for her Glock that was in the tub with her but strangely in wasn't there, and before she knew it T2 was smacking her in the head with the butt of his shot gun causing her to lose conscious.

About thirty minutes later Ma Ma was awaken by T2 as he constantly smacked her while throwing water in her face.

"Sleeping beauty, wake your pretty ass up this party just getting started," said T2 with a wicked grin on his face. As she lay on the cold bathroom floor butt naked still drifting in and out of conscious, she tried to stop the blood that was rushing from her forehead but the wound was too severe. Silent cries escaped her lips as she cried out for Gator but she knew there was no way in hell he could save her, then she looked around for

146

Bianca but she was nowhere to be found.

"You looking for your home girl ain't you?" asked T2 as he poked her in the side of her head with the barrel of his shotgun. Bianca! "Bring yo ass up here, yo lil fuck buddy looking for you," yelled T2. A few minutes later Bianca entered the room and Ma Ma's heart sunk to her stomach as Bianca stood in front of her fully dressed holding a hand full her jewelry in one hand, and her custom made Glock in the other. Ma Ma had been deceived and played like a piano.

As her bloody, beaten body lay on the floor, she looked up, locked eyes with Bianca, and shot her a stare so cold and fierce that no words were needed. Sensing the animosity Bianca slowly walked over towards her with her expensive Jimmy Choo pumps clicking on the marble floor with every step she took, then squatted down beside her. Aww what's wrong baby?

"It ain't no fun when the rabbit got the gun now is it?" asked Bianca as she gently traced the barrel of the pistol up and down Ma Ma's bloody face.

"Let me let you in on a lil secret," said Bianca as she knelt down and put her lips to Ma Ma's ear. That lady who you gunned down in the streets like a dog that was my aunt, my fucking aunt! said Bianca as the tears began to flow freely down her face. Overwhelmed with anger and rage Bianca grabbed a fist full of Ma Ma's hair and began banging her head against the edge of the tub with so much brute force it caused her to lose conscious before T2 quickly snatched her off of her.
Slow down Bianca we can't kill her just yet, we gotta get the combination to the safe first.

"I know Gator got at least 200 grand in this muthafucka," said T2 excitedly as he began to rub his hands together. Disappointed that her opportunity to avenge her aunts' death would have to wait, Bianca slowly stood up from her squatting position and began

violently stomping Ma Ma in the face until smoke
snatched her up and carried her downstairs so they could
finish searching the rest of the condo.

Smoke had been working on this plan for
months. Bianca was his side piece and once he found out
that Bianca and Ma Ma were cell mates he began to put
his play into motion. Bianca wanted to kill Ma Ma once
she found out who she was in the jail but Smoke put a
stop to it, he had a better idea.
Instead of killing her in the cell and gaining nothing out
of the ordeal but a stiffer prison sentence, Smoke
suggested that she play it cool and befriend her. That
way, when they were release, Bianca could get close to
her and rob her blind of everything she and Gator were
worth. That way everybody was winning. Bianca could
avenge her aunts death while getting a nice piece of
change, Smoke and Gator would become a few hundred
grand richer, and Tammy would hopefully get what her
soul was searching for by having Ma Ma out of the
picture.

Aight pretty lady you got two options, play nice
and give me the combination to the safe, and I'll make
sure you have an open casket burial, or you can play that
tough girl act that Gator got you hooked on and I'll make
it to where they'll need dental records to identify your
body.

"The choice is yours," said T2 as he knelt down
beside her. Ma Ma picked her head up off the floor and
looked him square in the eyes as she mustered up the last
bit of strength her battered body had to offer.
Fuck you, you pussy ass nigga! Your whole life you
wanted to be Gator, well let me tell you something,
you'll never be Gator, you too fucking weak and your
bum ass can't make a dollar out of 15 cent. If you go'n
kill me, then kill me, said Ma Ma as she spat a mixture
of thick blood with saliva in his face then tried to wrestle

the shotgun out of his hands. Ma Ma was too weak and
didn't have enough energy as T2 quickly overpowered
her and began beating her in the head the butt of his
shotgun once again until she was on the verge of losing
conscious.

Oh you think shit a game?

"Let me show you how serious I am," said T2 as
he held the shotgun to her head while unbuckling his
pants. You been giving all that good pussy to Gator, let
me remind you what a real man feel like. With all her
might Ma Ma tried to fight him off but it was to no avail
as he overpowered her 5'6 135 pound frame, pinned her
down to the ground, and brutally raped her. As the sweat
from his forehead dripped down on her, mixing in with
the blood on her face, the memories of her being
molested as a young child began to resurface. After six
long antagonizing minutes of fighting, crying, and
screaming, her mind, body, and soul, went completely
numb as she lay on the floor in a pool of her own blood
staring up at the ceiling wondering why God was
allowing this to happen to her.

Hearing all of the crying and screaming, Smoke
made his way upstairs to see what was going on but
what he saw next made his jaw drop. T2 had the look of
a madman in his eyes as he brutally raped Ma Ma's
battered, bloodied, limp body, before Smoke snatched
him off of her.

"Come on T2 tighten the fuck up, that ain't what
we here for!" barked Smoke as he looked down at Ma
Ma feeling bad for her.

"Did you at least get the combination to the safe
yet?" asked Smoke. Hell naw she playing hardball.

"I don't know why she going so hard for a nigga
who don't give a fuck about her," said T2 as he wiped
the sweat off his face with the back of his hand while
still breathing heavily from his sexual assault. She think

he out of town laying low with the fam, the whole time he at Tammy crib laid up with that bitch. He the reason she in this shit in the first place, "I ain't never in my life seen a bitch put a bounty on her own sister's head just so she can have her man to herself," said T2 as he began zipping his pants back up.

Ma Ma couldn't believe her ears. It felt like someone had ripped her heart out of her chest and set it on fire, while repeatedly stabbing it. She was all out of tears to cry as she closed her eyes praying that they would hurry and kill her. She had came to the conclusion that death would be better than what she was going through.

"Well if she ain't gon' talk we might as well just kill her and get the 50 grand from boss Lady," said Smoke. Call Bianca in here so she can see it, said T2 as he picked up his shotgun and turned up the stereo to drown out the sound of the gunshot. As Bianca stood behind T2 looking over his shoulder eagerly waiting on him to end the life of the person responsible for her aunts death, Smoke intervened.

"Naw bruh, let Bianca do it," said Smoke. T2 looked back at Bianca and gave her the shotgun with a look of approval on his face, but before she could pull the trigger Ma Ma held up one finger gesturing for them to hold on.

Oh now you wanna talk? "Look bitch you got about five seconds go get right or I'ma paint this pretty marble floor with your brains," said T2 as he snatched the gun out of Bianca's hands. Take me to the safe, said Ma Ma in a weak, barely audible voice. Smoke picked her up and carried her to Gator's man cave where the five foot tall steel safe was located.

Aight Ma Ma don't try no funny shit, said T2 as he held his shotgun to the back of her head while she attempted to open the safe. Trying to by herself sometime and come up with a plan, Ma Ma stalled and fumbled with the combination until T2 caught on to her.

"Come on now it don't take this long to open up a fucking safe," said T2 as he jammed the cold steel into the side of her head causing her neck to jerk. My fucking eyes are swollen shut, I can barely see, what you expect? Pleaded Ma Ma.

With that being said T2 grabbed the lamp off of Gator's desk and held it up to the safe so she could see the numbers better. As Ma Ma entered the last four digits of the combination to the safe, the heavy steel door swung open and she immediately went into action. Thinking fast and quick on her feet, she grabbed the snub nose .38special that was kept in the safe for scenarios just like this, and in one quick motion spun around sending four hot slugs into T2's chest while the fifth slug found a resting spot in Bianca's lower back as she ran for her life barely escaping through the front door. As she went to fire on Smoke the only sound she heard was CLICK! She had ran out of bullets.

Smoke reached down, picked up T2's shotgun, and aimed it at her head. She was all out of options, there was nothing she could do now but close her eyes and accept her fate. Anticipating the loud boom and forever darkness, Ma Ma was puzzled when she didn't hear the gun go off. Instead she opened her eyes and there stood Smoke in front of her with his hand extended out to her.

"Come on lil moma let me take you to the hospital, you done been through too much shit tonight," said Smoke with a look of sincerity in his eyes. Ma Ma sat there with a crazed look in her eyes staring into his soul wandering what he had up his sleeve and why he hadn't killed her. At this point she didn't have anything to lose so she took his hand and accepted his offer. Making their way out of the front door, Smoke took off his jacket and placed it over her naked body. Before she could get one foot out the door she paused in her tracks then slowly turned around as if she forgot something. You good? asked Smoke. Ma Ma wanted to shoot him in his face for asking a dumb ass question like that as she shot him an ice cold evil stare before limping back into the room where the safe was located.

Once inside she closed the door behind her and went into the real safe that was located behind the wall in the closet. She knew she was on borrowed time so she typed in the password then quickly emptied out all of its contents into a book bag. Once the safe was cleaned out she made her way to the kitchen and began searching through the drawers nonstop until she found what she was looking for.

With a butcher knife in one hand, and a bottle of lighter fluid in the other, Ma Ma had a look in her eyes of someone possessed as she made her way into the guest room where T2 was laying on his back holding on to dear life. Smoke didn't know what she was up to so he took a few steps back closer to the door. The way she stared him down a few minutes ago still had him pretty cautious as he watched her closely.

Come on Ma Ma we gotta get the fuck outta here! Yelled Smoke as he heard the police sirens off in the distance. His words fell on deaf ears as she knelt down beside T2 who was hanging on to dear life with every short breath he took. Staring into his glossy eyes as they began to roll in the back of his head, flashbacks of how he brutally raped her was all she saw as she unbuckled his pants and began to saw his dick off with great force before shoving it down his throat.

"Let's see if you rape somebody else you bitch ass nigga," said Ma Ma as she stood up, drenched is body with lighter fluid, then set him on fire giving him a one way ticket to hell.

"Take me to Richmond, fuck the hospital," said Ma Ma as she limped out of the front door.

CH/15.

~

Gator sat on the plush velvet sofa sipping a cup of syrup as he surfed through the channels. Ma Ma had been on his mind the entire evening and Tammy sensed it so she made her way upstairs and let him be. T2 had texted her earlier in the evening informing her the everything was in place, so she knew it was only a matter of time before she got the news she had been eagerly anticipating.

Over the last few weeks Gator had been contemplating on purposing to Ma Ma once things died down in the streets. Yea it was a huge step but he figured why not? If there was anyone in the world he wanted to spend the rest of his life with, it was her. Being that Tammy was four months pregnant and still hadn't got an abortion, he figured she never had any intentions on getting one in the first place. He didn't know how that situation was going the play out with Ma Ma, he just hoped and prayed that she would have some understanding. It was times like this where the heart felt words of his favorite rapper Boosie really played a role in his day to day life "What if he had another baby, put you in a situation, would you forgive him or leave him and hate him?"

Gators thoughts were interrupted as the constant ringing of the doorbell woke him up out of his halfway nod, causing him to spill his cup of syrup in his lap. It was almost 2:30 in the morning and neither he nor Tammy were expecting company, shit nobody even really knew where she lived. Grabbing his Glock from under the pillow on the sofa he cautiously made his way to the front door. By this time Tammy had gotten out with of her bed and made her way down the steps to see who was at her door this time of night. She was praying to God it wasn't T2 she had called him a few times earlier to see how the job had went but his phone kept going straight to voicemail.

Gator peeped through the blinds but didn't see anyone so he slowly opened the door with his Glock drawn ready to send shots through whoever was on the other side but what he saw next made him fall to his knees in pure agony. Ma Ma lay on the doorstep curled up in a fetal position wearing nothing but an oversized black hoodie with a book bag strapped to her back. Gator quickly picked her up and carried her in the house but when he got a good look at her face he lost it. It looked as if she had been hit by a train, both eyes swollen shut, a huge gash going across her forehead that was bleeding profusely, dried up blood coming from her nose, lip bust open down the middle two times its normal size, and last but not least a trail of blood running down her inner thigh.

Gator was lost for words as rage overwhelmed his body causing him to shake as tears welled up in his eyes. Baby girl what happened?

"Who did this shit to you?" asks Gator as he tried the hold back his tears and keep his composure. Drifting in and out of conscious, Ma Ma used the last drop of strength she had to push out one word before fading the black and falling unconscious. While looking up at Tammy who was standing at the top of the steps with a look of pure shock on her face, Ma Ma uttered the name "T2."

Eleven days later Ma Ma had finally awaken at the hospital. With her head wrapped in bandages and bruises all over her face and body, Gator still manages to find the beauty in her as he leaned over and softly kissed her on her lips.

"Damn baby I thought I lost you," said Gator as he held on yo her hand while gazing into her big beautiful eyes. Just the sight of her laid up in the hospital bed like that made him sick to his stomach as he began to clinch his fist while imagining the excruciating pain she had to endure at the hands of his enemies.
Baby girl I put that on everything I love when I find that nigga T2 he gon' wish he was never born.

"I got Jux and Murdock shaking down the whole city killing everything that he ever loved or cared about until they tell us where he's hiding out at," said Gator in a calm assertive tone as tears began to well up in his eyes. Ma Ma tried to speak but her throat was so parch she was unable to get any words out. Sensing she was in dire need of some water Gator rushed over to the sink and poured her a tall glass before placing it to her lips so she could sip.

Looking around making sure there were no nurses around, through a cracked raspy voice Ma Ma uttered the words, "I killed him," with a smile on her face.

"You killed him?" asked Gator in disbelief. Ma Ma slowly nodded her head up and down before replying, all I remember is he was laying on the floor taking his last breaths then I cut his dick off and shoved it down his throat before I set him on fire. Gator's eyes grew wide as he listened to the gruesome details Ma Ma was sharing with him. Truth be told he thought T2 was still alive and well in the streets but to find out he was murdered and how he was murdered gave him a whole new level of respect for the woman laying before him. Gator's thoughts were interrupted as the doctor entered the room and cleared her throat to get their attention. Mr. Spencer could I have a word with you in the hallway please? Asked the slim pale face nurse as she jotted something down on her clipboard. Sensing it was something important Gator kisses Ma Ma on the forehead assuring that he would be right back as he left her side to go speak with the nurse.

Hi Mr. Spencer my name is Doctor Brawnson, I've been assigned as the lead doctor to overlook the care of your girlfriend. I need to ask you something, so you know what happened to her? Naw actually I don't. I was at a friend's house and she just showed up on the doorstep in the middle of the night, "I don't even know how she got there," said Gator with sincerity in his eyes. The slim pale face doctor looked at him as if he knew mode than what he was revealing but decided to keep her thoughts to herself.

Well Mr. Spencer your girlfriend was brutally assaulted. She suffered blunt force trauma to her head and we had to perform surgery to stop the brain from bleeding. The trauma was so severe that she suffered swelling of the brain and an adequate amount of memory lost. However there is about a thirty percent chance that she'll eventually gain her memory back but nothings guaranteed.

Before I let you go there's one more thing Mr. Spencer. The pale face doctor looked down at the ground then back up at Gator as if she dreaded what she was about to tell him. You girlfriend was raped. She was raped so brutally that it damaged the chances of her ever being able to give birth again, I'm sorry Sir.

The doctor had just confirmed Gators suspicions causing him to feel lightheaded as he took a seat in one of the waiting chairs. He had noticed the blood trail down her inner thigh when she showed up on the doorstep but his heart wouldn't allow himself to believe that someone had violated in such a cruel manner. Unable to withstand any more heart breaking news, Gator walked off and made is way to the parking lot where he sat in his Porsche truck and fired up the blunt he had in the ashtray. As he lay his head back on the headrest while blowing the grade a smoke out of his nose, the words of Boosie ran through his mind, "Too much for one nigga to deal with."

Gator made arrangements for his mother and sister come stay with Ma Ma at the hospital for a couple days while he hit the streets to see what the business was. Poncho was set to be released in a few weeks so he decided to pay him a visit down at the jail but first he had to check on his condo. Ma Ma said that she had killed him and set him on fire in their home but he saw nothing on the news about T2's murder so he decided to check into it himself.

As Gator pulled up to the Gated community he circled the block just to make sure the feds weren't doing surveillance on his home. Once inside the smell of burnt plastic and bleach was so potent that he had to cover up his nose as he walked through the condo. Making his way to the guest room which he turned into his personal "man cave" where the safe was located, he noticed the entire floor was almost burned to a crisp along with a few dried up blood stains on the wall. He could tell that someone had tried to clean up the crime scene but who? And where was the body?

As he made his way through the rest of the condo it looked as if a tornado touched down and caused hell with clothes scattered everywhere and almost every piece of furniture broken and flipped over. Once upstairs he noticed two wine glasses sitting on the edge of the tub but what really had him perplexed was the fact that that hot tub was still halfway full with rose pedals floating in the water. What the fuck? Was Ma Ma cheating on me? Gator thought back to the last conversation he had with her on the night of her attack, who was she with? and just like that it hit him, BIANCA! The more he thought about the conversation they had, he began remembering little pieces like her telling him bout the door being unlocked but he brushed if off. Something wasn't right and Gator was going to get to the bottom of it even if it killed him.

It had been a few months since he last came to visit his right hand man Poncho. Truth be told, Gator had so much shit going on in the city he felt the law might try to snatch him up if they saw him down at the jail so he tried his best to avoid it. Being in the critical type of situation he was in he had to roll the dice and try his hand on this one. If he knew anyone who could give him the info he needed it was Poncho.

Making his way from the back Poncho looked like a caveman in his baggy orange jumpsuit with a nappy fro and so much thick facial hair that a comb couldn't get through it. Poncho was given one year for possession of an illegal bulletproof vest that they pulled off of him in the hospital. The feds wanted him for murder and drug trafficking charges but they could never get enough to make it stick so the smallest thing that could place him behind bars they were on it like flies on shit. That high powered Calico did quite a bit of damage to him but the vest ultimately saved his life. A permanent limp, two fingers missing and thirteen staples across his neck was better than a permanent dirt nap any day.

Big bruh what it do my nig? Said Gator as the two bumped fist through the glass window.

"I'm coolin like a fan mane, couple more months and I'm up out this bitch," said Poncho with a grin on his face. Yea you already know we gon" do it big for you, that ain't no question, "how you holding up tho, you good?" asked Gator.

"Come on lil bruh you already know what the business is," said Poncho with a hint of arrogance behind his words.

"Look mane fuck all that, what going on with Ma Ma she aight?" asked Poncho with a look of concern in his eyes. Yea she just woke up earlier today. You know she was in a coma on life support for 11 straight days.

"A fucking coma bruh, fighting for her life, my baby almost died behind this shit mane," said Gator as his blood began to boil and his hands began to shake. Poncho fell silent as he shook his head from side to side while feeling great sympathy for Ma Ma. That nigga T2 gotta go, "it ain't no way in hell he supposed to be still walking this earth," said Poncho as he looked Gator square in the eyes. That's a done deal, baby girl threw him a party that same night. Poncho had a look of surprise mixed with confusion on his face. He had hear T2 was missing but everyone thought he was just ducked off laying low.

"That's aight mane, that's aight," said Poncho with a look of approval on his face. He knew Ma Ma could hold her own but going up against a certified killer like T2 he didn't think she would stand a chance. Your old lady a true soulja mane, "I can't count how many times she done put that work in and bailed you out," said Poncho as they both shared a laugh. Yea mane she definitely a rare breed, once all this shit blow over I think I'ma purpose to her, "go on and turn in my Playa card mane," said Gator with a straight face.

Poncho leaned back in his seat and looked at his right hand man as if he were speaking a foreign language. Hold on bruh you serious mane?

"Serious as a heart attack," said Gator with that same straight face. Before I hang it up and make it official, I gotta do some homework and hunt down everybody who was involved in this shit, "then I'll be truly at peace," said Gator with a stern look on his face. Poncho looked at him puzzled, "I thought T2 was the

160

only one behind that shit." Naw bruh, that's what I thought too, but the more I looked into it the more it was more than one person, maybe even an inside job. Over the next thirty minutes Gator explained everything to Poncho in full detail until he felt where he was coming from.

Times up let's go! Yelled the short stubby guard as he blew his whistle trying to clear out the visitation room.

"Yea bruh you right that definitely sound like an inside job," said Poncho as he stroked his beard. Just do me a favor and wait until I get home before you make any moves, but until then go spend some time with your girl she need you mane. With that being said, the two of them stood up and bumped first through the glass window before parting ways.

For the next six days Gator stayed at the hospital with Ma Ma day in & day out, the only time he would leave her side was to shower and change clothes. Tammy had stopped by a few times to check up on her but it was more out of guilt than anything. Seeing her sister laid up in the hospital like that really took a toll on her and it showed every time came to see her. The hospital was releasing her the next morning so due to the circumstances the three of them decided it would be best if they just stayed at Tammy's place for the time being, at least just until Gator and Ma Ma found a new place. Pulling up the Tammy's home Gator wandered if he was making the right decision. He didn't want Ma Ma shacked up in some hotel and going back to their condo was definitely out of the question so it seemed like this was his last option.

As Ma Ma made herself comfortable in the lavish guest room upstairs, Gator made his way downtown the kitchen where Tammy was to clear the air and get some understanding between the two.

161

"Look Tammy we gotta talk," said Gator as he sat down on the barstool in the kitchen. As she turned around to face him Gator could tell she had been crying because her dark green eyes were now puffy and red as she held a glass of wine in her hand.

What's wrong girl, you aight? Asked Gator. Yea it's just that I feel so fucked up about what happened.

"You don't understand Gator my sister shouldn't be going through no shit like this," said Tammy as she padded her tear filled eyes with a napkin to prevent the tears from falling down her face. Her guilty conscious was eating her up inside and as bad as she wanted to confess she just couldn't.

The two of them locked eyes for a brief moment before Gator looked away. He knew the type of power Tammy possessed over him but enough was enough. It was time for him to draw the line and let it be known that Ma Ma was his main priority.

"You ain't gotta avoid eye contact with me I know what you came down here to talk to me about," said Tammy as she took a sip from her glass of wine.

"So you know we can't fuck around no more then," said Gator as he made firm eye contact with her letting her know he was serious this time. Tammy twirled her straw around in her drink then looked out the window before replying, "yea I understand we can't fuck around any longer and I'm willing to accept that, its gon' be hard but I'm willing to do anything to protect my sister's heart. This was actually going smoother than Gator had expected, he wondered where was all of this do the right thing shit at when she was fucking and sucking his brains out for the past year.

Feeling like now was the best time to put all of his cards on the table, Gator decided to address the elephant in the room. So now that we got some understanding, what up with this baby situation? Tammy

162

looked at him with pure malice in her eyes as she fell silent while trying to keep herself calm. If looks could kill Gator would've been a dead muthafucka. Well to answer your question, "I'm almost five months pregnant and being this late in my pregnancy I doubt any doctor will perform an abortion," said Tammy as she tried her best to hold her tongue and avoid saying what was truly on her mind.

Gator sat there shaking his head from side to side while staring out the window, wondering why she was trying go fuck his life up. Sure both of them were to blame for having the affair, but Tammy was the one who had the power clean it up and fix it, she just refused to. Look Tammy Ma Ma done been through too much shit as it is, "ain't no way in hell I can tell her I'm having a baby with her sister that shit will kill her," said Gator with a great deal of emotion. Tammy shot him a piercing stare with those devilish green eyes before replying, "that ain't my problem, now is it?" then casually stood up and left Gator sitting in the kitchen alone with his head spinning.

CH/16.

~

Over the next few days the three of them enjoyed each other's company as if they were one big family. Gator hoped Tammy comments the other day was just her speaking off of emotion because the last thing he wanted to do was put his hands on her or worse. Both of them had a lot to lose if Ma Ma found out about the affair so the best thing for Tammy to do was act like it never happened.

Gator had took some time off from the trap and just focused on the love of his life, she had been through so much he felt he owed her that and much more. Ma Ma and Tammy were getting along like best friends. Looking at the two of them working side by side in the kitchen to prepare the meal for dinner Gator sat back and thought to himself, "Damn what if I could have both of them at the same time?" That thought was quickly erased out of his head and replaced with images of Ma Ma killing the both of them if she ever found out about their secret love affair.

The next day Poncho was scheduled to be released from the city jail. His original release date was still a month away but due to overcrowding they released him a few weeks early. His old lady was throwing him a little get together at their home in Grist Mill with just his family and close friends, since he had been shot up like that she decided against throwing him a big party at a club.

His old lady Keyana was cool and laid back but she ain't take no shit. She was originally from Chicago but she had been living in VA, ever since she was

164

thirteen. Her and Poncho met at a local high school football game their freshman year and the two have been together ever since.

Ma Ma had been cooped up in the house ever since she came home from the hospital so Gator decided to bring her along with him so she could get a breath of fresh air and a change of scenery. Ma Ma kept it simple in a black Dolce` & Gabbana jumpsuit with a matching pair of Christian Louboutin heels, while Gator matched her fly wearing a black Cashmere sweater, grey Ferragamo pants, with a pair of black suede Balmain boots. Ma Ma still looked gorgeous as ever even with that long scar going across her forehead. She actually embraced it calling it her "war wound."

The two of them pulled up to Poncho's around 7:30 and once inside they were greeted with daps and hugs from Poncho's family and close friends. Gator and Poncho had been so tight for so long that Poncho's family was like his family so it was all love. No bullshit, no hating, just an old fashion good time over some southern hospitality soul food, Earth Wind & Fire, and plenty of Cognac.

After a friendly game of dominoes Gator and Poncho made their way outside to the patio so they could chop it up one on one. Once outside the cold night air felt good to Gator's body as it cooled him down a bit. All of those shots of Cognac had his body heat rising as he began to fan himself, so some crisp night air along with a fat blunt was exactly what he needed.

"My nig welcome back mane how it feel to be up out that cage?" asked Gator with a smile on his face. Bruh you already know I'm loving every second of it, as soon as this lil get together is over with I'ma go in here and give Keyana the business! Eight months without no pussy I'm like I dog in heat right now you heard me.

"Hold on bruh you been home all day and you

165

mean to tell me she ain't gave you no pussy yet?" asked Gator. Mane hell naw, replied Poncho as the two shared a laugh.

I made some phone calls and reached out to some people after you came to see me and word got back on who else was involved in that situation. Gator was all ears as he eagerly waited on Poncho to break the news to him.

"Some bitch name Bianca who she was locked up with, and Smoke," said Poncho as he flicked the ashes from the blunt before passing it to Gator. Gator shook his head from side to side then took a long pull from the blunt while thinking out loud, I knew something won't right with that bitch, I told Ma Ma to fall back and play her from a distance, and Smoke, that was T2's lil flunkie so that's not surprising, but I thought he would've had enough sense not to cross me.

"I know where Smoke moma live at and as far as Bianca I don't know too much about her but I can put a couple dollars on her head to get her snatched up," said Gator as he began to strategize. Okay cool that sound like a plan, but the situation get a lil deeper than that, said Poncho. You see, Bianca and Smoke are just the peons in this situation, "the person that we need to focus on the most is the person who orchestrated the hit and put the bounty on her head," said Poncho with a straight face.

Gator put his drink down and looked at Poncho with a state of confusion on his face. What the hell you talking bout bruh? Poncho paused for a second and gathered his words in his head before he spoke again, he knew this was a touchy subject for his childhood friend so he made sure to present it to him the right way. Look lil bruh, I don't know what enemies Ma Ma got out their but somebody wants her dead, and whoever it is they serious about it cause the price tag was $50,000.

Gator sat there in deep thought as he picked his brain wondering who would want Ma Ma dead and pay such a high price. The first thought that came to his mind was Angel's people but he quickly disregarded them from the equation because he knew they didn't have that type of money. Then he thought about the other handful of dealers in the city who were getting that type of money but what would they accomplish by getting rid of Ma Ma? If anything they would've put the hit on him since he was the one flooding the city with his high grade heroin making it hard for them to profit off of their bullshit ass dope.

"I don't know Poncho, I don't know," said Gator as he stroked the hair under his chin while staring off into the clear night sky. Yea, we'll figure it out lil bruh don't stress yourself over it. One thing for sure, two things for certain, what's done in the dark will eventually come to light.

The next morning Gator hit the streets early with his mind made up. Before leaving the house he gave Ma Ma five grand and told her and Tammy to go enjoy themselves for the day. As much as he loved Ma Ma, him sitting in the house laid up with her all day wasn't going to bring her justice so he had to go for what he knew. Poncho was on some be patient shit, Gator knew his right hand man wasn't telling him anything wrong but all that shit flew in one ear and out the other. Pulling up across the train tracks around 9 in the morning Gator spotted Jux and Murdock on the porch of one of their trap spot already waiting on him. Gator hoped out if his Porsche truck and joined his comrades as the three of them came up with a master plan to bring Smoke of hiding. Gator didn't bother bringing Poncho into the mix due to the fact that he had just gotten out and needed to spend time with his family, but in all actuality he knew that Poncho would disapprove of what he had in mind.

Later on that evening the three of them pulled up out Smokes neighborhood in Newsome Park. They were still in Murdock's brand new Audi A7 so they parked a few blocks away then walked to Smoke's mother house so no one could identify what they were driving. One thing Gator learned in the streets, is that when you're out there head first selling dope, robbing, murdering, and thuggin foreal, you need to move your moma out the hood the first chance you get.
Being that it was night time in the fall the temperature had dwindled down a bit so there wasn't many people outside.

There were a few young hustlers along with about five or six junkies sitting on the stoop a few doors down but Gator wasn't concerned, him and his men would be in and out. God forbid any of them wanting to play hero because Gator and his men had enough fire power to knock down their whole project building. Gator knocked on the door with Murdock and Jux right behind him. The sound of the "Ohio Players," could be heard blaring through the stereo in the apartment so Gator knocked a little louder this time. He was trying to avoid kicking in the nice woman's door but if need be then he would.

As soon as he was about to kick the door off the hinges he heard a female voice on the other side of the door asking who is it.

"It's Jay!" shouted Gator over the loud music so the woman could hear him.

"If you looking for Smoke he ain't here," said the woman on the other side of the door. I can't hear you! Yelled Gator. Frustrated with the person on the other side of the door, she quickly opened it just enough so they could hear her. I said if you looking for Smoke he ain't, before she could get out another word Gator shoved his Glock in her face and forced his way through the front door with Jux and Murdock right behind him.

Once inside the apartment Jux searched downstairs while Murdock searches upstairs.

"Bitch where yo muthafukin son at?" barked Gator as he viciously smacked her in the face with his pistol causing her to spit a couple of her bloody teeth out on the ground.

"I don't know, I swear to God I don't know!" pleaded the woman as she held on to her swollen jaw fearing the worst. Feeling like she was playing games, Gator repeatedly pistol whipped her until her face was covered in blood.

"I'm gon' ask you one more time, where yo son at?" asked Gator in a calm assertive tone.
By now the woman's voice was almost at a whisper as she was on the verge of losing conscious.

"You ain't gon' believe what I found," said Murdock as he made his way down the steps with a crying toddler in his hand who looked just like Smoke. Please that's my grandson he's only four years old please don't hurt him! In one quick motion Murdock smacked the young boy across the face with the butt of his Mac90 sending him flying across the kitchen floor. Now I'm gon' ask you one more time, where he at? The woman didn't reply she just sobbed uncontrollably as she reached out to her grandson who was still laying on the kitchen floor.

Being the level headed one of the crew Jux intervened before things got out of hand and took a turn for the worst.

"She don't know where he at bruh let's slide off before somebody call the law," said Jux letting the two hotheads know that they had did enough. "Yea you probably right," said Gator as he stood up from his squatting position and took a step back from the

169

traumatized woman. When you talk Smoke tell him Bossman stopped by. Gator put his Glock to the terrified woman's leg and let off two shots before leaving the apartment. He didn't have any intentions on killing her he just wanted to send a message, which he did loud and clear.

CH/17.

~

    The weekend was just one day away so Gator was preparing for his trip to Baltimore while Ma Ma sat on the bed Indian style with her face screwed up. Come on baby girl don't act like that, you know I would take you with me but it's only the fellas this weekend,

    "Poncho ain't taking his old lady with him," said Gator trying to drift the attention to Poncho instead of himself. Fuck Poncho, he the reason you going out of town in the first place.

    "That niggas did eight punk ass months and y'all celebrating like he just came home from a ten year bid," said Ma Ma as she spoke with her arms folded across her chest.

    Gator couldn't help but crack a smile as he admired his girls' feistiness. Girl you a trip, you know I love you right? Yea whatever, said Ma Ma as she cut her eyes at him. Knowing how to get her off of his back and back on his good side Gator walked over and handed her the blunt he had just finished rolling.

    "Here spark this and lay your head back on the pillow," said Gator as he went to go close the bedroom door.

    Ma Ma did as she was told and within seconds she could feel his soft lips caressing her pretty feet as he slowly made he is way up her inner thighs. Licking circles around her inner thighs then making his way to he pussy where he began planting soft kisses on her pussy lips causes her breathing to switch up as she anticipated his tongue slow dancing up and down her clit until she spilled her sweet juices all over his face. With every kiss, lick, and blow, her pussy got warmer and warmer. Unable to withstand the foreplay any longer she grabbed the back of his neck shoving his face into her warm fat pussy that was screaming his name.

Gator ate her pussy with passion and persistence for a full thirty minutes straight without coming up for air not one time. As she lay on her back with her head propped up against the pillow and her legs wide open Gator licked a trail from her pussy to her asshole causing her to bite down on her bottom lip as she gently massaged her golden brown nipples. She had never been to heaven but she felt this was as close as she was going to get as she reached her second orgasm. Needless to say, after Gator worked his tongue out like he was at the gym then hit her with the dope dick for an hour straight, she was no longer trippin about him going to Baltimore, she just wanted him to hurry and come back.

After putting Ma Ma to sleep Gator made his way downstairs to grab a bite to eat. After giving her the business like that it had consumed most of his energy so a late night snack and a Newport was exactly what he needed to shake back. While entering the kitchen he notice Tammy sitting in the living room munching on a peach with a glass of wine in her hand so he decided to check on her.

"It's almost three in the morning what you doing up this late down her by yourself?" asked Gator as he took a seat down beside her on the sofa. The smooth voice of Anita Baker could be heard playing softly on her iPhone, Gator could tell she had a lot weighing on her mind.

"What's on your mind girl talk to me," said Gator as he let his hand rest on her thigh then took the glass of wine out of her hand.

"I got so much shit going on in my head right now I don't even know where to start," said Tammy as she wiped away a single tear that slid down her cheek.

Its gon' be aight lil moma whatever you going through
you ain't gotta go through it by yourself, we all in this
shit together ya heard me.

Tammy gazed into his eyes with a look so fierce
it was as if she could see through is soul. With those
almond shaped, dark green eyes, he could never truly tell
what she was thinking but he knew something was
weighing heavy on her. Without another word being said
she gently kissed him on the lips then made her way
upstairs to her bedroom and closed the door behind her.

The following morning Gator, Jux, Murdock,
and Poncho, met up on Childs ave then hopped on
interstate64 and made their way to Baltimore. Poncho
rode with Gator in his midnight blue Rolls Royce
Wraith, which he only pulled out for special occasions,
while Murdock and Jux rode together in Mudock's
cocaine white Audi A7. Jux and Murdock had the guns
in the Audi with them so they led the way while Poncho
and Gator trailed them. This was a tactic they had been
using for years to avoid the car in front from being
pulled over. Even though they were taking a trip to go
relax and enjoy themselves, there was no way in hell
they were going to Baltimore unarmed.

There were some things that had transpired over
the course of Poncho being away in the hospital and
incarcerated so Gator felt now was the best time to bring
it to his attention being that they had a three hour road
trip ahead of them. Gator put his Wraith in cruise control
and let and let it coat up the interstate as he reclined his
seat while taking sips from his cup of syrup.

"I think I fucked up bruh," said Gator as he
glanced out the driver side window.

"What you talking bout?" asked Poncho. Tammy
mane, you know I been fucking her for over a year now,
it was supposed to be a onetime thing but I couldn't
shake her. No matter how hard I tried to keep my dick

out of her I always found myself right back in between her legs, now I done fucked around and got her pregnant mane.

Poncho raised his eyebrows then turned music down to make sure he heard right. Hold on, hold on, you did what?

"Yea bruh, she five months pregnant and she keeping it," said Gator in a tone that revealed his worries. Poncho leaned back in the mahogany brown leather seat and slowly shook his head from side to side. I told you bruh, "do not start fucking with that bitch," just keep it strictly business. Now if she get in her feelings and feel like you tryna play her she can get on some bullshit and stop doing business with us. Poncho did have a point, Gator never thought about it in that aspect. To find another plug like Tammy and her people would be like trying to find a needle in a haystack, especially in Virginia.

Now what about Ma Ma? All three of y'all living together and you think she ain't go'n find out y'all fucking?

"Hell naw," replied Gator sharply. Plus I told Tammy I was done fucking around with her, we came to and understanding she was cool with it. Once again Poncho shook his head from side to side while thinking to himself how unaware Gator was to how the female mind works.

Look lil bruh, all of that fairytale shit about her being "cool" with y'all not fucking around no more is bullshit. That girl betrayed her own sister for your affection and on top of that you put a baby in her so why would she just willingly agree to being cut off?

"Women are smarter and more calculating than you what you may think and if I were you I'd get Ma Ma out of that house ASAP because a women's intuition is very strong and they can feel when something ain't

right," said Poncho with a straight face.
Now what about the baby?

"You think the baby ain't gon' come out looking like you?" asked Poncho with a smirk on his face. Once again this was something that Gator hadn't considered.

"Yea you right I ant even think about that," said Gator as he began to feel more worried about his future with Ma Ma. I'm telling you bruh you gon' start listening to me one of these days, 'I ain't gon' always be here to pull you up out that water so you better tighten up and stop playing with fire,' said Poncho.

Once they arrived in Maryland Gator called the Marriott to make sure their room was ready and just as he expected, it wasn't. They informed him that the sweet would be ready in a couple of hours so to burn some time they figured they would just ride through the city. Baltimore wasn't your typical city that you would ride around sight-seeing. With all of the project buildings and rundown houses lined up in rows, Gator thought to himself, "Shit I might as well be back around the way." Pulling up to a rundown corner store with a heavy amount of drug activity in the front, Gator hope out of his Wraith and made his way inside to get a box of blunts and a pineapple Fanta. Once inside he laid eyes on this beautiful yellow bone stallion who stood at about 5'10 with long fire red hair that resembled curly fries, and beautiful exotic looking tattoos all over her body. Making her way to the counter the two of them briefly made eye contact as she placed her items on the counter for the clerk to ring up.

"I'm sorry lady we don't accept anything larger than a $20 bill, read the sign," said the Arab clerk with a hint of aggression behind his words as he rejected the woman's $50 bill. Observing the confusion and frustration on the woman's face Gator intervened and offered to pay for her items. Pulling out a large dope man knot Gator thumbed through his bankroll with gold and diamond clusters on almost all of his fingers until he found a $10 bill.

Thanks I appreciate it, "these muthafuckas always tryna give somebody a hard time," said the red hair woman as she made her way out of the store with Gator beside her. Yea you right, you ain't never lied about that, my name Gator nice to meet you. The red hair woman looked at Gator with a look of uncertainty on her face then replied, "My name is Justice, nice to meet you too."

Gator went to shake her hand but before he could fully extend it he thought about a saying that his old head Jay Cofield installed in him back in the day, "hug a woman tight, never shake a woman's hand." With that piece of game embedded in his mind he leaned in for a hug and she accepted with open arms. Feeling as soft as a butter biscuit and smelling like a fresh batch of cotton candy Gator had to snap back into reality and let her go once he realized he was still hugging her. He thought the overextended hug might have caused her to feel uncomfortable but once he release her from his warm embrace her facial expression said otherwise. So Gator where you from? Cause I can tell you ain't from around here said Justice as she studied his attire which consisted of a dark blue Burberry sweater, grey Evisu jeans, and a pair of dark blue Balmain boots, with his clear frame good Versace glasses.

Damn lil moma I stand out like that?

"You definitely do," replied Justice with a grin on her face. Gator cracked a smile flashing his shiny good teeth before replying, "I'm from VA, Hampton VA. Me and my people down here for the weekend we doing a lil celebrating, we gon' hit Eldorado's tonight, "you should come fuck with us," said Gator as he undressed the beautiful high yellow stallion with his eyes. Justice began smiling and shaking her head from side to side.

"What wrong did I say something funny?" asked a curious Gator. Naw it's just that, Eldorado's that's where I work at.

"Oh shit well that's a plus, I'ma see you tonight then lil moma," said Gator with a hint of excitement behind his words.

"Yea you definitely will," said Justice as she programmed her number in his phone before climbing into her Lexus jeep and pulling off.

CH/18

~

Back at home Tammy and Ma Ma treated themselves to a day at the spa filled with pampering and much needed relaxation. Tammy had been feeling like a ticking time bomb lately as her emotions took her on a rollercoaster ride. Part of her wanted to do the right thing by protecting her sister's feelings and shielding her from the heart breaking truth that she was pregnant with Gator's child, while the other part of her wanted to knock her head off her shoulder every time she caught a glimpse of Gator showing her affection.

Rubbing her stomach while getting her pedicure, thoughts of her child growing up without a father took over her thought process as she glanced over at Ma Ma. To her surprise Ma Ma was staring back at her with a look so fierce it causes Tammy to quickly look away. Ma Ma was deeply consumed in her own thoughts. Lately she had been feeling like something was off about her sister but she just couldn't put a finger on it.

As Tammy maneuvered her G Wagen Benz truck through the busy city streets of downtown Richmond, Ma Ma decided to break the silence. You know Tammy I never got a chance to ask you who the lucky man was, I mean you never even talk about him. Lucky man?

"Girl what you talking about?" asked Tammy. Your baby daddy, not one time have I heard you speak of him, "he must not be shit," said Ma Ma with an inquiring mind.

Yea you can say that again.

"You know how these niggas do, butter you all

178

up for you to give them the pussy, have you thinking
everything is peaches and cream then as soon as the
word pregnant come out they get amnesia about the fact
that their dick was living in your pussy for the last 11 or
12 months," said Tammy as the two shared a much
needed laugh. Yea well fuck him you don't need him,
plus it ain't like you hurting for money so you'll be aight.
That's why I'm glad me and Gator got a relationship the
way we do, "I mean we go through our lil rough patches
from time to time but at the end of the day we know
where each other heart lies," said Ma Ma as her heart
began to beam with joy inside. Tammy looked at her
sister through her $700 Fendi sunglasses and cracked a
smile while thinking to herself, "Only if you knew baby
girl, only if you knew."

The two of them made their way back to
Tammy's place around eight in the evening. Tammy was
tired from all of the ripping and running they had been
doing all day so she decided to take a hot shower while
Ma Ma prepared the dinner. Making her way through the
front door Tammy place he red suede Dolce` & Gabbana
pursue on the kitchen counter then let her long sexy legs
lead her to the shower. Gator hadn't given her any dick
since Ma Ma came home from the hospital so she
planned on pulling out her purple vibrator and playing
with her pussy in the shower until her fingers were
drenched in her warm thick cum.

The constant ringing of Tammy's phone was
beginning to irritate Ma Ma as she chopped up the
vegetables and seasoned the catfish so she grabbed the
phone and took it to Tammy in the shower. Here Tammy
your phone been ringing nonstop for the past five
minutes you might wanna answer it, said Ma Ma as she
entered the bathroom. Stepping out of the shower with a
towel wrapped around her body she check her phone and
noticed she had eight missed calls, all from Smoke. Not

knowing if Ma Ma got a glance at the name on the caller ID or not she quickly erased his name and number out of her phone as she made her way down the hall to her bedroom to return his call. The last thing she needed was for Ma Ma to be snooping around trying to play detective.

As Tammy dialed his number he anxiously picked on the first ring.

"Bitch what the fuck you done got me into! Yo nigga Gator!" before he could continue his rant Tammy stopped him in his tracks. Hold on, hold on, first of all you need to watch you're fucking mouth and remember who the fuck you talking to.

"I ain't one of them bum ass bitches you be dealing with I'll get yo ass erased," said Tammy in a calm but assertive tone.

Yea aight, like I was saying, your boy Gator trippin.

"I don't know what you and T2 done got me into but I don't want no parts of this shit," said T2 in a much more respectable tone. Him and his boys ran up in my moma spot, pistol whipped her, shot her two times, and pistol whipped my four year old son!

"Wait, wait, hold on you said they did what?" asked Tammy making sure her ears weren't playing tricks on her.

"Yea you heard right," said Smoke confirming what we thought she heard. Word is they gon' kill everybody who had something to do with that shit and whoever get in the way. I know how you feel about Gator but you need to put your feelings to the side and think about your life, that nigga Gator is a threat you need to get rid of his ass before you end up like T2.

"In the mean time you need to send me some money so I can fly my family down here where I'm at," said Smoke with heavy desperation in his voice.

Aight I got you just calm down, "where you at so I can Western Union you the money?" asked Tammy. I'm in Stone Mountain Georgia but I don't know for how long. Tammy paused for a brief moment as she put a play together in her head.

"Okay I'll take care of it, give me a couple hours and I'll call you with the address of the Western Union you'll need to go to," said Tammy giving him a sense of comfort.

"Aight Tammy good looking out," said Smoke feeling a bit better about his situation.

"Yea don't worry about," replied Tammy. Hey Smoke before you hang up let me ask you something. How did she make it out of that house alive anyway? There was a brief moment of silence on the other end before Smoke replied, "To be honest with you Tammy, I don't even know."

Tammy hung up her phone then threw it on the bed and began to casually lotion up her body as if she didn't have a care in the world. She was far from stupid she knew Smoke was feeding her bullshit. Smoke was a certified killer along with T2, ain't no way in hell she was supposed to walk out of that house alive unless somebody let her.

She now saw Smoke as a liability and had to eliminate him. If Gator got to him before she did she was sure as hell that he would fold like a chair and tell him everything just the try to save his own ass. Thinking fast and using her resources reached out to her people in Decatur who owed her a favor or two, and just like that Smoke would be taken care of in a couple hours.

CH/19.

~

Back in Baltimore Gator and his team pulled up to Club Eldorado's and killed the parking lot. Stepping out of his $300,000 Rolls Royce coupe, with Murdock parked beside him in his $90,000 Audi A7, all eyes were on them as they walked to the front of the line draped in every designer from Fendi, to Ferragamo, to Bally. Gator knew they would have a hard time getting past security with their small arsenal of firearms so they gave the two bouncers $700 a piece to let them in without being frisk. Once inside them four young hustlers were like kids in a candy store, they had never experienced anything like this before. The strip clubs back home were mediocre hole in the wall clubs where the strippers couldn't even get naked, this shit right here was elite!

Two stories with about six stages, velvet plush carpet draped throughout the entire club and all types of beautiful women from all sorts if different ethnics walking around ass naked. Making their way to the second floor where they had a VIP section reserved, they began to order up their bottles and singles. Two bottles of Peach Cîroc, two bottles of Hennessey, and $40,000 in ones stuffed in two separate milk crates filled to the brim.

Gator had forgot to call justice and let her know that he was in the building so he pulled out his phone and began to text her. Before her could finish the text her looked up and the bartender was in route bringing them their drinks. All he could see was a pair of sexy butter cream legs approaching their table holding their bottles in the air with sparkles flying. It wasn't until she placed the bottles on the table that he realized who she was.

"Hey sexy," said Justice as she placed their bottles on the table dressed in a red silk one piece bathing suit, with black fishnet stockings, and a sexy pair of red bottom high heels on. Her bright red curly hair was now straight and sleek as it hung down the middle of her back giving her more of an elegant look. All of this threw Gator for a loop, when she said she worked at Eldorado's he automatically figured she was a stripper.

"Damn Baby girl you putting on ain't you," said Gator as he stood up to give her a warm welcoming hug, and once again he found himself having a hard time letting her out of his arms. Damn girl you smell so good and your body feel so good in my arms it's like I don't even wanna let you go. Justice blushed a little showing her deep sexy dimples as Gator finally released her from his enticing embrace.

"You ain't have to let go of me so soon, you could've held on to me a little longer," said Justice as she twirled her finger around her hair while gazing into his cloudy red eyes.

The two of them flirted back N forth for the next few minutes making one another smile and blush as if they were high school sweethearts. Poncho noticed Gator off to the side boo loving then nudged Jux on the shoulder who had two beautiful women on his lap already.

"Look at like bruh over their all booed up, we ain't even been in the club 15 minutes yet," said Poncho.

"Aye Gator! Gator! Tighten up lil bruh, all this ass over here you trippin mane!" yelled Poncho over the loud music.

Gator Glanced over at his boys who were getting "well acquainted" with a handful of beautiful Baltimore women, then he casually turned his attention back to Justice as if he wasn't fazed. Well it looks like your boys need you over there so go enjoy yourself just make sure you get at me before you leave, said Justice as she kissed him on the cheek then made her way through the crowd to continue serving drinks. Gator was mesmerized as her big yellow soft ass bounced with every graceful step she took walking away.

Snapping out of his trance gator back to the VIP section where the party was just getting started. As the women they were partying with took shot after shot, while throwing back ecstasy pills like they were skittles, things began to heat up a bit. Pieces of clothing began to slowly come off piece by piece and the more turned up they got, the more Gator and his team showered them with ones. Seeing the amount of money being showered on the women they just met in the club who weren't even strippers, caused the actual strippers to step it up a notch and turn up for the attention of the young hustlers.

Everything was going down, nothing seemed to be off limits. Gator and Murdock made it rain on the two honey brown stallions who were giving them the show of their lives as they the shorter one of the two held on to the other one's waist while she was in the doggy style position and began stoking her from behind as if she was fucking her. Soft brown thighs with a light mist of sweat smacking up against her friend's soft phat ass laced in baby oil had the two young hustlers' full attention as Gator popped another rubber band off a stack of ones. Gator just so happened to glance up and what he saw next further reminded him that he was no longer back home in a mediocre titty bar. Off in the corner he spotted Jux and Poncho laid back on the plush sofa getting a nice dose of oral treatment from two beautiful Dominican looking women who looked like they could be sisters. Focusing back on the two women in front of him who were beginning to arouse him, Gator hit the blunt then said to himself with a smile on his face,

"damn this what I been missing the whole time."
As the night went on the X-rated show continued.
Strippers squirted water out of their pussy four feet into
the air, Twelve inch dildos being used in deep throat
contest, I mean the list goes on. Gator sat back and
thought to himself, "shit fuck Hampton I can get used to
this Baltimore shit.

As the night came to an end both crates of
money were empty. Between the four of them they had
threw a total of forty grand in one night and if you ask
Gator that forty grand was definitely "week spent." It
was close to four in the morning but the party was far
from over. Poncho had arranged for a handful of women
they met in the club to meet them back at their room
including the two exotic looking Dominican women.
With a party pack of double stack ecstasy pills and a
little over an ounce of purple Kush left, the four young
hustlers from across the tracks had plans on making a
movie tonight that would be talked about for years to
come.

Making their way out of the club headed for the
parking lot, Gator spotted Justice putting her bags in the
trunk of her dark green Lexus jeep. As soon as he saw
her it dawned on him that he was supposed to touch
bases with her before he left but he was so caught up in
the new scenery of new women it totally slipped his
mind.

"Damn lil moma that's my fault, I was so caught
up fucking with my boys I forgot to come kick it with
you," said Gator as he was walking up on her.
Yea I see you were occupied, did you enjoy yourself?
Asked Justice with a slight grin on her face.

"Yea I definitely did, I just might fuck around
and make Baltimore my second home," said Gator as he
sparked a Newport. A lighthearted smile spread across
her face as she replied, "yea that would be nice, and

these Baltimore girls wouldn't know what to do with you.

Gator cracked a smile as he undressed this beautiful woman in front of him with his eyes. It was something about her that stood out something peculiar, something about her that gave of an alluring vibe that made Gator want to touch, taste, feel, and learn everything about this woman. So what you about to get into? Asked Justice. Gator looked over at his boys who were standing in front of Murdock's Audi conversing with about five or six half naked women all rolling off ecstasy down for whatever.

The look on Gator's face said it all he didn't even have to answer her question. Well you go have fun, don't let me get in the way of y'all men's night out, just call me before you head back to VA. With that being said Justice gave him a hug followed with a friendly kiss on the cheek before climbing into her Lexus jeep.

Turning around and making his way back to where his friends were gathered, something in his body just wouldn't allow him to walk away from this woman and possibly never see her again. Having a change of heart Gator walked back to her jeep, leaned in through the driver side window with a grin in his face and told her, "I'ma fall back and chill with you tonight lil moma."

"What about your boys?" asked Justice not wanting to be a party pooper. Shit they aight, "I see them muthafuckas damn near everyday back home, this might be the last time I get to mingle in your presence," said Gator stroking her ego. Aww look at you making me feel all special, said Justice as she began to blush showing off her heartwarming dimples.

With his mind made up gator made his way over to his boys who were beginning to get lil too rowdy while rapping along the Project Pat album "Mista don't play," and informed them that he wouldn't be joining them tonight and that he would be hanging out with Justice instead. Murdock was the first to speak on it. Bruh we got six pieces of new pussy lined up ready to back to the room and get buck wild and you mean to tell me you ain't going?

"That bartender girl got my young boy nose wide open," said Poncho as they all shared a laugh including Gator. Look mane y'all take y'all time ima catch y'all tomorrow, said Gator as he dapped up his childhood friends. Before he turned to walk away Murdock pulled out his black .40cal Sig from his waist and handed it to him. Meet us at the room around three, that's when we rolling out, said Murdock.

About twenty minutes later they arrived at her place in a quiet neighborhood on the outskirts of the city. Once inside Gator made himself comfortable as he took a seat on the charcoal black suede sofa and began rolling a blunt.

"You can make yourself at home I'ma go get out of these clothes," said Justice as she placed her purse on the kitchen counter then made her way down the hallway.

Putting the finishing touches on four gram blunt, Gator sat back and let the purple Kush marinate in his lungs as he slowly blew the smoke out of his nose. Waiting on Justice to return from the shower, the words of Boosie ran throw his mind, "her pussy might be clean if her house clean." With that thought in mind Gator began to scan her living room for any signs of filth so he could get a better understanding of the woman be was dealing with. He even checked her kitchen and peeped into her bedroom to make sure everything was legit and just as he hoped, everything was squeaky clean. Thinking about his boys and knowing they were having the time if their lives it dawned on him that he still had a few ecstasy pills on him. He didn't know if she fucked around or not so he popped half a pill while she was in the shower. About 15 minutes late Justice emerged from her bedroom wearing a white see through long sleeve shirt, with a pair if sexy white laced panties, and bra to match. The enticing smell of Almond Shea Butter flowed from her soft body as she sat down next to Gator who was mesmerized by her beauty and style. Her long red hair was now tied up in a bun exposing her baby hair giving her a slight look of innocence.

You rollin ain't you? Asked Justice as she sat on the sofa Indian style beside Gator looking into his eyes. Naw why you say that? "Cause you can't stop grinding you teeth and you chewing the hell outta that gum," said Justice with a grin on her face. Gator cracked a smile and threw his hands up gesturing be had been caught. Yea yo got me, I'm rolling like a muthafuckaa, said Gator as he rubbed his hand over his freshly cut fade.

"You got some more?" asked Justice.
This was music to Gator's ears. Rolling off ecstasy is okay when you're the only one high, but when your partner gets down with you it's ten times better.

"Yea I got a few more left," said Gator nonchalantly. Reaching into the pocket of his boxer briefs Gator pulled out a small bag of red Bart Simpson ecstasy pills and dropped one in her hand.
As she went to throw the pill back Gator sat up and stopped her. Hold on lil moma you gotta take your time with that, that's a triple stack just pop half of it. Justice looked at him with a wicked grin on her face then threw back the whole pill and began to chew it as if it were a delicious piece of sweet candy. Gator sat there in awe thinking to himself, "oh this bitch a straight savage."

Over the next couple of hours the two of them got acquainted very well with one another. They talked about everything from past relationships, to family, to dreams. Justice was a nurse throughout the day and a bartender at night, who at the age of 23 had dreams of one day owning her own clinic to assist the families in poverty without healthcare.

Sitting in the couch like that with her legs crossed Indian style had Gator in a trance as his eyes traveled from the pretty pedicured toes with white toe tips, to her thick yellow thighs spiced up with colorful tattoos, then finally to her fat pussy as it bulged through her white laced panties like a small fist. Justice sensed his hormones arousing because hers were as well. Every time Gator would open his mouth to speak or roll a blunt, her eyes would be glued to his sexy full lips as she imagined what it would feel like to ride his face and release her sweet nectar all over his mouth full of gold. Both of their minds were on the same thing so Justice leaned over and blew him a shotgun. That was all it took as Gator grabbed hold of her hips and guided her onto his lap. Once she was on his lap the two began passionately tongue kissing while she anxiously fumbled with his farragamo belt buckle to unleash his throbbing manhood.

Wrestling his thick manhood out of his Armani boxers, Justice got on her knees and went to work making a sloppy mess. She normally didn't give head unless she was in a relationship but since this was Gators last day in town she wanted to make sure he would never forget her name. Licking the tip of his dick while slurping the spit back up was driving Gator crazy! Seeing his blissful facial expression made her go even harder so she continued her relentless super head attack until he filled the back of her throat with his warm thick cum.

The ecstasy gave her an extra boost of nastiest that she never knew existed within herself. Once he erupted in her mouth she gargled the slowly spit it back on his dick before slurping it back up and swallowing it all.

"Got damn lil moma," was all Gator could say as she navigated as much of his dick as she could down her slippery throat and let it marinate in her mouth while she moaned and massaged his balls. This lil stunt got Gator back hard instantly so as soon as she pulled him out of her mouth she slowly got off her knees and straddled his lap.

Slowly riding his dick Justice made sure she felt every inch of him deep inside of her as she as she kissed on his neck while whispering sweet nothing in his ear. After about fifteen minutes of deep, passionate, slow grinding, Justice felt herself about to cum so she picked up the paste as she held on to the back of his neck for leverage and reached and orgasm that felt like it lasted a lifetime. Still sitting in his lap with his cum soaked dick inside of her Justice began licking circles around his ear lobe as she whispered in his ear, "Follow me upstairs." If Gator thought his night of pure pleasure was coming to an end he was sadly mistake, Justice was the true meaning of "lady in the streets, freak in the sheets."

Once inside her bedroom Justice turned on some old R&B then got fully undressed as she planned on giving him the "Red light special" all night long. I want you to hit it from the back, said Justice as she positioned herself in the middle of the bed doggy style with an arch in her back that was out of this world. Gator couldn't wait to slide inside her warm juicy pussy from behind, just the sight alone of her phat yellow ass high in the air like that gave him an extra boost of stamina as he went for round two.

For the next twenty minutes Gator wailed away like a porn star as big yellow ass bounced uncontrollably with every stroke. She had a beautiful tattoo going across the top of her ass crack that read "Taste the rainbow" in bright colorful ink with a large colorful rainbow over top of it. Gator kept glancing at the intriguing piece of art every time she threw her as back and the ecstasy was beginning to get the best of him, he had to see what that pussy taste like.

The erotic sound of her ass cheeks smacking against thighs along with his cream covered dick being swallowed with every stroke pushed Gator over the edge as he pulled out and began eating her pussy from front to back like an ice cream cone while at the same time licking her asshole as well. This drove Justice crazy! As she bit down on her bottom lip while moving her hips to the rhythm of his of tongue. After getting an appetizing taste of the rainbow, Gator went to continue pounding her pussy from the back but getting her asshole licked like that brought out the inner freak inside of her. Hold on baby I wanna try something else with you, said Justice through partial moans as she searched through her nightstand drawer. Finally finding what she was looking for she handed Gator a small pink bottle of lube oil and told him to lube her asshole up. Gator did as he was told and within a few minutes he was balls deep in her ass as she looked back at him saying all types of filthy shit causing his dick to grow even biggest inside of her. No more than ten minutes later Gator erupted deep in her ass causing his knees to tremble and taking his breath away as she continued to slowly throw her ass back making sure he filled her asshole up with every last drop of his warm thick cum.

Over the course of the next couple of hours the two of them explored each other's body while taking each other places sexually that they never knew existed. Tammy had did some things to Gator that made his toes curl and fall asleep in the pussy but Justice made Tammy seem like a Sunday school teacher. From fucking in the shower to getting her pussy ate on the kitchen table, this was definitely a night that they both would never forget.

Towards the end of their journey they began making love. Gator didn't know if it was the ecstasy or the sensual chemistry they had built over the last few hours but they were definitely intrigued with one another. The constant ringing of his phone woke him up out of his deep peaceful sleep. Glancing at the clock on the nightstand it read 3:27pm. And he knew right then and there it was time to bring his blissful night of rapture to an end. Dialing Poncho's number he looked around and notice Justice wasn't in the bed with him so he got up to see where she had slid off to. He was in unfamiliar territory with about $13,000 in cash on him so he had to be on point.

Searching around the room for his pistol Gator's palms began to sweat. His pistol was nowhere in sight nor was is jeans with the $13,000 in them. Cursing himself for being so naive and falling victim to the pussy, Gator put on his boxers and grabbed the closest weapon in sight as he made his way down the hallway with murder on his mind. Once he hit the hallway he could smell the aroma of fried bacon in the air as Justice put the finishing touches on their breakfast.

Dressed in Gator's dark blue Burberry sweater with a pair of purple Victoria Secret panties on, Justice stood at the counter looking beautiful as ever with a new glow on her face as she pour him a glass of cranberry juice. Noticing the crazed look in his eyes and the hand held lamp that he was clutching in his hand, Justice asked, "what's wrong Gator you aight? and why the hell you got my lamp in your hand like that?" asked Justice as she sat down at the table and began pouring maple syrup over her thick pancakes. Gator stood there for a minute observing the scene and her body language, she didn't seem to show signs of someone who had ill intentions. The more he observed the scene he noticed his pistol on the top of the refrigerator and his pants folded up on the arm of the sofa.

Feeling a sense of relief Gator sat the lamp down then put on his pants which still had his large knot of money inside the pockets. I see you finally woke up said Justice as Gator sat down next to her and began to cut into his thick piece of turkey ham.

"Yea I wish I ain't have to leave so soon but I got the squad waiting on me," said Gator with a bland expression as if he really didn't want to leave.

A look of great disappointment showed all throughout her body language as she stared of the window while playing with her baby hair on the side of her hairline. Well I'm keeping your sweater just in case I don't see you again, "so whenever I start thinking of you I can bury my face in it and smell you," said Justice with a slight smile on her face trying to make light of the situation. Gator sat there eating his breakfast while thinking to himself, "shit baby girl trippin, that Burberry sweater ran me $1,400." Yea you definitely gon' see me again, said Gator with an assertive tone.

Finishing up his plate Gator got up and the two embraced for what seemed like forever as Gator gripped a hand full of her ass while softly kissing on her neck. He was in a bitter sweet state of mind now that he was sober because holding and kissing her like that reminded him of Ma Ma and his guilty conscious began to peek its head out of the dark hole it had been hiding in. Make sure you call me when you make it back to Hampton and don't be no stranger, said Justice as she watched Gator walk to his car hoping this wasn't the last time she would see him.

CH/20.

~

Floating his Wraith down the interstate Gator was consumed in his own thoughts unable to get his mind off of Justice. Poncho picked up on it and decided to fuck with him.

"Damn lil bruh, ol girl must've had some good ass pussy, look like she got you zoned out, contemplating on leaving the wife and kids," said Poncho as the two shared a laugh. Poncho I'm telling you mane shawdy on another level. She took a nigga to the moon and back, had me feeling all crazy inside, I ain't even wanna leave.

For the next ten minutes Gator gave Poncho the whole rundown on the mind blowing sex he and Justice had and he also let him in on the strong connection they shared that had him feeling some type of way. That's aight lil bruh just make sure you play her from a distance and don't let her come in between you and Ma Ma.

"You already got one situation to fix with Tammy you damn sure ain't got room for another one," said Poncho. "Yea you definitely right," said Gator as he plucked the ashes from the blunt into the ashtray.

You know what's so crazy bruh? Between me and you I still ain't told her about what went down that night and that somebody put a hit on her.

"I just love her so much I feel like she done been through too much as it is so I just been keeping it to myself away from her," said Gator. There was a few seconds of silence between the two as Poncho took a sip from his cup of syrup before speaking. I feel you bruh, I know that's a fucked up feeling to have to break some news like that to the woman you love but don't you think she deserves to know? Those are some big secrets to hold from a person and I'm telling you mark my words, "its better if she hears it from you than someone else."

Pulling into the driveway of Tammy's estate Gator reminded himself that he needed to stop procrastinating and purchase another house. He didn't mind living with two beautiful women but Poncho was right, he was definitely playing with fire. Stepping out of his car Ma Ma pulled use beside him in her S560 bumping her Lachatt CD, "Murder she wrote."

"Bout time you made it back, did y'all have fun?" asked Ma Ma as she retrieve a few bags from her backseat before placing a soft kiss on his lips.

"Yea it was aight, it would've been a lot better if you were there with me," said Gator trying to stroke her ego. Ma Ma looked at him with a smirk on her face then rolled her eyes. She knew when Gator was feeding her bullshit, the only person who probably knew him better was his own mother.

Once inside Gator sat down at the mini bar in the kitchen while Ma Ma stocked the refrigerator and cabinets with the food she had just purchased.

"Where Tammy at?" asked Gator as he pour himself a double shot of Hennessey. Hell if I know, she said she had to make a run. You know how Tammy is she so damn private I don't know what be going on with that girl and she my damn sister.

You know she just now telling me about her baby daddy and I had to force that out of her. Gator damn near choked on his drink as he tried to keep cool and regain his composure. Oh yea what she say? Asked Gator trying to see how much she really knew. Nothing really, just that he ain't around band he ain't shit, "you know how y'all niggas do," said Ma Ma as spoke to him with her back turned while reaching for something in the top cabinet.

Gator wiped away the pellets of sweat that began to accumulate near his hairline as he breathed a sigh of relief. He was definitely playing with fire and could feel the heat. One thing he knew for sure was that he owed Tammy a big one for keeping their dirty little secret between the two of them.

"Come here baby come sit down," said Gator as he pour her a drink.

"Look baby its a couple things I need to talk to you about," said Gator as he held on to her hand while gazing into her beautiful eyes. Oh Lord I don't like the way this sound already, "Gator please don't tell me you got another bitch pregnant," said Ma Ma fearing the worst.

"Naw hell naw you trippin," said Gator with so much confidence he began to believe the lie himself.

"Oh okay, so what's on your mind lil daddy?" asked Ma Ma feeling like a weight had been lifted off of her shoulders. I know you don't really remember what went down that night or the details surrounding why it happened but I feel like you deserve to know. Ma Ma was all ears as she took a sip from her glass while staring into her soulmate's dark brown eyes.

Gator looked away as he contemplated on being truthful with her. She had been through so much the last thing he wanted her to know was that someone put a $50,000 bounty on her head. The words of Poncho gave him the courage he needed as he took a deep breath and let her know what the business was.

Aight look baby, somebody put a hit on you.

"Gator stop playing with me, what you really wanna talk about?" said Ma Ma dismissing what she just heard.

"Naw baby I'm dead serious," said Gator with a straight face. By looking into his eyes Ma Ma could always decipher if he was serious or not and by the way it looked he way in no joking manner.

Wait what? What you mean somebody put a hit on me?

"I thought that transpired behind you and T2 being at war," said Ma Ma with a look of confusion on her face. Naw baby it's a lil deeper than that. Somebody put a $50,000 bounty on your head and whoever it was figured that since me and T2 were already at war it would make sense to get him to do it.

Somebody? What you mean somebody? All them fucking connections and resources you claim you got out there and you can't even find out who tried to kill your fucking girl! Said Ma Ma as she stood up with tears in her eyes. Gator felt her pain so he just let her vent. Instead of putting up and argument he stood up, pulled her in close to his chest, and let her cry on his shoulder as he whispered in her ear, "I got you baby, I got you." Ma Ma sat their perplexed as she tried to figure out who would want her dead. Throughout her short 20 years on this earth she had been the center of a few shysty situations, from home invasions and homicides, to committing homicides herself, so to be honest she didn't even know where to begin. One thing she did know was that with or without Gator she would get to the bottom of it even if it killed her.

Do you think it was Angel's people? Asked Ma Ma as she padded her eyes and wiped the tears away. It could be but I highly doubt it, her people ain't playing with that type of paper. Speaking of Angel, your girl Bianca, that was her niece she was in on it too, said Gator hating to be the bearer of disappointing news. She was playing you the whole time baby, befriending you and try a get close to you so you would get comfortable and let your guard down.

Ma Ma sat there in silence trying to hold back tears of rage wondering how she could be so naive and let

Bianca deceive her the way she did. Everything between the two of them was nothing but a lie; the companionship, the laughter, the moments of intimacy everything. The more she thought about it the more she hurt inside and was no longer able to hold back the tears. She had been hurt so much throughout her life it was beginning to turn her warm bubbly heart into a cold piece of steel.

Don't worry bout it baby I'ma take care of it, "I'ma kill every muthafucka who had something to do with that shit, you got my word," said Gator as he held on to her soft freshly manicured hand then placed it over his heart. Feeling the solid drumbeat of his heart while staring into his intense dark brown eyes Ma Ma saw nothing but determination and courage staring back at her. It was that very moment that she knew Gator would go to hell and back for her. Little did they know the person responsible for all of their pain and misery was right up under their nose.

The sound of the front door opening interrupted their slight moment of intimacy as they both drew their weapons and made their way to the front door.

"Damn y'all it's just me," said Tammy as she strolled through the living room carrying shopping bags on both arms.

"My fault sis," said Ma Ma as she and Gator lowered their pistols.

"Just know if anybody ever tried to run up in your spot we got you covered like makeup," said Ma Ma with a wicked grin on her face.

"Yea I can see that," replied Tammy. Placing the bags on the living room couch Tammy began to pull out the things she had got for Ma Ma. I hope you like Jimmy Choo and Dolce & Gabbana, said Tammy as she lay out two pair of Jimmy Choo high heels along with three Dolce & Gabbana dresses for her sister.

"I know how you like to get all dolled up and be on your fly girl shit so we gon' hit the club and kill em once I drop this baby," said Tammy as she placed her hands on her knees and began to make her ass clap letting Ma Ma know she hadn't lost it. The two shared a laugh while Ma Ma tried on her $800 heels before replying, "You better bet it."

"You playing with fire lil bruh," were the words that kept replaying over and over again in Gator's head as he stood off to the side wondering how things would unfold once Tammy had the baby.

The vibrating of his phone snapped him out if his thoughts and it just so happen to be Poncho. My round what's tha word?

"Tell me you around a TV," said Poncho. Yea, why what's up? asked Gator. Turn to channel 3 this shit gon' trip you out.

Gator stepped into the kitchen and turned on the 25inch flat screen that hung over the mini bar. 19 year old Douglas Peterson from Newport News Virginia was found shot to death in his car outside of a Western Union parking lot in Stone Mountain Georgia. Fuck! Gator crossed his arms over his chest and began stroking the hair under his chin as he continued to watch the segment.

Hearing him make an outburst like that, Tammy and Ma Ma made their way into the kitchen to see what was going on. What's wrong baby everything alright? asked Ma Ma as she walked up behind him placing her arm on his shoulder. Hell naw, somebody done killed that bitch ass nigga Smoke before I could get to him. Shit that's a good thing ain't it? asked Ma Ma. Naw not really, I needed him alive so I could get him to talk and tell me who put the hit on you before I killed him myself, said Gator with a look of frustration on his face. As the news continued to play they showed the black

Nissan Altima he was gunned down in and whoever was behind it was definitely about their business. Every window shattered to pieces with at least 75 bullet holes throughout the entire car. Off in the distance a slight smile spread across Tammy's face as she thought to herself "good job." Thinking that she had all of her loose ends tied from her murder for hire gone bad, she felt like she was in the clear and could now move on with her life. After all, the two people she hired to do the hit were now dead, but little did she know there was still a missing piece to the puzzle out there who she knew nothing about.

Over the next few weeks no one really brought up the issue and Gator was taking Poncho's advice by just waiting it out and eventually Bianca would pop back up on the scene. Being that Tammy was due in a few months Gator put his foot on the gas concerning the new house. He linked up with some contractors who Jux plugged him in with and came up with a plan to build him a mini mansion from the ground up deep in the fox hill area of Hampton. He was hoping and praying that they would be finished by the time Tammy had the baby because there was no way in hell he was going be able to live under the same roof with her, Ma Ma, and the baby.

His relationship with Tammy was sailing along pretty smooth. He never thought in a million years that he would be making that 3 and a half hour trip once a week to see her but it was something about her that he just couldn't shake. He was actually getting closer to her then he planned, so he kept telling himself it was just sex, nothing more, nothing less, but deep down inside he knew it was way more to it. It would be times where they would talk on the phone for hours at a time, lay in the bed and just hold one another while sipping syrup and talking about life.

It was as if she was becoming his remedy. She

knew all the right things to say and do to free him of his stress and worries, while at the same time bringing him into her world. Gator didn't know where their relationship was going but he knew one thing, it couldn't go too far.

Over the course of the next few months Gator let her into his world by opening up to her about the situation with Ma Ma and how someone had put a hit on her. Justice was the only woman who he could confide in without worrying about hiss business being all through the streets of Hampton. It seemed as if the more she learned about Ma Ma the more she wanted to meet her.

She herself had been through a similar tragedy in her past dealing with her ex-boyfriend but unlike Gator he wasn't a hustler, he was a jackboy. He made a living by orchestrating home invasions and robberies on high class drug dealers but one day his luck ran out and shit got real as he met his match. In the retaliation to the robbery they shot up his mother's house, grandmother's house, then when they found out where he was actually laying his head they went to pay him a little visit but he was nowhere to be found.

Instead, what they did find was Justice all alone as the three masked men kicked in her backdoor and brutally assaulted her until she gave up his whereabouts. Being the stand-up loyal woman she was raised to be, Justice kept her mouth shut and endured the traumatic pain and suffering. She would rather die in agony, then become a coward and betray her love. Badly beaten and bleeding profusely she managed to drag her battered body to the phone and dial 911 for help but once they arrived they searched the apartment and recovered several illegal firearms. Still remaining loyal to her man and sticking to the G Code, she wore the charges resulting in a three year prison bid. Needless to say throughout her entire bid she never received one visit, one red cent, or even a single piece of mail from her boyfriend, so hearing how Gator held Ma Ma down through her entire bid she respected him even more for that.

CH/21.

~

Sitting on the floor in the living room getting her hair braided, Ma Ma gazed out the window as she inhaled the Kush smoke and let her mind wonder. Picking up on her daydreaming state of mind Tammy decided to intervene and see what was on her sister's mind. What's on your mind girl, "you been quiet all day, you aight?" asked Tammy. Yea I'm just thinking, thinking how the fuck I let that bitch play me like that. I actually allowed myself to open up and have feelings for this bitch, and the whole time she was deceiving me, rocking me to sleep and I couldn't even peep it.

A single tear cascaded down her soft pretty face and she just let it flow, she was filled with so much heartache and rage she didn't even give a fuck. Hearing this information caused Tammy's antennas to go up as she subtly dug for more. From what she knew the only two people involved were T2 and Smoke who were now both dead.

I thought it was just those two dudes Gator was beefin with, "I ain't know somebody else was involved," said Tammy as she dipped her finger in the tub of hair grease then applied it to Ma Ma's scalp. Yea, neither did I, Gator just brought it to my attention a couple weeks ago nor it's been lingering in my mind ever since.

"You remember Bianca don't you?" asked Ma Ma as she reached back to pass Tammy the blunt but quickly pulled it back remembering she was pregnant. Tammy sat there for a minute trying to recollect as she finished up the last braid on Ma Ma's head. Bianca?

"Ain't that the pretty brown skin girl you introduced me to at your party?" asked Tammy. Yea that's her, replied Ma Ma in a dry tone. Sensing Ma Ma's vulnerability, Tammy felt this was the best time to slide in and put her play into action.

I don't know why you ain't been told me about her you know I got resources all throughout the south, what's her last name? Ma Ma sat there wrecking her brain until it popped up, Fitzpatrick, "Bianca Fitzpatrick," said Tammy in a calm assertive tone. Tammy wrote her name down on a piece of paper then stored it inside her little black book. Now all she had to do was make sure that her men got to her before Gator did.

Several weeks had flew by and there were still no signs of Bianca. Tammy kept her foot on her men necks pushing for them to search harder but every time they got a lead it turned out to be nothing. Tammy wrecked her brain for weeks trying to figure out how this young girl from around the way with no connections could be so elusive. There was no contact with family, no trace of credit card use, no contact with law enforcement, it was as if she just vanished.

Trying to clean up her mess and track down the last surviving person who could link her to her sister's murder attempt had Tammy stressing like never before as she soaked her beautiful 5'8 honey brown frame in the hot tub while caressing her belly. That doctor had informed her to try to maintain a stress free life while pregnant but that was easier said than done. As the warm water relaxed her body she felt a sharp pain in her stomach. At first she thought it was just the baby kicking but the second time around it was way too intense. She experienced that same sharp pain about fifteen minutes later and she knew what time it was, she was having the baby.

Slowly pulling herself out of the tub she yelled

for Ma Ma knowing she didn't have enough time the make it to the hospital. This baby was coming, and it was coming now! What's wrong?

"I heard you screaming from all the way downstairs," said Ma Ma as she burst through the bathroom door. I think I'm having the baby right now! yelled Tammy as she breathed heavily while lying on the bathroom floor.

Thinking fast Ma Ma ran to the hallway closet and retrieved a handful of thick, soft, towels the lay on the bathroom floor while at the same time dialing 911. Aight sis I got you just take deep breaths and stay calm. Ma Ma had never been in this type of situation. before but she knew if she freaked out then Tammy would do the same so she tried her best to remain calm and assure her that everything would be fine. With the help of the operator guiding her step by step over an excruciating 13 minutes, Ma Ma successfully helped her sister bring her first child into the world on her bathroom floor. Minutes later the ambulance arrived and escorted them to the hospital with Ma Ma trailing behind.

About thirty minutes away on the outskirts of Richmond, Gator and Poncho sat in a high class sports bar eating hot wings & shrimp while watching the football game. The Ravens was Poncho's favorite team and they were playing in a playoff game so he was deeply tuned in while Gator tried the get his mack on with the sexy slim Latina waitress. Gator wasn't really into sports as much as Poncho was, he would just bet money on the opposite team and try to get up under Poncho's skin. Tonight they had five grand on the game and things were looking good for Poncho.

The vibration of his cell phone put a halt to his flirtatious conversation he was engaged in with the sexy waitress. Seeing it was Ma Ma he quickly stored the woman's number in his phone then returned her call.

"My sweet lady, what's the word?" asked Gator as he took a sip from his long island ice tea.

"Baby you ain't gon' believe what I just did," said Ma Ma with a great deal of enthusiasm behind he words.

"What you do?" asked a now curious Gator. I just help Tammy deliver her baby at home on the bathroom floor.

Gator fell silent as his head began spinning, thinking he heard wrong he asked her, "hold on you did what?" Yea I did it all by myself too, well except for the help of the operator. We on our way to the hospital now so you need to come up here. Come to the hospital for what? That ain't my damn baby, replied Gator in a sharp tone making himself seem guilty. Gator don't act like that, you know me and you are the only family she has in Virginia and at times like this, people need family by their side.

Gator stood up from the barstool and hung up on Ma Ma as he looked up at the ceiling running his hands over his fresh fade. What's wrong bruh?

"I know you ain't mad cause you bout to lose five grand," said Poncho with a grin on his face. Hell naw bruh I gotta go to the hospital, Tammy just had the fucking baby. Gator's last statement took all of the laughter and joking out of Poncho as he shook his head from side to side trying to imagine what his right hand man was going through.

Hold on let me get this straight, so she called you and told you to come to the hospital? Asked Poncho trying to get a better understanding of the situation.

"Naw Ma Ma called me, she up there with her," replied Gator. Poncho looked at him I disbelief as he grabbed a napkin to wipe the BBQ sauce of his hands then replied, "that sound like a set up lil bruh don't do it." Gator sat there in silence for a brief moment before

206

replying, "I know, that's why I'm taking you with me," said Gator with a stern look on his face as he made firm eye contact with Poncho.

Mane hell naw I ain't getting involved in that shit.

"I told you from the jump to let that pussy get past you and keep it strictly business, you ain't wanna listen to me," said Poncho as he leaned back in his chair. Poncho wasn't going to let his right hand man walk into a situation like that by himself, he just had to hit him with a dose of that "I told you so" medicine. Gator hopped on I64 and floated his Porsche truck to downtown Richmond. He didn't know what lie ahead of him so he popped two xanez bars to calm his nerves and prepare him for the sticky situation he had gotten himself into.

Back at the hospital Tammy cradled her 7 pound baby boy in her arms as Ma Ma sat there by her side suffering in silence. Thinking of the gang of women who attacked her for no apparent reason causing her to lose her unborn child had her so full of hatred and heartache that her hands began to tremble as she wiped away the tears that were forming in her eyes. Even though Tammy wasn't to blame for her losing her unborn child she still felt some type of way but she refused to let it show.

"So what's his name?" asked Ma Ma as she put on a false smile to keep from crying.

"Sincere," replied Tammy through her half closed cloudy eyes. Aww that's a sweet name, honest, pure, and true. As the two sisters admired the beautiful baby boy the pain medication began to kick in causing Tammy to look her sister in the eyes and break down crying.

What's wrong sis you okay? Asked Ma Ma fearing that she might be having complications from the pregnancy. I'm sorry, I'm so sorry, said Tammy as she lay back with tears in her beautiful dark green eyes.

"Sorry about what?" asked a confused Ma Ma. The tears began to flow like a river as she continued uttering the words "I'm sorry."
Tammy's heart went out to her sister in every which of way imaginable. She was sorry for all of the pain and heartache she had caused her younger sister and she felt like the more she held it in the more it ate her up inside. She openheartedly wished that she could take everything back but she couldn't.

About twenty minutes later Gator and Poncho entered the hospital room. Ma Ma sat in the chair by the bed cradling the baby while lay sound asleep from the heavy dose of pain medication.

"You wanna hold him?" asked Ma Ma as she stood up and extended the baby to Gator. Gator glanced over at Poncho for an answer who slightly nodded his head.
As Ma Ma carefully placed the baby in his arms Gator looked into the babies eyes and saw himself. What's his name? "Sincere," replied Ma Ma. Over the next couple of minutes Gator held Sincere in his arms and smile as he saw a miniature version of himself recreated and born all over again. Ma Ma picked up on Gator's interaction with the baby and her mind began to wonder but she quickly erased that thought from her head knowing such a thing would never happen.

CH/22.

~

Over the next few weeks Gator tried to stay as far away from Tammy's place as he possibly could. Him being around his son gave him a typical urge he want to embrace the fact but he just couldn't. Luckily for him the contractors had informed him that the wiring and plumbing would be complete around noon the next day. Ma Ma had no idea that he had built her a home from the ground up so he planned on giving her the surprise of her life, Lord knows she deserves it.

Making his way through the front door of Tammy's place to pick up Ma Ma, Gator spotted Tammy in the living room looking peaceful and beautiful as ever as she fed Sincere while talking to him in baby talk. Instead of going straight upstairs to Ma Ma like he intended to he walked into the living room and sat down next to her on the sofa. I ain't seen you up this early in a while, said Gator. Yea Sincere makes sure I'm up bright and early, as soon as the sun rise, "he rise," said Tammy with a warm smile on her face.

"Let me hold him real quick," said Gator as he placed his cup of syrup on the coffee table. Holding his son in his arms and having him stare back at him with those big dark green eyes had Gator feeling some type of way. He hated the fact that he couldn't claim his own flesh & blood, but due to the circumstances that's just how it had to be.

They both sat there in silence consumed in their own thoughts as Tammy held back her tears. Truth be told she still loved Gator and still wanted to have a family with him but it just wasn't going to happen and she had to accept it. Damn Tammy, what we gon' do? Asked

Gator as he held his son realizing that shit was real and no longer a game. By now the tears were beginning to flow down her face as she grabbed a tissue off the coffee table and padded her eyes.

You know Gator I try to be so strong while holding everything into place because that's the role I had to play my entire life, but to be honest with you I don't know what to do, I just wish things were normal between us, said Tammy as the tears continued to flow freely as she quietly sobbed. Gator put Sincere in his high chair and began consoling the mother of his child. Holding her in his arms with her head resting on his chest, Gator tried his best to comfort her while assuring her that everything would be okay.

Forty five minutes later Ma Ma was showered, dressed, and ready to roll. You still ain't told me where we were going, said Ma Ma as she flipped down the sun visor and began to apply her lip gloss. You'll see when we get there, just sit back and enjoy the ride. Gator passes her the cup of syrup and let the Teena Marie song "Out on a limb," ease their mind as he floated his Porsche truck down the interstate headed to Hampton. After a well-deserved breakfast at one of Ma Ma's favorite diners, "Tommy's," He navigated his way through the Fox Hill area of Hampton until he reached his destination. Pulling up in the driveway of a beautiful five bedroom brick house with a castle like structure, Ma Ma looked around while silently wondering what they were doing there. She doubted they were there to make a play because this definitely didn't look like the Trap.

These are some beautiful homes out here especially this one, they got that whole modern day castle thing going on that shit is so beautiful, said Ma Ma as she admired the unique style of the home they were parked in front of. You see, Gator was a smooth young dude who was very attentive. All of those nights when the two of them would sit in the car together pulling all-nighters in the Trap, high off ecstasy and codeine while sharing their dreams with one another, it may not seemed as if Gator was paying attention but he was. Ever since they were 16 he knew she was infatuated with homes of this structure and style and always dreamed of living in one one day but he played it so nonchalant like he didn't even care.

Ma Ma was so mesmerized by the beautiful homes surrounding her that she never noticed Gator reach into his pocket and pull out a small black jewelry box. So what are we doing out here? I thought you had something special planned for me, said Ma Ma as she snapped out of her daydream state of mind. Gator didn't reply, he just looked at her with a slight smirk on his face. Turn around I got something for you. Ma Ma looked at him a little strange then hesitated before turning around, she knew Gator had something up his sleeve she just didn't know what.

Feeling the 4 carat crushed diamond necklace being placed around her neck sent chills down her spine while giving her pussy a warm tingling feeling inside.

"Oh my God baby its beautiful!" said Ma Ma as she traced her fingers up and down the cold piece of ice. As she turned around in her seat to give her man a kiss she examined the necklace a little more that's when she noticed key hanging next to the pendant. Looking at the key then back at Gator who had that same mischievous smirk on his face, she put two and two together and her eyes began to water up as she thought to herself how Gator was making her dreams come true.

Once inside her jaw dropped as she took in the beautiful sight of the twenty foot ceiling draped with gold plated chandeliers. The more she examined the house the more she began to realize it was built with her in mind as she notices her initials engraved in the glass shower door with a pearl outline. Needless to say she made sweet love to Gator in almost every part of their new home while at the same time doing a little extra just to show his much she appreciated him.

Over the next few days Ma Ma spent most of her time furnishing the house. Gator had given her a nice piece of change so she could turn their house into a home and she did so without disappointing. With her unique style and elegant flavor, one would have thought she was a professional the way she had the place decked out.

It was Friday evening and also Gator's 22nd birthday. Poncho and Jux kept trying to pursue him to fly down to Miami with them for the weekend to do it big but Gator decline. On his birthday he just wanted to chill with his old lady and enjoy the fruits of his new home while sipping syrup and inhaling blunts of Kush until he dosed off. Not to mention he had spent a little over $260,000 getting the home built so the last thing he wanted do was go out partying and spend more money. As Gator sat at the mini bar sipping a Starbucks coffee cup filled with codeine, he got a phone call from Justice. Ma Ma was a few feet away from him at the stove preparing his birthday dinner so he showed some respect and declined her call. Being persistent and calling right back Gator felt it was important so he went on and took her call.

Hello? "Hey sexy, happy birthday!" said Justice with a hint of excitement in her tone. Thank you I appreciate it, "I ain't know you remembered it was my birthday," said Gator with a slight smile on his face. Come on now Gator I could never forget "anything" pertaining to you, said Justice as she thought back to all of passionate breath taking sex they had. So what you got planned for tonight? asked Justice. I'm laid back tonight, "I got my old lady in the kitchen throwing down for me then after we eat she gon' put that good snap back pussy on young nigga," said Gator with a grin on his face as lustfully watched Ma Ma prepare his meal.

"Don't be telling everybody my damn business," said Ma Ma as she turned around with her face screwed up. Who is that anyway?

"Just an old friend from out of state," said Gator. With that being said Ma Ma turned back around and continued putting her "New Orleans bounce" on her special gumbo while at the same time paying close attention to this friendly phone conversation Gator was having.

"So when you gon' let me meet this Ma Ma girl? asked Justice. Why you wanna meet my girl so bad?

"You must wanna taste that pussy ugh?" Said Gator in a calm, cool collective tone. Justice erupted in laughter on the other end of the phone before replying, "naw it ain't nothing like that she just seem so trill and I feel like we got a lot in common, that's all." Gator's last comment made her stop what she was doing and come sit down next to him to see what was going on. The extra strong cup of codeine he was sipping on had him feeling so good and relaxed that he spoke freely on the phone with Justice as if Ma Ma was nowhere in sight.

"So who you got on the phone talking bout they wanna eat my pussy?" asked Ma Ma as she stood in between in legs grilling him while he sat on the barstool. Nobody girl, "look you gon' burn the food you all over here in my conversation," replied Gator through his half closed eyes with a slight grin on his face. He was definitely feeling the effects of the codeine and California weed, besides it was his birthday he could do no wrong.

"Aight Gator don't let your lil friend get you fucked up," said Ma Ma as she walked off to attend to the food. Hearing her thoroughness in the background

213

Justice said to herself, "yea I definitely got to meet this bitch."

Well look lil moma I definitely appreciate the birthday shout out, I'm bout to kick back and get my grub on so you take your time and be easy out there. Okay baby you too, oh Gator before I forget, we got a new girl who just started working at my club last week and when she showed me her ID I noticed it said Hampton, Va. I remember that situation you had informed me about so I figured this information might be useful to you. This caught Gator's attention as he put his cup down and paid close attention to what she had to say.
Her name starts with a B, I believe it was Baneeta or Bianca, some shit like that.

"What about her last name?" asked Gator? She bad real funny last name that I would never forget because it just didn't fit a black person, "Fitzpatrick." A wicked grin began to form on Gator's face. because he knew it wasn't too many chocolate covered Bianca Fitzpatricks from the city of Hampton. Okay cool, well look I'ma call you tomorrow first thing in the morning so we can finish this conversation, good looking out girl. As Gator ended the call be walked up behind Ma Ma, wrapped his arms around her waist, and made a trail of soft kisses from the top of her spine to the top of her neck sending chills all throughout her body.

"I love you girl," said Gator as he whispered in her ear while gently nibbling on her earlobe causing her to let out a small sigh. Taking it a step further Gator turned her around, picked her up by her waist and sat her on the kitchen counter.
Knowing what was on his mind Ma Ma slowly spread her soft smooth caramel thighs wide open and began taking off her laced panties giving him full access to her warm, delicious, love box. The sight of her neatly

trimmed fat cat with the "slippery when wet" sign tatted on her inner thigh had Gator's mouth watery as he navigated his head in between her thighs and began tongue kissing her clit for a full ten minutes without coming up for air. As she bit down on her bottom lip while popping her pussy in his face, Ma Ma wanted Gator to taste her essential flow of juices and he did so with great pleasure.

Gently massaging her wet asshole with his thumb Gator continued to make love to her clit causing her to grab the back of his neck with a grip so tight he couldn't escape. While rubbing on her nipple with her free hand Ma Ma moved her hips to the rhythm of his tongue as she felt herself on the verge of an orgasm.

"I'm about to cum daddy don't stop," were the words that escaped her soft pretty lips as she applied more pressure to the back of his neck and within seconds she was releasing her sweet nectar drowning him in her honey flavor juices as her body began to twitch. Bringing his head up from between her legs Ma Ma wiped his face off then began passionately tongue kissing him with her arms wrapped around his neck.

"Baby I wanna feel you inside me," said Ma Ma as she looked into his eyes while unbuckling his belt. Hard as a piece of steel while the taste of her sweet pussy still lingered on his tongue, Gator looked around for the perfect place to lay her down and give the business. Carrying his queen from the kitchen counter to the kitchen table Ma Ma aggressively knocked everything off the table to give her man some room to work.

Sitting on the table with her legs wide open Gator began to tease her as he rubbed the tip of his thick manhood up and down her cum soaked clit causing her body to yearn the sensation of his thick chocolate dick inside of her warm wet pussy.

"You ready for this dick?" asked Gator as he continued to massage her clit with the tip of his throbbing manhood.

"Yes daddy please just put it inside," said Ma Ma as she grabbed the base of his thick manhood guiding him inside the softest place on earth. Entering her tight, juicy, warm, love box like that had Gator feeling like he was in heaven as he started off slow then gradually picked up the paste. With her pussy hugging on to his dick like a skin tight glove Ma Ma matched the rhythm of his strokes thrusting her hips back N forth while staring into his eyes as she bit down on her bottom lip. For the next 15 minutes Gator filled her pussy with long deep strokes before erupting deep inside of her as his body collapsed into her arms.

Damn baby why you keep doing me like this?

"You gon' make me kill a bitch fucking with you," said Ma Ma as she gazed into his intense dark brown eyes while trying to catch her breath. Yea well you just might be in luck, I think I found our girl Bianca. This was music to her ears as she revisited that cold place of deceit and betrayal in her heart with vengeance on her mind.

"Where is she?" asked Ma Ma as she snapped out of her sinful daydream while slipping back into her panties. Baltimore, I'ma link up with Murdock first thing in the morning so we can come up with a plan to snatch her up. Ma Ma sat there on the kitchen table pondering in silence as her bare legs swung back N forth before replying, "take me with you, I wanna kill her myself." Gator could tell by the cold malice behind her words that she meant business so there was nothing else to talk about. The way she jumped out and handled her business when they had to shut down that block party out Portsmouth, showed Gator everything he needed to know. After their delicious finger licking birthday dinner was consumed, Ma Ma grabbed her man by the hand and led him up stairs where she would continue to give him a night filled with Thug Passion.

The following morning Gator woke up bright and early and called Justice. He didn't like going into situations in the blind so he wanted to gather as much Intel as he could so he could have a better understanding of what he was up against. While waiting on Justice to call him back with the rundown he and Ma Ma got dressed then made their way out Park Place to link up with Murdock. Stepping out of his cocaine white Audi A7 Murdock jumped in the backseat of the rented Tahoe as the three of them made their way to Spruce St where Gator kept his arsenal of weapons.

As the trio searched through the duffle bags choosing which guns they wanted to carry along on the mission Gator's phone began to ring.

"Sweet lady tell me something good girl," said Gator as he passed Ma Ma the blunt then made his way down the hallway to continue his conversation. He knew whatever justice had to bring to his attention was going to be vital to his operation so he made sure to give her his undivided attention.

Well I got good news and I got bad news. The good news is I got the drop on where she lay her head at, the bad news is the house where she's staying at his full of killers, and I mean straight savage cutthroat killers. They call themselves KKM, short for Killa Klan Mafia. This caught Gator's attention, he had heard of the ruthless gang when he was younger doing time upstate in the juvenile facility. If the rumors he had heard upstate were anywhere close to being true then knew he had his hands full.

"What she doing running around with them?" asked Gator. From what I know they pimping her out. Word is she needed protection from some wild niggas

217

back in VA who were trying to kill her, so once she
linked up with one of the KM's she started fucking with
him and in return of his protection she allowed him to
pimp her out. It's about six or seven of them in the house
at all times with two lookouts on the porch, said Justice.
Gator stood there rubbing the hair under his chin while
thinking to himself, "damn this might be a lil harder than
I expected."

"Well look let me put something together and
I'ma hit you back in bout an hour," said Gator as he
ended the call. With the odds stacked up against him
Gator knew he had a tough road ahead of him, but if it
meant bringing justice to the one responsible for Ma
Ma's brutal attack then he was all for it.
Contemplating on how he was going the get past a gang
full of killers on unfamiliar territory had Gator in deep
thought as he took pulls from the hush filled blunt
dipped in codeine as he leaned up against the
refrigerator.

"So what's the word my nig?" asked Murdock
who was eagerly waiting to get it in. We gotta think this
one through bruh, she running around with a gang full of
killers in a city that I'm unfamiliar with, "some Killa
Klan Mafia niggas," expressed Gator.

Murdock stood up from the raggedy sofa then
threw the two bags of guns on the table in front of Gator.
Mane fuck them niggas! They ain't the only ones who
know how to catch bodies! You see these muthafuckin
straps we got? Mac90's, Calicos, Carbine15's, mane fuck
a Killa Klan Mafia! said Murdock with a great deal of
emotion as if he were preaching. A devilish grin spread
across Gator's face as he felt every word his comrade
was preaching.

Murdock was reckless and didn't give a fuck
that's what Gator loved the most about him. He was
going to ride with Gator till the wheels fell off no matter

what the odds were. With Murdock amping him up it put
the ice back in Gator's veins that he needed to take on
the ruthless gang, even if they were outnumbered. They
had been outnumbered plenty of times in the past and
they still prevailed so with his mind made up he called
Justice back informing her that they were on their way.

CH/23.

~

       Floating the Tahoe up the interstate Gator wrecked his brain until he came up with the best plan he could think of. It was times like this that he wish he had Poncho or Jux with him so he could get their outlook on the situation but the few times he had tried calling them he got no answer. They would give him more sensible advice unlike Murdock who was just as reckless as he was, if not more.

       Pulling up to Justice's home Gator was also rolling the dice by bringing Ma Ma around her but due to the circumstances he didn't really have a choice, he just hoped thing would play its course and run smoothly. If things got out of hand between the two of them he would cross that bridge when it got there but as of now he had bigger fish to fry.

       "I see you ain't waste no time," said Justice as she opened the door and welcomed Gator and his people into her home.

       "Yea I couldn't let this opportunity get pass me," said Gator as he gave her a friendly hug before introducing her to Murdock and Ma Ma. As Justice went to shake Ma Ma's hand she looked her up and down then walked right past her leaving her hand extended and hanging. Murdock made brief eye contact with Gator giving him that "I told you so" look. Sensing the tension in the air Justice made her way into the kitchen and pour them all glasses of Hennessey as they sat at the table listening to Gator give them the game plan step by step. After everything was set in motion and ready for execution they still had a couple hours until it was time to move so they just sat around talking shit waiting on the clock to strike 9pm. As Gator and Murdock sat in the living room checking the magazines in all of the guns he began to wonder if he was making the right decision by bringing Ma Ma around Justice. Even though they hadn't physically or verbally got into an altercation a blind man could see that it was unwanted tension between the two.

"I give it to you bruh, you got some big balls introducing your old lady to your mistress, ain't no way in hell I would've pulled a move like that," said Murdock as he cautiously watched the two women in the kitchen going over their role for the mission ahead.

"Naw bruh you see it ain't that you wouldn't pull a move like that, you "can't" pull a move like that," said Gator in a jokingly manner as the two shared a laugh. Before Murdock could respond with a slick comment the ringing of Gators phone cut their conversation short as he realized it was Jux.

Big dawg what's the word my nig? Ain't shit coolin mane, enjoying this Miami life. Beautiful women every time you turn your head, palm trees everywhere with big ass oranges dangling from them, not to mention the 75 degree weather in December, "lil bruh you trippin I don't know why you ain't slide down here with us," said Jux with a hint of excitement behind his words. Yea well after I finish taking care of this lil situation I'ma definitely take a vacation, I might not even come back to this raggedy ass city, said Gator thinking out loud. Situation? What you got going on now lil bruh? Asked Jux. You remember when you and Poncho kept telling me to be patient and let things come to me? Well I think this is as close as its gon' get, I found Bianca.

"Oh yea, where she at?" asked Jux as he put down the martini he was sipping on and paid close attention to the Intel he was receiving. Baltimore, I got the drop on her and where she lay her head at but she

living in the Trap with a gang full of niggaz who go by
Killa Klan Mafia, "you ever heard of them?" asked
Gator.
Yea I heard of them, they run the Northeast part of the
city. They say they're the reason people started calling
Baltimore Maryland, "Bodymore Murderland," they
known for killing shit that's all they do.
    "Yea I heard the same thing," replied Gator in a
dry tone.
    Well look mane I called you earlier to get your
opinion on whether or not I should move on them but
it's too late now, I'm already in Baltimore locked and
loaded.
    "So what's your plan?" asked Jux.
    "Shit it ain't much too it, we gon' run up in that
bitch, kill everybody in that muthafucka, then snatch up
Bianca and get her to tell me who orchestrated the hit,
simple as that," said Gator with a bit of arrogance
behinds his words. Jux shook his head from side to side
while thinking to himself how young and reckless Gator
still was.
Look lil bruh you gotta be rational, it's more than just
one way to skin a cat, said Jux. I feel what you saying
but at the same time I want to send a message, a message
so bold and fierce that their great grandkids gon' get
nervous and start to sweat when they hear my name. Jux
couldn't help but crack a smile as he thought back to the
time when they jumped out of the van with Scream mask
on and turned the warm sunny block party into a bloody
massacre. He was definitely a firm message sender when
it came to laying down law.
    I don't know Gator I still think it's too risky, you
know sometimes you just gotta sit back and look at the
bigger picture. Somebody sent T2 to kill Ma Ma and she
ended up killing him, the other dude who was involved
karma caught up with him and he ended up getting

smoked too. You and Ma Ma are alive & healthy, you getting plenty money, and you just got that big ass house built for you and your old lady. Mane shit I would be somewhere with my feet up right now feeling like I won. Gator took in everything Jux was saying and he did have a point but it was too late now. Gator had already made up his mind and his team was counting on him.
Ending the conversation with Jux Gator made his way to the kitchen to have a word with Justice. To his surprise they were actually having a civilized conversation over a glass of Hennessey. Ma Ma had finally let her guard down just enough for Justice to get one foot in the door. She felt like if she was trill enough to put her life on the line and go on a mission with them that had no guarantee she would make it back alive, then she was trill enough to be given a chance.

"It's about that time ladies," said Gator as he entered the kitchen and gave Ma Ma a kiss on the forehead. Here baby take the keys and go start the car up, I gotta have a word with Justice before we slide out. Ma Ma shot him a curious look as she cut her eyes at him. She knew this wasn't the time or place to be questioning him about petty shit like that so she did as she was told without putting up an argument while Murdock followed behind her with the arsenal of firearms in a forest green duffle bag.

I ain't never get a chance to tell you but I really appreciate you jumping out there and helping me with this situation.

"You know the average woman wouldn't even entertain the idea of involving herself in a situation of this magnitude and here you are right here on the front line," said Gator feeling proud inside along with a few other feelings he didn't know how to describe. Yea, well I guess I ain't your average woman, and that shit they did to your girl was fucked up! I feel like everybody who

had something to do with that shit should feel her pain,"
said Justice as she sat on the edge of the kitchen table.

"Yea you definitely right about that I couldn't
agree more, said Gator.
Reaching into his pocket pulling his large Dope man
knot, Gator counted out $7500 then handed it to her.
What's this for? asked Justice with a look of confusion
on her face. It's for your services, you ain't have to do
none of this shit but you still came through for me. Naw
Gator I ain't do it for the money I did it out of love and
respect.

"It ain't every day that I run into a rare nigga like
yourself so I just want you to know that my love and
respect for you is genuine," said Justice as she gazed into
his eyes felling a connection that was out of this world.
Justice fucked him up with that last one as he put the
money back in his pocket and cracked a smile flashing
his full set of shiny gold teeth. Her not accepting the
money showed a lot about her character and Gator
respected that.

"I don't know what I'ma do with you girl," said
Gator as he took a good look at her admiring her beauty
on the inside and out. Justice took a step closer, so close
that she could feel the heat and smell the $600
Ferragamo cologne seeping from his pores then replied,
"just love me."
The four of them jumped in the Tahoe and within twenty
minutes they were creeping down N. Vincent St.
checking out the scene. There were two lookouts on the
porch just as Justice informed them there would be so
Gator parked about six houses down from his target and
put his plan in motion.

"Aight ladies y'all know what time it is, as soon
as y'all give us the signal we going in," said Gator as he
turned around in his seat making firm eye contact with
the women. After checking the clips to their Rugers and

making sure one was in the chamber, they secured their pistols to their thigh holsters then made their way down the secluded side street.

Walking as if they were drunk while slurring their words, these two beautiful women looked to be the perfect victims of a free good time, and the two young hustlers on the front porch took the bait. What's good with y'all? "What y'all getting into tonight?" Yelled one of the young hustlers as Justice and Ma Ma walked past wearing skin tight miniskirts with sexy enticing high heels to complement their provocative outfits.

"We just now leaving a party off Myrtle we tryna find something else to get into," said Justice with a face full of sweet seduction. The two young hustlers had a word with one another amongst themselves then signaled for the two sexy drunk women to come join them.

So what's up y'all tryna go inside? "we got plenty liquor, weed, molly, whatever y'all want," said one of the young hustlers as he greedily eyed Ma Ma's 5'6 caramel frame while licking his lips and rubbing his hands together.

"Naw we good lil daddy we already fucked up we just want some quick dick," said Ma Ma eyeing the young hustler right back. The two young hustlers looked at one another with smiles on their face before replying, "well shit come on let's get this shit poppin!"

Turning around and making their way to the front door the women abruptly stopped them.

"Naw we ain't tryna go inside we don't want y'all friends all in our business," said Ma Ma. So where y'all wanna go? Ma Ma looked around for the most excluded area then replied, "Shit you can just fuck me on the side of the house." The way she licked her lips while seductively staring him up & down was enough to make the young hustler cum in his pants before he even got a taste of the pussy. Without another word being said the four of them made their way to the side of the house in the dark shadows of the night and began to make out. Hard as a rock and eagerly ready to get a taste of some new pussy, Ma Ma and Justice bent over right in front of them pulling their skirts up and in one quick motion snatched their pistols from their thigh holsters then went to work. With guns aimed point blank in their face and their paints down to their ankles, they knew they had fuckd up. You just couldn't resist the pussy could you, said Justice as she handed both men zip ties forcing them to tie their own hands together.

Y'all bitches don't know who y'all dealing with, "if y'all let us go now I'll act like this shit never happened," said the young hustler in a tone of arrogance." Ma Ma looked at Justice then smirked. You right lil daddy I don't know who I'm dealing with, could you please enlighten me, said Ma Ma as she walked up on the young hustler who showed no signs of intimidation even when tied up with a gun to his head. The young hustler locked eyes with Ma Ma showing not one ounce of fear as he proudly replied, Killa Klan Maf, SMACK! His words were cut short as Ma Ma repeatedly smacked him in the face with the butt of her gun causing him to spit out a mouth full of blood along with a few broken teeth as he fell to his knees.

"You think I give a fuck who you are or who you run with?" asked Ma Ma as she knelt down beside him tracing the barrel of her Ruger alongside his bloody face. Well evidently I don't, because if I did I wouldn't be standing here in this pissy ass alley ready to paint the side of this house with your brains now would I? Justice stood off to the side observing Ma Ma hoping she wouldn't fuck up the plan. If she let off a shot this close to the house it would alert the rest of the gang inside and possibly get them killed. She wanted to intervene but she wasn't sure how the hotheaded trigger happy Ma Ma would react.

As Ma Ma shoved her pistol down the young hustlers throat Justice took a gamble and decided to intervene before things got out of hand.

"Ma Ma come on girl leave that shit alone we gotta stick to the plan," pleaded Justice. Ma Ma looked up and shot Justice a stare so cold it sent chills throughout her entire body. I was just having a lil fun, damn girl loosen up, said Ma Ma with a wicked grin on her face. With both men hog tied and gagged, the two women emerged from the side of the house giving Gator the signal.

Armed with a semi-automatic Saga 12 shotgun, Gator jumped out of the Tahoe and casually made his way to the front door with a heavily armed Murdock right beside him. With Justice and Ma Ma positioned near the back door to prevent anyone from trying to flee the scene everything was in order. As Murdock positioned himself to kick the door in Gator stopped him in his tracks then went to turn the knob. His intuition was on point as the slightest turn of the knob opened the door for them.

"Y'all know what time it is, everybody on the muthafuckin ground!" barked Gator as he stormed through the front door with his shotgun aimed at all three men in the living room on the couch. This tactic normally worked in his favor but he was on different stomping grounds now as one of the men went for his Tech9 sending a barrage of gunfire wildly through the air before Gator sent two powerful slugs through him that lifted him off his feet sending him flying through the entertainment stand. Joining the action Murdock began firing on the other two men with his Carine15 but by now they had somehow retrieved their weapons from under the cushion of the couch turning this home invasion into an all-out war.

Trading gunfire back & forth as the two men ducked behind the raggedy sofa giving Gator and Murdock what they came looking for, caused Gator to rethink his decision making. Hot bullets from an M16 flew past Gator's head as he and Murdock took cover in the tiny kitchen.

"I ain't know they was strapped like this," said Gator as he tried to wipe away the dust in his eyes from the sheetrock that was exploding near him with every shot they sent his direction.

Not wanting to feel like a sitting duck, Murdock stood up and let his Carbine15 rip in the direction of the two Baltimore men. Just his luck he was right on time as one of the men tried to sneak up on them Murdock caught him in his tracks sending multiple bullets ripping through his torso. With just one of the three men remaining he felt it was now or never as he jumped up from behind the couch like a madman recklessly firing shots from his M16 but was met with three shotgun slugs to the chest and one to the lower part of his face knocking off his entire chin. Hearing one of the men still gasping for air taking his last breath, Murdock walked over to him ready to take him out of his misery but before he could make it to his body two loud BOOM'S echoed through the small house as Murdock hit the floor with a thud.

Looking at his comrade's lifeless body lying on the floor with the entire right side of his head split open from a Mac11 Gator lost it. Slamming a fresh clip into his Saga12 shotgun with tears in his eyes, Gator made his way through the hallway and went berserk as he fired round after round into the door where the fatal shit came from leaving holes in the door the size of bowling balls. Looking at the bowling ball size holes in the door the man in the room didn't know what the fuck Gator was gunning at him with and he damn sure didn't want to find out.

Feeling like it was either do or die the man behind the door sprinted across the room sending a barrage of shots in Gators direction before catching a crucial shotgun slug to his arm almost decapitating it. Gator caught two slugs to the chest knocking him to the ground with a third and fourth bullet going through his hip and lower abdomen. Checking his chest to feel for blood Gator was saved by his vest but he wasn't as lucky when it came to his other two wounds.

While putting all of his weight on one leg he mustered up as much strength as he possibly could to finish the job. Limping into the room with his shotgun in hand and murder on his mind, he unapologetically watched the man who tried to killed him go into shock as his left arm hung on by just a few bone ligaments. Trying to reach for his Mac11 that was a few feet away did him no justice as Gator stood over top of him pumping slug after slug into his face leaving his head resembling an exploded watermelon.

Hearing the sirens off in the distance Gator snapped out of his trance and began searching through the rest of the house for Bianca but she was nowhere to be found.

Remembering that he had Ma Ma and Justice positioned outside by the backdoor he went to check and see if they had her back there but when he opened the back door no one was in sight. WTF? A million thoughts ran through his mind as anger, confusion and rage overwhelmed him.

Hopping on one leg feeling like he had been hit by a Mac truck, Gator made his way to the front of the house while mumbling to himself, "I can't believe I put my trust in these bitches." Making his way past Murdock's lifeless body he had to look the other way as his childhood friend lay on the hardwood floor with half of his head blown off. Before he could open the front door it flew open and he was staring down the barrel of two pistols. Luckily for him it was Justice and Ma Ma coming to see what was taking him so long.

"Come one Gator we gotta go!" yelled Ma Ma. Seeing that he was shot Justice and Ma Ma helped carry him out of the house but before they could make it off the front porch Ma Ma frantically asked, "Hold on where's Murdock?" The look on Gator's face said it all and without further explanation Ma Ma knew he didn't make it. Putting him in the backseat of the Tahoe Justice quickly pulled off making her way to the nearest hospital. Gator was in so much pain and distress he didn't even notice Bianca in the seat behind him hog tied and gagged.

"He's losing a lot of blood back here Justice we gotta get him the hospital fast!" yelled Ma Ma from the backseat. Justice glanced behind her in the backseat and noticed his whole lower half covered in blood, she had a life altering decision to make and time wasn't on her side. Risk taking him to the hospital and being confronted by law enforcement, or take him to her place and try to save his life with her mediocre nursing skills. Justice weighed her options and did what she felt Gator would want her to do in a situation like this as she bust a u turn and headed to her place.

Carrying him through the front door and placing him on the kitchen table, Justice quickly ran upstairs to get her medical bag.

"It's gon' be okay baby just stay awake," said Ma Ma as she stood by his side applying pressure to his wounds with tears in her eyes. Ma Ma was frantic inside but she tried her best to stay calm while assuring Gator that everything would be okay.

Racing back downstairs with her medical bag in hand Justice went to work. Aight Ma Ma help me take off his clothes so I can see if he's hit anywhere else. After a

230

quick examination of his body the only place he had been hit was in his hip and stomach but the shot to his stomach had opened him up pretty bad and he was losing a lot of blood. Turning him on his side she could see that the bullet had went straight through but the evening exit would in his back was the size of a golf ball.

Aight Gator this is gon' burn a lil bit, said Justice as she doused his wounds in alcohol then began removing any pieces of bullet fragments she found to prevent his wounds from getting infected. Once she finished cleaning the wounds she the stapled the holes shut and gave human shot of morphine for the pain which put him straight to sleep. Now all she had to do was pray the bullet didn't strike any main arteries causing internal bleeding and that he would ultimately wake up.

CH/24.

~

The next few days were filled with dread and anxiety as Ma Ma and Justice waited patiently for Gator to wake up. Ma Ma took out her pain and frustration on Bianca as she assaulted her hours at a time while tied up in Justice's basement. Every time she would pass out Ma Ma would throw a bucket of ice water in her face to wake her up then continue her vicious assault.

Justice spent most of her time watching over Gator. From monitoring his heart rate, to checking on his pulse by the hour, even sitting down by his side at night expressing her love for him as if he could hear her. She could never forgive herself if he didn't make it so she did everything in her power to keep him alive.

Sitting on the bed beside him gently caressing the side of his face, Justice began talking to Gator hoping her words would reach his heart. It's only been six months Gator but I swear it feels like I've known you all my life. The first day I met you that store I could tell you were different, it was all in your mannerism, your confidence, the integrity in your eyes, and that walk that just yelled out "I'm that nigga." A smile spread across her face as she wiped away the single tear trickling down her cheek.

Don't take this to the head but to be honest with you, "you make me feel like all of the guys before you were either a mistake or just a distraction," said Justice as she began to blush a little showing her deep dimples. I don't know Gator, I just feel like if I lose you I'll be losing a part of myself as well so you gotta pull through.

232

I'm falling in love with you and as much as I know it ain't right I just can't help it.

After getting the heavy load off of her chest that she had been carrying around for the last few months, Justice kissed him on the forehead before turning off the light. She knew if Gator didn't wake up in the next couple of days that it was a high possibility that he wouldn't make it. Even though she was a certified nurse the equipment and medicine she had in her home wasn't substantial enough the save lives.

As she went to leave the room the sound of a muffled cough stopped her in her tracks. Turning around on her heel she slowly walked back to the bed and noticed Gator attempting to open his eyes as he continued to cough. Seeing that he was in dire need of water she ran to the kitchen and retrieved him a tall glass of cold water before rushing back to his bed side. Devouring the cold glass of water as he hadn't had any in years, he then looked up at Justice with a slight smile on his face and uttered the words, "I think I'm falling in love with you too."

Tears began to well up in her eyes as she said a small prayer thanking the man upstairs then suddenly punched Gator in the arm. Damn what the fuck was that for? asked Gator as he held on to his arm. I thought you was unconscious, so you heard everything I said? asked Justice as she wiped away the tears with the back of her hand. Gator didn't reply, instead he held on to her hand while gazing into her dark brown eyes with a slight smile on his face. No words were needed to acknowledge the fact that he had indeed heard every heart felt word she dropped on him.

"Ma Ma hurry up and come upstairs he woke!" yelled Justice as she checked his vitals while positioning the pillows on the bed so he could sit up. Running up the basement steps like she was a track star for the Hampton

233

Cabbers, Ma Ma stormed into the room and once she saw Gator alive and well she broke down crying. Gator was her knight in shiny armor, he was the only thing in her life that seemed right. Seeing the love of his life she's tears of joy to see him alive touched a special place in his heart as he motioned for her the come sit on the bed with him. Hugging him as tight as she could while planting soft kisses all over his face, this was in fact a moment that she wanted to last a lifetime.

"Don't you ever scare me like that again, you had me in this bitch going crazy," said Ma Ma as she wiped her tears away while sitting on the edge of the bed. In the process of her wiping her tears away Gator noticed the bloody brass knuckles she had on her hand then he looked at her tee shirt noticing spects of blood on that as well. Ma Ma what the hell you got going on?

"What you mean?" asked Ma Ma with a confused look on her face. Gator looked at her hands then back at her, she was so caught up in the moment she had forgot she still had the bloody brass knuckles on.

"Oh I was giving our friend downstairs a lil tune-up," said Ma Ma with a wicked grin on her face. Gator sat their perplexed for a minute wondering what the hell she was talking about then it dawned on him,

"Bianca?"

"Yea baby who else," replied Ma Ma.

"Oh shit I thought she got away, I ain't even know y'all snatched her up," said Gator as he adjusted the pillow his back was propped up against.

"Yea that lil bitch tried to be slick and climb out the window," said Justice as she gave him a hand full of painkillers with a glass of water.

Did y'all get her to talk? I've been trying as you can see, said Ma Ma as she held up her bloody brass knuckles. She won't give up a name, all she keep saying is that it was a woman. She claims she never met her and

234

whenever T2 or Smoke spoke of her they would always refer to her as "Boss Lady," said Ma Ma as she picked a few prices of lint out of his hair.

Gator sat there in deep thought trying to figure out who this mysterious "Boss Lady" woman could be as he threw back a hand full of Percocet. You been beating her ass for two straight days and all she keep saying is "Boss Lady?" Yep, replied Ma Ma gesturing she didn't know what else to do. Gator sat there in silence for a minute then looked over at Justice and said, "Shit she might be telling the truth." Y'all help me downstairs, I wanna talk to her myself. With Ma Ma and Justice helping him out of bed and giving him a Cain to walk with Gator slowly made his way downstairs to the basement. He felt if he could be in her presence while looking into her eyes he could get a better feel if she was being truthful or not, or so he thought. Once he made it to the bottom of the steps he was able to get a glimpse at Bianca and he thought he was trippin. Got damn Ma Ma what the fuck you do? A devilish grin spread across her face showing much pride in her work.

Gator sat down in a chair across from her and tried looking into her eye but they were both swollen shut. Bianca, Bianca! Gator shook her leg trying to get her attention but she was unresponsive.

"Ma Ma I think you done already killed the bitch," said Gator as he began to check for a pulse. Naw she ain't dead yet, hold on. Ma Ma returned with a mop bucket full of ice water then threw it in her face causing her to wake up in a panic while frantically breathing as if she were drowning.

Look Bianca it's me Gator. I'ma give you one last time to come clean about who put the hit together, if not I'ma let baby girl beat your as for a whole week straight until you come correct, "now what its gon' be?" asked Gator in a calm but assertive tone. Barely audible with a trail of thick blood running out the side of her mouth, Bianca made one last attempt to save her life, "Boss Lady," that's all I know. Bloody, battered, beaten, with her face swollen like a pumpkin, it was no way in hell she wasn't telling the truth. Aight y'all looks like she telling the truth, go ahead and send her home Ma Ma.

This was music to her ears as she went and grabbed her .38special off the top of the washer machine and proceeded to take her out of her misery before Justice stopped her in her tracks. Naw Ma Ma we can't do it like that, that shit gon' be too loud, "hold on I'll be right back," said Justice as she ran upstairs. A couple minutes later Justice came strolling down the steps with a 12 inch butcher knife in hand then casually handed it to Ma Ma. Ma Ma looked at the knife then looked at her pistol. She had never stabbed anyone to death, but since it would be a more slowly painful death she was all for it.

Walking up on Bianca with the knife clutched tightly in her hand and malice in her eyes, Ma Ma released years of pain and pinned up aggression as she brutally stabbed Bianca over and over again in the chest, face, and head, until her body finally stopped moving. She didn't know what they did to her on the night of her attack but she knew whatever it was it had to be heinous because no matter how many times she asked Gator what happened he just wouldn't tell her. Imagining all of the horrible things they could've done to her on top of beating her in the head so viciously that it gave her partial memory lost, had her overwhelmed with rage as the tears began to flow while she shook uncontrollably still clutching the blood drenched knife.

As Justice stood off to the side observing the wild scene unfold she thought back to when she was brutally assaulted and left for dead a few years ago. Just the mere thought of it caused her eyes to well up with tears and her stomach to turn. She felt Ma Ma's pain as if it were running through her own body as she walked over to and motioned for her to hand over the knife. As Ma Ma placed the blood soaked knife in her hand Justice turned around as if she were going to get rid of it but what she did next shocked everyone in the room. Justice began viciously stabbing Bianca as well, letting go of years of resentment and hatred towards the ones who violated her. Once she felt like she got it all out of her system she dropped the knife and without a single word being said they began to hug and console one another as the tears flowed freely. Right then and there a bond was forms between the two of them that could never be broken, altered, or dismantled.

For the next couple of day Gator and Ma Ma hung out at Justice's place on the outskirts of Baltimore while Gator tried to regroup and gain some strength back. All he had been thinking about was Murdock and how Jux had told him that the situation was too risky and to leave it alone. Only if he would've listened and took his advice his childhood friend would still be with him. Interrupting his thoughts was Ma Ma as she entered the room and sat down beside him on the bed.

"How you feeling baby, you aight?" asked Ma Ma as she softly rubbed on his leg. Staring out the window in a daze Gator replied, "I'm fighting the storm right now baby girl, I can't even front." Ma Ma glanced at the half empty pill bottle on the nightstand then back at Gator who was still staring out the window. She could tell Murdock's death hit him hard that was his round, his whody, his thug

Ma Ma hated seeing her man down like that so she tried her best to ease his mind and bring a little joy into his world. She did everything from erotic strip tease shows, to making sweet love to his dick and balls until her jaws locked up. They were scheduled to hit the interstate and head back home once Justice got off work, so until then they just laid in the bed together, got high, and reminisced on all the good times they shared together.

As the young couple lay back in bed enjoying one another's company, a frantic, distraught, Justice came storming through the front door. We gotta get the fuck outta here! Yelled Justice as she quickly began to pack a few of her belongings. What's going on girl? asked Ma Ma as she walked into Justice's bedroom. I just killed one of the Mafia niggas!

"They know where I work and they probably know where I live at," said Justice as she fumbled with her suitcase while breathing heavily. Hold on Justice calm the fuck down, what happened? asked Gator as he made his way into her room while limping on his cane. Taking a few deep breaths Justice finally calmed down and regained her composure. I was at work and two of them showed up in my club looking for me so I slid out the back door. When I got to my car I could see them running towards me so I'm fumbling with my keys trying to get the door open and before I knew it he was right up on me so I shot him with the gun you gave me.

"What about the other guy?" asked Gator? I shot him too but I don't think he's dead cause when I jumped in the car he started shooting back.

Time was of the essence and Gator had to come up with a solution fast. He was in no shape to go to war nor did he have the man power so he made the most logical move he could think of. Ma Ma go grab the guns out of the closet and load them in her car, she going back to VA, with us.
Arriving at his home back in Hampton Gator stepped out of the backseat of the Lexus jeep and stretched his legs. It felt good being back home minus the fact that his comrade didn't make it back with him and he had two

.45caliber bullet holes in him. Once inside he told
Justice to pick a room and make herself at home, he had
a lot on his mind right now and some much needed sleep
is what his body yearned for.

CH/25.

~

Tammy sat in the plush chair at her salon getting her routine pedicure and manicure. This was normally something the she indulged in once a week but ever since she had given birth and became a mother she didn't really have time for pampering. Laid back in the reclining chair with her feet soaking in warm water she decided to call her people and see how the search for Bianca was coming along. It had been two whole weeks and she still hadn't heard anything.

"KC, tell me something good, how we looking lil daddy?" asked Tammy as she sat back enjoying her foot massage a little too much causing her pussy to get slightly moist. Well we had the drop on her since she used her real name to get a job at a club, but by the time we connected all of the dots and figured out where she was at it was too late, somebody beat us to the punch. What? "Hold on KC I'm not understanding you," said Tammy as she sat up in her chair and signaled for the woman massaging her feet to give her a minute. Yea I think your boy Gator got to her before we could. When we pulled up on her street damn near the whole block was blocked off with yellow tape and I counted at least four body bags being carried out of the house.

"I mean we can keep looking if you want but I got a good feeling that was her in one of those bags," said KC her most trusted henchmen from her hometown Memphis.

She knew there was no need for her men to keep searching. That was Gators M.O, kill you and everybody you're with just to send a message. Feeling as if she had done everything she could Tammy hung up the phone and continued her pampering. She was done with trying to tie up loose ends and refused to let it stress her any longer. Whatever the outcome turned out to be she was willing to accept it in whatever way need be.

It had been almost three months since Gator got shot and things seemed to be going smooth for the young playa from around the way. He had gained most of his strength back but due to the large caliber bullet cracking his hip bone he still had to walk with a cane for some time being. Gator was the slight bit discouraged by the cane, he actually embraced it. He had went online and ordered a 24carat gold Versace cane with a Medusa head as the handle.

Justice was still living with him and Ma Ma. It was supposed to be temporary just until things died down in Baltimore but the three of them were getting along so well and had been through so much over that short period of time that they were beginning to form a family like bond. Part of him felt like Ma Ma would be open to at least considering a three way relationship he just had to find the audacity to bring it to her attention.

It was a beautiful spring morning, Ma Ma and Justice needed a girl's day out so they jumped in her S560 and hit the city. It was a slow motion day for Gator so he lounged around the house shooting pool while smoking blunt after blunt by himself. He had been thinking about Sincere lately so he decided to give Tammy a call and check in on his lil one.

Pretty lady what you doing girl? asked Gator as he held the phone to his ear with his shoulder while pouring a pint of codeine inside a two liter Mountain Dew. I'm sitting here with Sincere, he acting like he wanna start walking but he so fat he keep tipping over, you should see him it's hilarious, said Tammy as she began laughing on the other end.

"Don't be laughing at my son," said Gator with a grin on his face. Oh now he's your son? Look Tammy we was doing good don't even start that shit. I'm about to slide through there so I can see my lil man so make sure you don't go nowhere.

"Yea aight," was Tammy's response before she hung up leaving Gator with a bitter taste in his mouth. A couple hours later Gator pulled up to Tammy's place wondering how long he could keep this secret away from Ma Ma. He knew sooner or later he would have to open up to her about his infidelities but he wanted to put on hold for as long as he possibly could. This wasn't a simple mistake like he forgot to take the trash out, or he left the toilet seat up, he was the father of her sister's child.

For the next hour or so the three of them enjoyed the company of one another as if they were one big happy family. Once Sincere tired himself out Tammy put him in his crib while she and Gator talked downstairs.

"So what you been up to?" asked Tammy as she sat down next to him on the sofa with her legs crossed. Rocking a polo sweatshirt with a pair of pajama shorts Tammy was still breath taking.
Gator's eyes roamed up and down her long sexy butterscotch legs remembering how she used to warp those same legs around his waist when he was deep inside her guts. Gator! Yea what's up? "I asked you what you been up to," said Tammy snapping him out of his lustful daydream. Same old shit you know me, tryna make a dollar out of fifteen cent.

"It's something I wanna talk to you about but I ain't feel comfortable discussing it over the phone," said Gator as he looked into her almond shaped dark green eyes making sure he had her undivided attention.

"Talk to me, what's on your mind?" replied

Tammy as she leaned back and took a sip from her glass of wine.

Well we found that girl Bianca up in Baltimore. Long story short we put the pressure on her and got her to talk but all she kept saying was a woman who goes by the name Boss Lady is the one who ordered the hit. I know you well connected throughout the South and East coast so I was wondering if you ever ran across someone who goes by that name.

Tammy put on a show as she paused for a minute while acting like she was really thinking if she knew a Boss Lady.

"Are you sure she was telling the truth?" asked Tammy. Yea I'm pretty sure, Ma Ma beat that girl ass for two straight days with brass knuckles, damn near killed her. If that wouldn't make her come clean I don't know what would.

"Well I'll look into it don't stress yourself over it, sometime you just gotta learn when to left shit go," said Tammy as she placed her hand on his knee while gazing into his deep dark brown eyes.

Well look I ain't gon' hold you up I gotta slide back on my side of town and handle some business, you take care of yourself baby girl. The two stood up to embrace one another and as Gator was releasing her from his arms she looked up into his eyes and asked, "so when you coming back to your son?" She had caught him off guard with this question and had him playing defense as he scrambled to come up with a quick response.

"Soon baby girl soon," were the words that rolled of his tongue as he kissed her on the forehead before walking out the front door.

Once outside in the driveway Gator climbed into his Porsche truck and lit the half smoked blunt from the ashtray. Thinking about what Tammy just asked him had him fucked up in the head as he blew the high grade smoke out his nose while stroking the hair under his chin. While letting the purple haze ease his mind he sat back and admired $600,000 home, along with her $160,000 Mercedes Benz G Wagen truck, and $120,000 Audi A8.

"I give it to her she a true boss bitch," said Gator as he flicked the ashes out the window.
Putting his car in reverse and backing out of her driveway Gator abruptly hit the brakes and began to think. Putting two and two together he began to wonder if Tammy could've been the one who sent the hit. She had ample enough money to hire a hitman, she fit the description of a "Boss Lady," and most of all, she had motive. The more he thought about it the more it made sense. If Ma Ma was out of the picture permanently he and Tammy could live a happy life together as a family with their son.

CH/26.

~

Over the next few days Gator wrecked his brain trying to figure out how he wanted to approach this situation. If he told Ma Ma would she even believe him? Not only that, she would want to know why, then he would have to explain to her the affair they were having and that Sincere was actually his son. Then there was the fact that he would have to murder the mother of his child because his loyalty lies with Ma Ma. With his head spinning and not knowing what to do, Gator popped two xanez bars and turned on some old Anita Baker until he nodded off into a coma like sleep.

As Gator lay sound asleep on the plush sofa Justice and Ma Ma sat at a popular sports bar on Mercury Blvd enjoying some drinks. Over the last few months the two of them the two of them had become inseparable. The Baltimore incident proved that they had each other's back while at the same time shedding light on their unfortunate past. It seemed as if Ma Ma had finally found that true friend who she could confide in and not have to worry about any backstabbing, besides, they both had the same blood on their hands.

"So how you like it down here so far?" asked Ma Ma as she took a sip from her Long Island ice tea.

"I can't even lie girl it's like an extended vacation which is exactly what I needed, but you know I can't run forever, sooner or later I'm gon' have to go back to Baltimore," said Justice in a more serious tone with a straight face. Ma Ma didn't like the way she expressed the word "run." It made her seem weak and passive so she quickly corrected her.

Naw you see Justice you got it all wrong, you're

245

not running don't ever say no shit like that you're just being smart and subtle. There was no way in hell we could've went to war with them after they tried to snatch you up at your job. With Gator shot up and Murdock dead we would've been totally outnumbered, so instead of fighting a war with a wounded army we retreat, regroup, then come back ten times stronger.

Ma Ma was speaking to her like a cold calculating General who was commanding a war while Justice paid close attention thinking to herself, "this bitch wicked, wicked but smart." Can I asked you something Ma Ma?

"Yea gurl anything," replied Ma Ma as she twirled her straw around in her drink. Where did you get that killer instinct and militant mind frame from? I mean you're so pretty and young most girls like that are the complete opposite, said Justice.

"First of all I'm only two years younger than you so please stop calling me young," said Ma Ma with a straight face. Justice didn't know if she was serious or not so she remained silent and let her continue. I really don't know I feel like that killer instinct was always in me. It seemed like after I killed the man who was molesting me it's like my mind, body, and soul, just became numb to homicide. Thinking back to when she was just ten years old having to endure the pain and humiliation of being molested by a man three times her age struck a nerve inside as her eyes began to well up with tears but she refused to let em drop.

Taking a second to pad her eyes with a napkin she then continued. Being militant minded that all came from Gator. A warm smile spread across her face as she thought about the love of her life. Gator taught me everything that I know.
When I was locked up he would always push the issue about reading and training my mind so he would go

online and order me books. Those books must've sat in my cell for three or four months before I even touched them, but once I started reading them I was so intrigued by them I couldn't put them down. They taught me how to master my emotions while training myself to think ahead, how to sit back and wait for the right moment to take action instead of giving in to my impatience impulse, and the one that I love the most, "it's more useful to be feared than loved." Yea I can definitely feel that," said Justice as the two women raised their glasses to share a toast.

After finishing her drink Ma Ma signaled for the waitress to bring them another round, now it was time for her to do the questioning. Aight Justice you got your inquiry questions out the way now it's time for mine. Justice looked at her with a slight bit of uneasiness on her face. She had a feeling of what she wanted to ask her but wasn't quite sure. With her poker face on and a voice full of confidence Justice casually responded, "Go ahead, asked away."

So Gator, you got a thing for him don't you? Ma Ma had a smirk on her face when she asked so that threw Justice off a bit causing her to fall silent and think about how she wanted to answer the question. Naw girl, me and Gator are just good friends and besides, that's "your" man, said Justice with a friendly smile on her face. The smirk quickly vanished from Ma Ma's face as she gave Justice the, "bitch is you serious" look.

Look Justice, I've seen the way Gator looks at you, it's not a look of lust but a look of passion. I like you Justice, I truly do. That shit you did back in Baltimore by going in that mission with us when you weren't obligated to, that shit meant a lot to me. That gesture alone showed me how Trill you are and that you stand firm on what you believe in so please don't get on no fake shit now that we're discussing my man.

Ma Ma had a point. Their bond had grown deeper than a man but at the same time Justice didn't want to put Gator in the hot seat by revealing her true feelings towards him. Taking a gulp from her glass of Remy Justice let the smooth dark liquor heat up her insides as she thought to herself, "it's now or never." She didn't know what the outcome would be but that was just a risk she would have to take.

Aight Ma Ma Ima be perfectly honest with you, I do have a thing for Gator. I've never met anyone like him, it's like when he touches me or even stands close to me I get chills all over, when he holds me and kisses me slowly I feel like I could die right there in his arms and be fine with it, when he's in my presence my heart beats at a different pace causing me to feel all mushy inside like I'm 16 again. Gator is special and rare, that's why when he kept talking about you and expressing his love for you I told myself I had to meet you. Any woman who is worthy enough for him to love and cherish that deeply is amazing, Trill, rare, and peculiar, all rolled into one.

Ma Ma sat there with a bland look on her face staring at Justice and Justice didn't know how to take it. She wasn't sure if Ma Ma was going to start crying or reach across the table and try to slit her throat. All she knew was that she had finally got it off her chest and she felt a hell of a lot better about herself because it was killing her inside knowing that she was having a secret affair with her man.

The two sat there in silence consumed in their own thoughts as Ma Ma was the first to speak. So do you love him? Once again there was an uneasy silence in the air. With tears welled up in her eyes Justice looked up and said the unthinkable, "yes I love him, and the more I get to know him the deeper in love I fall with him, I'm sorry Ma Ma." By now the tears were flowing down her face freely as she confessed to Ma Ma her deepest and most sincere feelings while feeling vulnerable as ever.

As Ma Ma got up from her seat to approach Justice she didn't know what to expect so she clutched her box cutter that she kept in her purse but surprisingly Ma Ma sat down right next to her and began consoling her. I'm sorry Ma Ma that shit was just weighing down in my heart so heavy I had to get it all out, said Justice as she wiped away her tears with the back of her hand. You don't have to be sorry, I'm just glad you kept it solid with me and I respect that.

"Now if you would've continued to lie about it and denied it, then I would've killed you," said Ma Ma with a straight face. I realize that Gator is gon' be Gator, "I'm just glad he chose a Trill bitch who I've grown to like, rather than one of them dusty ass bitches who give up the pussy for a twenty dollar bag of weed and a Chic Fila meal," said Ma Ma as the two shared a much needed laugh.

So you not mad at me? Asked Justice. There was a brief moment of silence between the two as Ma Ma pondered on her question before replying, "Naw I'm not mad at you." It's very rare that I run across a female of your caliber and to be honest I feel like we'll make a good team together.

"We got so much in common, shit even the same man," said Ma Ma. The tears were gone and replaced with smiles of trust and gratitude as they made a toast to forever stay true to one another.
The following morning Gator woke up in his California king size bed with Ma Ma snuggled up beside him. He had no idea how he made it from the living room couch all the way upstairs but somehow he did. As he laid eyes on his day one queen sleeping peacefully a wave of guilt hit him like a ton of bricks.

All of that misery and pain she endured on the night of her attack was a result of him betraying her love. Instead of getting dressed and leaving the house like he had planned to, Gator sparked a blunt, laid back and let the OG Kush ease his mind. With each pull from the Kush filled blunt he wondered how he could be so blind to the fact that the enemy was right up under his nose the entire time. All of that good pussy and body trembling head she was putting on him had that young nigga mind gone, that's how he was so blind to the fact.

Moments later Ma Ma woke up and laid her head on his chest while tracing her fingers up and down his six pack. Their chemistry was so strong one could feel when the other had something on their mind without even looking at each other.

"Whenever you're ready to talk I'm here baby," said Ma Ma as she listened to the rhythm of his heartbeat. Gator didn't respond, he just kissed her on the forehead then blew the smoke out his nose.

Later on that day Gator met up with Poncho at his home in Grist Mill. It was Sunday so Poncho invited Gator and Jux over to watch the game while his old lady cooked them a good ol southern meal. After the game was over with all three men were full to capacity from Keyana's special meat loaf, fried cornbread, collard greens soaked in vinegar and fatback, and her homemade banana bread cake to set it off. Keyana was a 24 year old from the inner city of Chicago, but the way she prepared a meal one would have mistaken her for a 60 year old woman from Augusta, Georgia.

Stepping into the den Gator began rolling a blunt while Poncho racked the balls on the pool table. Jux had left after the mouthwatering meal, he had a date with a beautiful second grade teacher from Williamsburg. How he managed to pull that one off neither Poncho nor Gator had the slightest clue, it seemed as if that was becoming the norm for their comrade.

Poncho had lost $1,200 to Gator from the game so he figured a quick game of pool would easily win him his money back since he was the more experienced player of the two. Before we get too deep in this game I gotta holla at you about something, said Gator as he watched Poncho knock in four balls in a row with ease. Poncho could tell by the tone in his voice that it was something serious so he put the stick down and sat on the barstool as Gator passed him the blunt.

"I found out who put the hit on Ma Ma," said Gator. Oh yea, who? You ain't gon' believe me when I tell you mane but, Gator paused for a minute before continuing, "It was Tammy." A look of pure shock and disbelief spread over Poncho's face as he leaned back in his seat repeating what he had just heard. Tammy? Yea bruh, I started connecting the pieces to the puzzle a few days ago and everything is coming back to her. You sure? Asked Poncho still trying to wrap his mind around the idea that Tammy was capable of such a thing, but the look on Gator's face said it all he didn't even have to respond.

Damn lil bruh that put you in a fucked up situation, I told you not to fuck that bitch, I told you mane, said Poncho with a great deal of emotion behind his words. Yea you right, never in a million years would I think she would take it this far just to get Ma Ma out of the picture, "I guess ain't know who I was dealing with," said Gator as he stroked the hair under his chin while staring at the ground. You think Ma Ma got an idea that it could've been her? asked Poncho. Naw hell naw, if she did I would be the first one to know, "trust me."

CH/27.

~

Sitting at the mini bar in his kitchen Gator took sips from his glass of Remy as he watched Ma Ma wash the dishes. Thinking back on everything she had been through Gator sat there wondering how she could hold in so much pain without showing it, while at the same time shining bright like the sun while moving so gracefully as if she were an angel who fell from the sky. Angel who fell from the sky yea right! She was more like a beautiful hazel eyed demon who escaped the pits of hell by getting the devil to fall in love with her right before she killed him. Gator began laughing to himself as the crushed up xanez in his glass of Remy had him feeling like he was walking on the clouds.

Hearing the laughter Ma Ma made her way to the mini bar and sat down beside him. You gon' let me in on the joke? Asked Ma Ma as she stared into his cloudy red eyes while taking a sip from his glass. Gator didn't respond, he just caressed the side of her face with the back of his hand and pulled her closer to him. Staring deep into her eyes he tried his best to find the slightest bit of distrust or hatred towards him but he couldn't. All he saw was a pair of hazel puppy dog eyes staring back at him that would kill and die for him.

Take your time with that drink baby girl.

"That's a grown mane drink you know how I do mine," said Gator referring to the crushed up xanez in his drink. Holding the drink up to the light while twirling it around, Ma Ma took another sip then called Justice into the kitchen. Bartending was what she did for a living so who else better to get the party started then her. Moments later Justice entered the kitchen wearing a pair of black silk pajama shorts with a matching top that was short sleeve with the first four buttons undone exposing her perfectly shaped breast that sat up firm in her black Fendi bra. Her fire red hair was tied up in a bushy ponytail giving off a more natural look while exposing her soft baby hair on her edges. Gangsta boo what's up girl? said Justice as she took a seat on the barstool next to the couple. Gangsta boo was the nickname she had given her after their little heart to heart a few weeks ago at the sports bar.

We need to borrow some of your bartending skills, Gator started the party without us.

"I don't know why he think he the only one who likes to get faded," said Ma Ma with a grin on her face. Justice looked over at Gator who shot her a slick smile flashing his shiny gold teeth then replied, "Say no more." Within minutes Justice was mixing and pouring drinks like she was back at her old job. A combination of VSOP Remy, Alize`, with a handful of crushed up xanez, and a splash of cranberry juice mixed all in one tall pitcher, they were sipping their own version of "thug passion." Gator plugged his phone into the stereo and went to his quiet storm playlist which consisted of all old love songs from back in the day. At just 22 Gator had an ear for music unlike anyone in his age bracket. His intent was to set a warm relaxing mood and that it did without disappointing.

The three of them laughed, flirted, revealed secrets about themselves, even cried. It was a slew of emotions going on but everyone was being themselves and wouldn't want to be anywhere else in the world at that moment. The Thug Passion had did away with all of their problems, stress, and worries, even if it was just for the time being.

By now the three of them had made their way to the living room and got more comfortable as their bodies sunk down into the plush mahogany suede sofa. As the beautiful Angela Winbush song "Your Smile," played softly in the background Ma Ma decided to fuck with Gator and ask him something that she had been going back N forth with in her mind lately.

"So Gator when were you gon' tell me that you that you wanted to practice polygamy?" asked Ma Ma as she sat on the sofa sideways with her legs stretched across his lap. Polygamy?

"What the hell you talking bout?" asked Gator with a confused look on his face. Ma Ma looked over at Justice who was on the other side of Gator and they both shared a smile as she told him to look it up in his phone. As curiosity got the best of him Gator pulled out his phone and began scrolling through the dictionary. Stopping on the word "polygamy," it read, (the practice of having more than one spouse at a time.)
After reading it he leaned his head back while thinking to himself, "is this bitch tryna a set me up?"

As he looked into her eyes trying to read her and see where she was going with it all he got was a nonchalant expression and her eyes told him nothing.

"Damn this girl is getting good at disguising her thoughts and emotions," said Gator to himself. Looking over at Justice she had the same expressionless look on her face as she blew the Kush smoke in the air then took a sip from her glass. Not knowing what to say Gator let the Thug Passion lead the way as he began planting soft kisses all the way from her pretty manicured feet with white toe tips, up to her juicy caramel thighs where he began planting kisses on her pussy lips through her laced boy shorts.

The Thug Passion had her feeling aggressive and wanting to take charge so after just a few minutes of him eating her pussy she ordered him to sit back on the couch as she began taking off her clothes piece by piece.

Dressed in nothing but her $30,000 Rolex and gold plated Chanel earrings Ma Ma straddled his lap and began passionately tongue kissing him while inserting his thick manhood into her warm, tight, slippery pussy that was screaming his name. Starting off slow then gradually picking up the pace, Ma Ma rode his dick like a bull rider from El Paso Texas while Justice sat right beside them with her legs cocked wide open playing with her pussy. Since Justice was in attendance that gave Gator an extra boost of stamina as he made sure to get every inch of him deep inside of her causing her to climax in the first 15 minutes.

Once Ma Ma reached her first orgasm the three of them made their way upstairs to the master bedroom where the real party began. The Thug Passion was running fluently through all of the systems as Gator lay on his back while Ma Ma rode his dick and Justice rode his face. The two women would rotate positions every 15 or 20 minutes while Gator just lay on his back and let them have their way with him. After their legs grew tired from the double team ride along, Gator began to hit Justice from the back while she tried her hardest to concentrate on eating Ma Ma's pussy. After three long passionate hours of pure ecstasy, the trio lay in the California king size bed drained of cum and energy while consumed in their own thoughts as they drifted off into a deep blissful sleep together.

CH/28

~

It was a beautiful spring day as Ma Ma jumped in her S560 and let it coast up the interstate to Richmond so she could spend some time with her sister and her nephew. It had been a while since she last saw them, five months to be exact so a warm visit was well past dew. Gator and Justice were out car shopping so she had the day to herself. Since Justice was part of the family now Gator informed her that she would have to upgrade that old ass Lexus jeep and ride like a true boss. Just the mere thought of Gator brought a smile to her face, she loved how he always wanted better for the ones he was close to and didn't mind lending a helping hand to bring them up in the world.

Once she arrived at Tammy's she waited in the living room for her to get Sincere ready, now that he was almost eight months old Tammy felt a little more comfortable bringing him out into the world. Holding Sincere in one arm and his bag in the other, Tammy made her way down the steps as Ma Ma rushed over and began planting kisses all over his little fat cheeks. Ma Ma would never admit it or let it show but deep down inside she envied her sister. Not for her beauty, status, or power, but the simple fact that she had a beautiful little son and she didn't. No matter how hard she tried she just couldn't seem to give Gator a child which in the end put a dent in her ego.

It was a beautiful day outside so they decided to hit Bush Gardens first. Not for the rides however, they were too cute to get on any rides so they just strolled through the theme park enjoying the scenery while turning heads. Next they let their presence be felt all through the Williamsburg outlet where Ma Ma splurged on her nephew in the Tru Religion and Polo store. Even though he was only eight months old Ma Ma let it be known that he was going to be the flyest eight month old that graced the earth.

Outback Steak house was their last stop as they got filled up on steak & shrimp while sipping martinis. Over the course of the meal Tammy had to excuse herself from the table on more than one occasion. Her guilty conscious was eating her up inside as she slid to the ladies room in an attempt to stop the tears of guilt and regret from flowing out her eyes.

Every time her mind would drift off and revisit the pain and agony she secretly put her sister through, she would get all choked up and have to pull herself together. Ma Ma had been nothing but good to her and after everything she had been through she still had a heart of gold. The guilt alone was driving her crazy and to be honest she didn't know how much longer she could continue living a lie.

Making her way back from the ladies room Tammy sat down and motioned for the waitress to bring them the check.

"Oh naw don't worry about it girl I already took care of it, I told you everything is on me today," said Ma Ma with an easy smile on her face showing her two gold crowns. Besides it's the least I can do for being MIA for the past few months.

"Between helping Gator run his business and taking care of our new home I barely have any time for my damn self," said Ma Ma as she searched for a $20 bill in her purse to leave for a tip.
Tammy was so caught up in her own thoughts and emotions she barely heard a word Ma Ma said as she packed Sincere things in his bag.

"Tammy did you hear me?" asked Ma Ma. Oh

I'm sorry girl my mind was somewhere else, what were you saying? By now the two had made eye contact and Ma Ma could tell she had been crying because her dark green eyes were now puffy and pink.

"You okay sis?" asked a concerned Ma Ma.

"Yea girl I'm fine, you bout ready to leave?" asked Tammy trying to avoid any further questioning. Ma Ma paused for a few seconds while studying her sister's body language before getting up and following her out the front door.

The hour ride back to Richmond was smooth and quiet with minimum conversation Ma Ma could tell something was bothering Tammy, she didn't have to reveal it, her body language and facial expression spoke a thousand words. You know Tammy if you ever need somebody to talk to I'm here for you. I understand you like to keep a lot of things to yourself but when things start to weigh down heavy on you, so heavy that it's hard to bare, its best if you just let it out and you'll feel better afterwards. Tammy looked over at Ma Ma in the passenger seat and couldn't help but smile as she thought to herself, "look at lil sis giving big sis advice on how to deal with her emotions. I appreciate the gesture but I don't think you're ready for what's weighing down on me.

Once Tammy put Sincere to bed she whipped up two Grey Goose cocktails for the two of them to sip on while they enjoyed the soulful sound of the "Waiting to exhale" soundtrack.

"This that real music right here girl yo lil ass don't know nothing bout this," said Tammy as she sang along to the Toni Braxton song "Let it flow." You forgot Tammy you're only five years older than me, and trust me when I tell you I know all about that old R&B, "Gator made sure of that," said Ma Ma with a warm smile on her face.

Over the next hour or so the two of them
listened to old R&B love songs just enjoying one
another's company over blunts of purple haze and
Tammy's special cocktails. Sitting on the sofa next to
Tammy with her legs crossed Indian style and a pillow
over her lap Ma Ma seized the opportunity to ask her
something a little more personal. They were family of
course but it seemed like Ma Ma always had to pry
information out of her half-sister for some strange
reason.

So Tammy, I know we don't talk or hang out as
much as we should but can I ask you something? The
constant flow of drinks and good weed had loosened
Tammy up a bit and had her feeling relaxed and
comfortable as she gladly responded, "yea sis what's on
your mind?" Ma Ma looked at her for a second then
smirked, "was it worth it?" What you mean was it worth
it? asked Tammy with a look of confusion on her face.
Look Tammy don't play dumb with me, I'm very
observant, I just wanna know was it worth it? asked Ma
Ma in a calm & easy tone.

The room fell silent as Tammy sat there trying to
study her body language. The slightest tap of the foot,
twitch of the eye, or change in breathing pattern would
tell her everything she needed to know but she got
nothing. Looks like you're having a hard time grasping
what I'm asking you, said Ma Ma with a grin on her face.
Tammy went to respond but Ma Ma quickly cut her off
as she held up one finger gesturing that she wasn't done
speaking.

Look Tammy let me explain something to you
so we'll both be on the same page. Do you remember
that time you were in the shower and your phone
wouldn't stop ringing so I brought it to you in the
shower? Tammy sat there for a minute trying to think,
she knew exactly what Ma Ma was referring to she was

259

just trying to buy herself some time. Picking up on the delay game Tammy was trying to throw her way Ma Ma took control of the conversion before she could even muster up a lie.

Since you having a hard time remembering let me help you out, I read the caller ID and it said SMOKE. That morning when Gator came to pick me up and surprise me with my new home, I just so happened to be on my way to the bathroom when I noticed you crying on his shoulder telling him how you just wish things could be normal between you two. Last but not least, back when I got jumped and they were viciously stomping my five month old pregnant stomach in one of them bitches mumbled the words, "This is for Boss Lady."

By now the tears had welled up in her eyes and began to slowly cascade down her face as she thought back to her unborn child being snatched away from her in such a cruel manner. No birthdays, no first day of school, no experiencing the baby take its first steps or speak its first words, Tammy had snatched all of that away from her younger sister with just the dial of a phone number. So I'm gon' ask you again, was it worth it? asked Ma Ma as she let the tears flow freely wanting Tammy to see and feel every ounce of pain she had caused her.

Look Ma Ma I'm truly sorry for everything that happened to you but you talking real crazy right now, you done had a lil too much to drink let's go upstairs so you can sleep it off. As Tammy reached over and grabbed her hand to walk her upstairs Ma Ma removed the pillow from her lap that was concealing a snub nose .357 then jammed it into her ribcage. Feeling the cold clump of steel pressed up against her warm flesh along with the emotionless look in Ma Ma's eyes was enough to make Tammy shit a brick. With her .380 upstairs in her bedroom Boss Lady was all out of options.

Like I said before we don't hang out as much as we should or converse as much as we should so let's talk. Now I'm gon' ask you one last time, was it worth it? The once cool, laid back, in control Tammy, was now a wreck as she frantically tried to think of a way to get out of this situation alive. Ma Ma I'm sorry, I, BOOM! Before Tammy could finish her sentence Ma Ma pulled the trigger on the powerful handgun sending chunks of Tammy's torso flying out her back.

As the smell of gunpowder filled the room Ma Ma slid over closer to Tammy who was clutching the hole in her chest while gasping for air, then whispered in her ear "breathe Tammy, breathe." The devil himself was on Tammy's shoulder as Ma Ma squeezed off another powerful round in her stomach followed by another one to the chest. Sitting up on the couch with her head leaned back, her once beautiful dark green eyes were now cloudy and red as they began to roll in the back of her head. With blood oozing out the side of her mouth the words "I'm sorry" tried to escape her lips but it did her no justice as Ma Ma put the barrel of the powerful .357 up under her chin and pulled the trigger leaving a hole in the top of her head the size of a plum and pieces of her skull and brain scattered on the wall.

The news of Tammy's murder took Gator by surprise leaving a bittersweet affected on him. Truth be told he really didn't know how to feel. Tammy was the mother of his child who since day one showed him nothing but genuine, solid love. Then there was the cold hearted, menacing, double crossing Tammy who put a $50,000 bounty on her own sisters head. The closed casket funeral was in her hometown of Memphis where damn near the entire city came out to pay their respect. Everybody who was somebody was in attendance, from drug lords, to high ranking gang members, to old school pimps who used to run with her father back in the day. The police didn't have any leads or suspects, but they did say whoever committed the murder was probably someone who she knew because there was no sign of forced entry. There was also two wine glasses sitting on the coffee table half empty leading them to believe the suspect was someone close enough to her that she would sit down in her home and have a drink with them. The part that really had Gator stressing and sick to his stomach was when news reporter stated that her infant son was missing from the home.

A whole month had passed since Tammy's murder and there was still no sign of Sincere. Gator Jux and Poncho had their people searching everywhere for Sincere. Between the three of them they put up a $150,000 reward for any information leading to his son's whereabouts but unfortunately he had heard nothing. Deep down in his gut he had his suspicions on who was involved but the situation was so delicate he kept it to himself, he didn't even tell Poncho what he thought and he told Poncho everything.

With Tammy out of the picture that meant no connect. He wanted to continue doing business with her people out of Memphis, the infamous "Vice Lords," but they refused to do business with him until he gave them the name of the person responsible for her death. In all actuality Gator didn't know who killed Tammy, and even if he did he wouldn't give them up just to continue doing business with them. Refusing to deal with the people in his own city Gator and Jux got together and linked up with his people in Patterson New Jersey. The dope wasn't as good as the dope he was getting from Tammy's people but it was a hell of a lot better than most of the dope in VA.

Making their way back from one of their monthly trips to Patterson, Gator and Jux sat in Chicken wing's house on Spruce and got the pack ready for distribution. Gator preferred quality over quantity so he only put 9 ounces of cut on every brick, turning his four bricks of heroin into five giving him a free $75,000 on top if his profit. Finally finished with a total of 180 ounces bagged up, Gator and Jux sat back and left the purple haze ease their mind.

"So what's the status on that situation?" asked Jux as he popped the seal on a pint of codeine and began to pour it into a Mountain Dew. Jux and Poncho were the only two people who knew Sincere was his son so their concern was more on finding Sincere then anything. The three of them had been thuggin together for so long and their bond was so strong if one of them were going through the struggle all of them were going through the struggle.

You know Jux, you and Poncho are like the two older brothers I never had. Y'all taught me everything I know from how to cook crack, to properly wash gunpowder residue off my hands, Shit y'all even taught me how to detect if a bitch was burning or not. By now Gator had a slight smile on his face as he pour himself a cup of syrup.

"Look my nig I'm telling you this because I trust you and I love you like a brother, between me and you I think Ma Ma did that shit," said Gator with a straight face letting Jux know he was serious.

Jux sat there looking at him for a minute before he responded. That was the last thing he expected to hear from his right hand man and truth be told he thought Gator had popped one too many pills before he started sippin his syrup. Hell naw bruh you trippin, "you think she capable of doing something like that to her own sister?" asked Jux.

"Half-sister," stated Gator firmly. To answer your question though, hell yea I think she capable of doing something like that and much more.

You see Jux y'all don't know Ma Ma like I know her. Y'all only know the pretty, soft spoken, loveable Ma Ma who won't hesitate to bust her pistol if her back is against the wall. Y'all don't know the wicked, cold, calculating Ma Ma, who will hide out in your garage for two straight days to even a score from three years ago. Not to mention on the night Tammy was murdered she was nowhere to be found. She came strolling in the crib around 2 in the morning, took a shower then went straight to sleep.

"Shit sound like to me she was getting her creep on," said Jux. I think you over thinking this whole situation bruh. Just cuz she ain't come home till 2 in the morning don't mean she killed her sister and abducted her 8 month old nephew. I don't know Jux maybe you right, maybe I am trippin, but I'm telling you I wouldn't put it past her.

Ever since Tammy's murder and Sincere's disappearance Gator had been spending less time at home and more time in the streets. It was as if the thrill of hustling and fucking different women every night was the only thing that kept his mind off of what he was dealing with. Gator had been on a three day flight hustling deep in the trenches of Hampton and Newport News with no sleep. The only thing keeping him awake and focus was the party pack of blue dolphin ecstasy pills as he squeezed around 110 grand out of the city over the course of those three days. All out of dope and in need of a long hot shower, Gator dropped Auriell off on Spruce St before making his way home.
Pulling up to his home deep in the Fox Hill area of Hampton, Gator noticed that Ma Ma's Benz was gone. In a way he was kind of relieved because he was still

rolling off the ecstasy and there was a good chance he would tell her what was really on his mind but without any proof he couldn't do such a thing. Once inside he was greeted by Justice with open arms. Being in her presence gave him a sense of peace and serenity which is exactly what he needed.

Where Ma Ma? asked Gator as he began to get undressed and make his way to the shower. She went to go make some runs for you, she should be on her way back, yelled Justice from downstairs. After a much needed shower Gator was rejuvenated and feeling like his old self again as he made his way downstairs and sat next to Justice on the plush sofa who was already rolling his blunt for him.

Putting the finishing touches on the Kush filled blunt resembling a long index finger Justice handed it to him then leaned in closer to smell him and said, "now that's the Gator I know." The two shared a laugh as Gator sparked the blunt and let the high grade Kush ease their mind, body, and soul. Whenever one was going through a trial or tribulation good weed and a thick cup of syrup was all you needed to reassure you that there would be better days to come.

With her head resting on his chest Justice looked up at Gator and said "I love you so much." Gator didn't reply he just kisses her on the forehead and continued rubbing his hand up and down her soft thick thighs covered in beautiful tattoos. I don't know what's going on between you and Ma Ma but I hope y'all fix it.

"I love her to death and I'm in love with you so if you ever need someone to talk to you can confide in me about anything," said Justice as she blew the smoke out if her nose then passed him the blunt. Her words were sincere and genuine as the rolled off her tongue and Gator knew she stood firm behind it but what made her think they were going through something?

"What makes you think we going through something?" asked Gator as curiosity got the best of him. Come on Gator I'ma female I can sense shit like this. Between you staying gone for three to four days at a time, and Ma Ma locking herself in her room crying herself to sleep it's pretty obvious something's going on. Gator sat there in silence as he took pulls from the Kush filled blunt, I mean what was he supposed to say? Was he supposed to tell her the reason he hasn't been home was because he felt Ma Ma was involved in Tammy's murder and Sincere's disappearance, and that Sincere was actually his son? Hell naw, he trusted Justice but at the same time he knows the type of bond she and Ma Ma share so some things are best left unspoken. Brushing off the conversation Gator continued caressing her thick yellow thighs without speaking another word on the situation.

Two blunts later Justice was sound asleep in his arms with her head against his chest as he surfed through the channels stopping on ESPN. They were doing a 30 for 30 special on Mike Tyson and Buster Douglas from the late 90's so Gator kicked his feet up and tuned in. About 15 minutes into the program the sound of keys jingling at the front door caused Gator to sit up and turn his head, then walked in Ma Ma with a few bags in her hand.

I see somebody finally made their way back home, said Ma Ma as she placed the bags at the bottom of the steps then made her way into the living room with Gator. Dressed in a burgundy and bage Dolce & Gabbana sundress, with a pair of Fendi sandals and her hair tied up in a bun she looked far from a killer. Sitting down on the sofa next to Gator she gave him a long tight hug followed by a kiss on the lips. Justice was still sound asleep right beside him so she tried her best not to wake her.

266

Where you been at? I been waiting on you for the past three hours, said Gator in a laid back but assertive tone. You been waiting on me for the past three hours while I've been waiting on you for the past three days. Ma Ma did have a point, Gator had no room to complain about her being gone for a few hours when he barely even made it home.

"Well since you must know, I did a few pick-ups for you," said Ma Ma as she pulled out a small folded up piece of paper from her bra and began to read off the names to Gator. JRock - 7,500, Mel Man 3,200, and Gangsta Fred- 4,500. Reaching into her Prada bag she pulled out two large stacks of money then threw them on Gator's lap as she rolled her eyes at him. Ignoring her antics Gator popped the rubber bands off the two bricks of money and began to thumb through them both making sure the count was correct.

Baby can I ask you something? Gator's mind raced 100mph as he pondered on what she could possibly want to ask him while at the same time playing it calm, cool, and collective. Yea baby go ahead. Ma ma paused for a few seconds as she gathered her thoughts while trying not to let a single tear fall from her beautiful eyes before asking, "do you still love me?" This caught Gator off guard as he scrunched his face up at her in disbelief before responding, "of course I still love you what type of question is that?" Once again there was that same awkward moment of silence from Ma Ma, she didn't reply she just kissed him softly on the lips then motioned for him to follow her upstairs.

Once upstairs Gator made himself comfortable while Ma Ma showered. It had been a little over two weeks since they last made love so Gator knew exactly what was on her mind, it was written all over her face. Breaking down the Kush weed on an old Three six mafia CD while sitting on the bed with his back resting against the headboard, Gator looked up and locked eyes with a breath taking goddess. Standing at the foot of the bed wearing a sexy two piece Chanel lingerie set that contested of a silk lavender bra with matching laced panties and a pair of lavender fishnet stocking, she definitely had Gator's undivided attention.

While standing up she placed her foot in the edge of the bed and began lathering her legs with oil putting on a small show for her man. Watching her slowly caress her beautiful legs and thighs Gator noticed her toe tips were even laced with a fresh coat of lavender nail polish as he thought to himself, "damn baby girl went above and beyond to please a nigga, that's aight." Feeling aroused Gator put the blunt down and attempted to make his way to the foot of the bed but was quickly stopped in his tracks.

"Naw baby it's all about you tonight, just sit back and enjoy the ride," said Ma Ma as she placed her hand on his chest and playfully pushed him back. Strolling through her playlist she stopped on the perfect song to set the mood the evening. With Xscape's song "Softest place on earth" playing softly through the surround sound, Ma Ma stood in the middle of the bed putting on a show for her man as she seductively dance for him, hypnotizing him with every wind, twist, and erotic gyrate motion her body had to offer. Her body moved so freely to the rhythm of the music as if she were a blessing sent from up above to rid him of all his worries.

Standing over top of him she squatted down and put her pussy in his face while slowly gyrating her hips giving him a whiff of her sweet pussy which gave off an alluring smell of fresh peaches. By now Gator's manhood was standing firm at attention as she bent over in front of him and touched her toes making her ass checks bounce one at a time. Her 21 year old Caramel body was soft, fresh, and flawless without a scar or stretch mark in sight causing him to fall in love with her youthful tenderness.

Backing up to the middle of the bed while keeping her hips moving to the rhythm of the melody she unbuttoned her bra and began slowly licking her honey colored nipples while never braking eye contact. Noticing Gator's erect manhood bulging through his Versace boxer briefs, she got on all fours and slowly crawled over to him them began stroking and kissing his throbbing dick through his boxers. All of the foreplay was driving Gator crazy as he sat back and inhaled the Kush smoke.

This was something new to him and to be perfectly honest he didn't know how much longer he could take it. Feeling his manhood on the verge of busting through his boxers Ma Ma could tell he was ready for her as she leaned over and pulled out a can of whip cream from her Chanel bag. A wicked grin spread across Gator's face as he watched on in lust while Ma Ma shook the can then covered every inch of his dick and balls with the tasty desert.

Over the course of the next thirty minutes Ma Ma ate his dick like a giant pop sickle on a hot summer day, licking him clean of every drop of whip cream. Satisfied with how well she handled the whip cream tactic she then stuffed as much of him as she could down her throat while humming an erotic melody and massaging his balls at the same time. Making a loud POP sound as she popped his dick out of her mouth she then paid attention to his balls as she covered them in saliva and made love to them for a full twenty minutes. Ma Ma was pulling out all of her special tricks for the love of her life as he sat back in a blissful mind state enjoying every second of it. All out of whip cream and yearning the sensation of his thick manhood inside of

her, Ma Ma straddled his lap then guided all eight inches
of him into her warm, tight, slippery pussy, she was here
to let it be known that her pussy was the "softest place
on earth." It had been almost three weeks since they last
made love and the tightness of her pussy reminded him
of the fact. Gripping her hips while planting soft kisses
on her neck Gator matched her stroke causing her pussy
to get wetter and wetter every time she came down on
his manhood.

The sound of ass cheeks smacking against his
thighs along with the sight of her pretty titties bouncing
in his face made his dick grow even bigger inside of her
as she bit down on her bottom lip while staring into his
eyes. Feeling the muscles in his throbbing manhood
expand inside of her tight pussy had her fat cat drenched
in juices as she tighten up her pussy muscles causing
him to explode deep inside of her while she shivered and
shook from her own orgasm as well. Both of them
climaxing together at the same time felt like pure ecstasy
to Gator as he closed his eyes and inhaled deeply trying
to savor every moment.

The feeling of cold steel being pressed against
his forehead caused him to open his eyes as Ma Ma held
her snub nose .357 to his head while continuing to
slowly grind on his cum soaked manhood.

"Stop playing girl get that fucking gun out my
face," said Gator as he closed his eyes again and went
back to enjoying the moment. What makes you think I'm
playing? By now Ma Ma was inches away from his face
as she licked a trail from the middle of his chin to the top
of his forehead while her pussy pulsated releasing its last
bit of cum with his dick still inside her. Before Gator
could repeat himself she smacked him in the mouth with
the heavy clump of steel causing blood the pour from his
mouth to show him she wasn't playing.

"I want you to shut the fuck up and listen," said Ma Ma

270

as she continued to slowly grind her hips while holding the powerful hand gun to his temple. You hurt me Gator, you hurt me to the core. How can the person who you love more than life itself be the same person who brings you pain and misery like never before? Ma Ma's tone was calm and assertive as she expressed to the love of her life what she had been holding in for months.

After the first couple weeks of Ma Ma being released from jail she began noticing small signs that something was off about her sister, then after the attempt on her life her suspicions grew even more. The caller ID incident, the crying on Gator's shoulder incident, all of that added fire to the flame making Tammy look guilty as charge, and would've caused your average person to react on sight in an irrational manner, but Ma Ma played it cool, gathered more solid evidence, then waited for the perfect time to strike. On that beautiful spring day when she went to go spend some time with her sister and nephew, it wasn't because she missed them and wanted to strengthen their bond, it was to connect the final piece to the puzzle. You see Ma Ma was patient, cold, and calculating. She waited almost a full year to determine if sincere was Gator's son or not, and those few hours that she spent with him face to face on that beautiful spring day told her everything that her heart was already insinuating.

Laying on his back staring down the barrel of the same .357 that blew Tammy's head off Gator thought about wrestling the gun out of her hand until he noticed she had the hammer cocked back. One light tap of the trigger with the hammer cocked back would leave his brains and thought scattered all over the Louis Vuitton bed sheets so he quickly disregarded that idea. Besides, Ma Ma was the love of his life there was no way in hell she would kill him, would she?

Staring into her hazel colored eyes Gator

couldn't find the sweet, loving, caring Ma Ma who would go to war with God behind him, instead what he saw was the devil himself staring back at him as a single tear rolled down her face and landed on his forehead. Let me ask you something Gator, did you know it was Tammy who put the hit on me? No better yet how long have you known? Gator went to respond but she put the barrel of the gun to his lips gesturing for him to remain silent. Did you know it was Tammy who orchestrated the attack on me that killed our unborn child? By now Ma Ma was seeing red as she clutched the handle on the gun so tightly her knuckles turned white.

Gator was speechless, he actually had no idea Tammy was behind the mob assault that caused Ma Ma to lose their unborn child. He was always suspicious about her assault in jail now it all made sense. Look baby put the gun down so we can, before Gator could finish his sentence Ma Ma viciously smacked him across the forehead with the gun causing it to go off knocking feathers out of the pillow he was laying his head on. With his ears ringing from the powerful blast along with the smell of gunpowder in the room, Gator knew he was still alive but for how much longer? Now he was actually considering the thought that she just might have what it takes to kill him.

"While I was locked away in that cold jail cell crying my heart out every night, wishing and praying I could lay next to you and feel your touch, you were balls deep in my sisters pussy without a care in the world," said Ma Ma with tears in her eyes as she looked down at the man who betrayed her.

"You know I had to save the best for last," said Ma Ma with a smirk on her face as she wiped away the tears with the back of her hand. Did you know Sincere was your son?

Gator's heart skipped a beat as the room fell silent. How

the fuck did she know all of this and how long had she known all of this? Everything that he had taught her about concealing her intentions, mastering her emotions, and waiting for the right moment to take action, she had used it all against him. Look Mr. Lover boy time is not on your side so I'm gon' asks you one last time, did you know? Before Gator could come up with a swift response the bedroom door swung open as Justice walked in.

Hearing the door open Gator assumed that Ma Ma would turn around and give him an opportunity to grab the gun out of her hands but to his surprise she never flinched a muscle.

"Did y'all hear that gunshot?" asked Justice as she entered the room still half sleep. Smelling the fresh gunpowder in the air then noticing Ma Ma pointing something in his face as she sat on his lap ass naked Justice began to put two and two together while asking herself "what the hell did I just get myself into?"

"Please Ma Ma put the gun down before you do something you'll regret, whatever it is y'all can work it out just please put the gun down," pleaded Justice as she stood by the door making sure to keep her distance. Why Gator why? All I ever did was love you and stay true to you, I never crossed you not one time, all I ever wanted was the same love in return, was that too much to ask? By now the tears were flowing down her face like a steady river but no matter what she wouldn't take her finger off the trigger.

"You were the only thing in my life that felt right, the only thing in my life that made sense, you gave me purpose to wake up every morning and live life, what happened to our love?" asked Ma Ma as her body began to tremble from rage, pain, heartache.
As Justice stood off to the side just a few feet away, her eyes began to well up with tears as she listened to her

273

pour her heart out. She knew the type of emotions true love could bring to the table and after everything Ma Ma had been through she was now at her breaking point, it's only so much a bitch could take. Gator didn't know how to respond, he just stared into her eyes hoping the find the slightest ounce of love she had left for him. He knew he had fucked up but he would never do anything intentional to hurt her, she was the love of his life and he loved her more than life itself.

All out of tears to cry Ma Ma looked down at him with a bland emotionless look in her eyes then uttered the words, "I love you." As Gator fixed his mouth to tell her he loved her too, the whole room shook as a single blast from her .357 freed her of all of her pain, misery, and heartache. Justice fell to her knees as a piercing scream escaped her lips, Ma Ma had did the unthinkable, and she had taken her own life.

She had every intention on evening the score by killing Gator tonight but something in her heart just wouldn't allow her to squeeze the trigger. Staring back into his intense dark brown eyes her heart began to melt as the thought of taking his life began to become a reality. Her love for him was so surreal she would rather take her own life and free herself of all of her pain, misery, & betrayal, then to be the one responsible for his death. Sincere was never found and four days later Gator was indicted on homicide charges from the Baltimore incident resulting in multiple life sentences.

One thing for sure two things for certain, the double cross is always lurking in the shadows. Let your intuition guide your reactions to prevail...